THE DEVIL'S WIRE

Deborah Rogers

Published by Lawson Publishing (NZ).
ISBN 978-0-473-33863-3

For Mum

1

The ironic thing is that tonight Jennifer is thinking about car crashes when she rounds the corner onto Pine Ridge Road. She could've sworn she was the only one on it, and that's why she's chosen the moment to reach down for the mandarin rolling loose in the foot well. The pothole she'd struck back on Tedder Street had sent the mandarins tumbling from the grocery bag and one had found its way here, to the front. She's being safety conscious because the thing might get trapped behind the brake pedal and she'd once seen a car crash and knew what a disaster it could be. That time, the car, a jeep deluxe something, had flipped right in front of her. It had hit the curb and skidded across four lanes worth of highway to land directly in her path, exposing its aging belly to the sunlight, dripping gasoline from its tank.

Worried the jeep might explode, Jennifer had tried to get the woman out, dragging her free through the smashed up windscreen, but the rescue guy later told Jennifer that the whole "car's going to explode because you've crashed thing" was an urban myth because gas tanks didn't blow up just like that, there needed to be fire first. Not that it mattered to the woman. She was dead by the time Jennifer pulled her into the ring of dirt by the side of the road.

So Jennifer knew what could happen when you were driving alone at night and a stupid mandarin was roaming free amongst the stone chips and twigs and stray pottery barn receipts. And she should really turn the stereo down because it's not helping her concentration. Then she

3

realizes the stereo isn't on and the music is coming from inside her own head, stuck on one of those loops that never seemed to stop, a ring worm or ear worm or worm something, the short point being she can't simply turn it off, that nondescript bassy crap that's good for cardio but not much else, and this uncooperative mandarin is really beginning to tick her off because it keeps slipping from her fingers but she's managing to still drive in a straight line. She tells herself to relax. That it's just one of those annoying but potentially dangerous things in life—a metaphor or simile or irony or whatever, for life's little mishaps—but she can handle it.

Then the mandarin disappears under her seat and now it's out of her reach entirely and it waits there, behind the lever, biding its time, like some sort of threat. An accident waiting to happen. Jennifer thinks about that as she straightens up and returns both hands to the steering wheel—an accident waiting to happen—and the meaning it implied, as if accidents weren't accidents at all but more like a sting, you know, *entrapment*, like a black toad sitting on a black stepping stone or a dog-eared mat missing one half of its Velcro stick or the unforgiving above-the-sink cupboard left slightly ajar. It was like the universe was setting you up all the time, with all these little accidents waiting to happen, and then Jennifer gets angry, because what was fair about that? And she thinks about her marriage and wonders whether that was an accident waiting to happen too.

And before she knows it, she's back to last night and his snipe about her hair. Oh, he made out like he was pissed because she was late, and she was, but then he said the thing about the hair. Well, screw you, she had wanted to say. *You don't own me. I'm not your little doll. I can do what I want.*

Maybe she was sick of the cobwebs growing out of her scalp. Maybe she was over being told forty was the new thirty or you-were-quite-a-looker-back-then or feeling like she was a favorite blouse beginning to soil at the cuffs. Maybe she wanted to feel refreshed, even if only for four to six weeks.

And what about him? Had he even looked in the mirror lately, with his whiter than white torso, that once taut college footballer's body now turning to fat? And if he thought he looked good with that beard, he was kidding himself. It was like the deal with McKenzie's food. He just didn't get it.

And last night when she got back from the hair salon, she could've screamed when she saw the state of the kitchen. The two half-stacked plates stippled with chili. The trail of nacho crumbs. The empty tub of ice cream beneath the dripping tap.

She had found him upstairs, getting ready to go out.

"You're late," he said, buttoning his shirt.

Jennifer held up the empty tub. "She's got an eating plan she needs to stick to, you know that."

"You never answered your phone."

"We've got to help McKenzie make better choices. It won't work if we're not on the same page."

He stood up and put on his jacket. "I don't like not being able to reach you. I was worried."

"Honestly, Hank, do you want her to get diabetes?"

He frowned. "Keep your voice down. She's twelve, Jen. Twelve-year-old's like ice cream. She can get back on her diet tomorrow."

He retrieved his keys and wallet from the side table. "I have to go. Chip Manderson wants to talk about a potential construction job on the waterfront. We'll pick this up again tomorrow."

"Don't do that," she said.

He faced her. "Do what?"

"Treat me like I'm a child."

He looked at her wrist and paused. "Where's your bracelet?"

She held his gaze and lifted her chin. "The clasp broke."

"Oh."

"It only just happened. I haven't had a chance to take it to the jewelers."

He looked at her awhile longer, studying her face. "I'm doing everything I can to keep this family afloat, Jen. What about you?"

Then he left but not before he said, "I'll never understand why women cut off their hair."

She should have said something, but she hadn't. She just let it slide. She was getting very good at letting things slide.

Outside her car window, the street lights cast a miserable gloom and Jennifer can barely make out the pines bordering the neighborhood. Why she let him talk her into moving here all those years ago, to this drab suburb of two-storey doer uppers, away from their perfectly good low maintenance apartment in Chicago, she doesn't know.

Hank had shown her the house online not long after the incident. We can grow vegetables in the backyard, he'd told her, go for hikes in the forest on the weekends. McKenzie will be able to play in the street with the local kids, and we can renovate the house exactly how we want. It's even got a fire place, Jen. Just think of those toasty winter nights, he'd said, and there's enough contract work out there to keep me going for years. Best of all, you can finally set up your practice.

He put in an offer without telling her so in the end she had no choice. But that was how Hank rolled. He knew best and she just went along for the ride.

She'd wanted to believe him, about their peaceful non-materialistic life in the upper Midwest, that they would live happily ever after, put that dark chapter in their lives behind them. What she got instead was a house that creaked in the night and damp that never left. Which was fitting because sometimes her life seemed like one big damp patch. But maybe it wasn't so bad. Maybe she was the one with the problem.

Damp patches make her think of Ivan and now she's worried because she should have been home more than two hours ago but at least she'd sent Hank a text and she couldn't have said no when Rosemary her receptionist stuck her head in the door after the last client left and asked Jennifer if she wanted to join in and celebrate the "big two-two", as Rosemary had put it, doing the victory fingers. They went to *The Green Parrot*, which smelt like hot sauce and feet and too much CK.

Rosemary introduced her to everyone. "Mandy, Liz, Kate, Sarah, Josephine, Samantha, Samantha's brother Chris, and Ivan. Everyone, this is my boss, Jennifer."

Jennifer took a seat next to Ivan who was too young and too good looking and dressed in blue jeans and a Che Guevara t-shirt.

"Hey," he said, doing the chin-tilt thing.

"Hi."

Then he picked up the pitcher of margaritas and poured her one and she sipped and licked salt from her teeth and pretended to look at the group of college kids on the dance floor. Ivan was watching her, she could tell. She shifted under the weight of his stare. Felt the backs of her thighs sweat in the vinyl seat. Stupid. He was just a kid. She stole a look. Nice eyelashes. Just the right amount of stubble. Lips that curled up in one corner. She imagined she could see the concave of flesh just beneath the hip bone—smooth, pale, porcelain soft.

"We're going for a boogie, wanna come?" shouted Rosemary.

Jennifer looked at her watch and shook her head. "I have to go."

"No, you don't," said Ivan, pulling her up.

"Steady there, big boy," she laughed.

And she let Ivan lead her to the dance floor, which was shoulder-to-shoulder full, and Liz held out the pitcher and filled up everyone's glasses and laughed as it sloshed over the sides and the music donkey-kicked Jennifer's breastbone and Ivan was dancing with his eyes closed and she imagined him shirtless and smelling of cigarettes and tasting of lime. And he kissed her. Or she kissed him. It was an accident waiting to happen. Rosemary pretended not to see. And Jennifer pulled away from Ivan's grasp and his "don't go" whisper and the image of them together in the back seat of his car or one-bedroom apartment above his parent's garage or a shop entrance stoop.

Jennifer turns the corner and sees her house up ahead and here comes the mandarin again, nudging her heel. And why couldn't Hank have just told her hair looked nice and none of this would have happened. Now she had kissed another man. Now she was in that category of spouses who occupied that moral grey area of the almost affair.

She feels a spike of guilt. Jennifer can almost guarantee that right now he'll be at home, pacing the length of the living room, pausing to check his phone, wondering where the hell she was. What exactly was she hoping to achieve with her little act of rebellion? She knew it was hard for him not being able to provide like he used to. She saw the way his eyes clouded over when he told her that the market was going turn any day now or that is was just a matter of time. And here she was, the disloyal, self-absorbed wife, kicking a man while he was down, a man who had supported her throughout her darkest hour.

Jennifer reaches for the elusive mandarin and it grazes her fingertips then slips away to circle her left foot beyond her reach, and she thinks of their first date when he told her he was in construction and how when he kissed her goodnight, she could smell sawdust on his skin. She thinks of later, before they were married and after, and how he never stopped looking at her like she was the center of his universe and how in the afterglow of making love, he'd look at her and say, "I can't believe you chose me, I must be the luckiest man alive". She thinks of him now shoving fistfuls of fruit loops in his mouth and the way he laughed like a four-year-old whenever he watched the jujitsu on TV and how he was a walking cliché with his Carl's Jr. addiction and beer and obsession with power tools.

He was a good person. Oh sure, he could be an overprotective, domineering hothead. But that was just his way. He took care of her. He had a good heart.

And he loved her and McKenzie more than anything else.

And she was a lousy wife.

And he was right. She hated her hair, too. Chocolate brown? What was she thinking? And why hadn't she asked for a shoulder length bob instead of a pixie cut? She needed to get things back on track, change her errant ways.

Nothing was more important than her mildly dysfunctional but perfectly formed three-person family.

Aha! She finally gets hold of that mandarin. Her fingernails sink into the skin and there's a burst of citrus and she feels like she's come through some sort of challenge. Pressing it to her lips she gives it a triumphant kiss. She doesn't realize there's something on the road before it's too late. She looks at the clock and sees it's just gone a quarter past eleven. It's funny, the things you notice.

2

Oh Sweet Jesus, a kid. Jennifer lurches to a stop and leaps from her seat and runs to the front of the Nissan. Nothing. She spins around, eyes raking the darkness for clues, thinking perhaps the child was catapulted into someone's front yard, but it is too hard to see.

Then, half-hidden by an overgrown buckthorn, she sees it. The huddled black mass of a dog.

"Hey, boy."

The animal is trembling. She reaches out but it shifts its glistening snout to avoid her hand.

"Come on, boy," she says, trying to coax it toward her.

Jennifer smells blood. The dog growls then seems to give up.

"What are you doing?"

Jennifer jumps and turns to see a short, red-headed woman fast-walking toward her.

"I said what are you doing to my dog?"

"It was on the road."

"You ran over my dog?"

The woman pushes Jennifer out of the way.

"Baby."

The dog thumps its tail twice. There's an accent Jennifer can't place.

"Don't just stand there, help me."

"I'll get my husband," says Jennifer.

"There isn't time."

Together they lift the dog. He's heavy and Jennifer nearly loses her grip when he arches his back.

"*Careful*," hisses the woman, "you're hurting him."

They put Baby in the back seat, and the woman gets in and cradles his head in her lap.

"What are you waiting for idiot! Move it!"

"I don't know any vet clinics," says Jennifer.

"Just go!"

Jennifer drives fast, faster than she normally would, even in an emergency, but the dog doesn't look good and it begins to whine.

"There's a clinic over by the school," says the woman.

"I thought I'd hit a child."

The woman glares at the rearview. "It's only a dog is what you mean."

"He was on the road. I didn't see."

"Well, that's obvious."

The woman turns back to her dog and dots it with kisses.

The outline of the school appears, its cream and red brick exterior lit soft like a museum closed for the night. The dog lets out two faltering cries. Jennifer turns into Barker Street and pulls outside the veterinary clinic. The gates are shut and there's a large brass padlock in place.

"It's closed."

"What are you talking about?"

"There's no one here. They probably don't work afterhours."

"Find another one."

"I don't know where else to go."

"He's *dying*," cries the woman.

Jennifer looks over her shoulder into the back seat. The dog is breathing hard now, its ribcage expanding with effort.

"Use Google maps," says the woman.

Jennifer hunts through her bag, but her phone isn't there.

"I don't have my phone."

"We need a proper telephone directory."

"Do they even make them anymore?"

"A gas station will have one. Hurry up would you."

Jennifer does a U-turn and the tires squeal and she guns it back in the direction they've just come from and pulls into the empty Sunoco forecourt. Jennifer looks over her shoulder and finally gets a good look at the woman, at the uncombed wildly frizzy red hair, the flecks of black mascara stuck in the creases beneath her eyes, the nose broken sometime back.

"How's he doing?"

"For God's sake, will you just bloody move it."

Jennifer gets out and half jogs into the building. An old man is sitting behind safety glass reading a battered copy of *Game of Thrones*, a steaming mug at his elbow. A badge is pinned to his faded knit polo. Martin B.

"Martin—" says Jennifer, breathless. "I need help."

He blinks at her.

"That ain't my name. I'm just wearing his shirt." He takes a careful sip from his mug. "You want gas or what? I ain't got all day."

"I need a phone book."

He mutters something she can't hear.

"What was that?" she says.

He puts his mug down.

"I said waste of time it's so old."

"It's better than nothing."

"Hey," he says, getting off his stool and backing away from the safety glass. "What's going on? Someone hurt?"

Jennifer follows his gaze to her hands outstretched on the counter. The left one is smeared with blood.

"I hit a dog."

He looks at her doubtfully then peers through the small rectangle window leading to the forecourt to look at the car.

"We need a vet. Hurry please, he's not in good shape."

The old man looks back at Jennifer and scratches the side of his nose.

"I'll see what I can find," he says finally.

He goes out back and Jennifer hugs her shuddering body and thinks of the lamb's wool pullover in the backseat somewhere beneath the dying dog. A moth throws itself against the naked light and drops into the old man's cup. Martin B, or whatever his name is, seems to be taking forever and Jennifer can't be sure he hasn't fled out the back door, across the corn fields, to the police station to report her as some sort of murderer but then there's a rust-induced groan and the door opens and pseudo-Martin appears with a phone book.

"Like I said, it's old. Three years at least."

He glances down at the moth in his mug, a look of disgust on his face.

"Will it fit?" says Jennifer, pointing to the safety glass opening.

The man tries but the directory's too big.

"Could you look it up for me and write it down."

He nods and leafs through the pages.

"Here we go," he says. "Big Spur Road. There's an emergency clinic there."

He tears out the page and passes it through the chute. Clutching the paper in her bloody fist, Jennifer rushes out the door and gets into the car. The smell of animal feces hit her and the dog has stopped whining.

"I don't think he's going to make it," says the woman, burying her face in Baby's fur.

"I found another place," says Jennifer. "Hold on."

She drives as fast as she can, ticking off street signs until finally the Big Spur Road sign appears on her left, but the clinic, sandwiched between a barber's shop and a Mom and Pop grocery store, lies in darkness.

"It's closed."

"Go see."

"There's no one here."

"For God's sake."

The woman gets out of the car and hits the clinic door with her fist for a full two minutes. A large black man with very thick glasses wearing a Cher in concert T-shirt appears. He comes and lifts Baby from the puddle of watery diarrhea and carries the dog inside the clinic to a small examination room.

"What happened?" he says.

Under the fluorescent light Jennifer can see a bone splinter protrude from the dog's left leg and she tries not to faint.

"She hit him with her car."

"It was an accident," says Jennifer.

"You should take better care," spits the woman.

"He was on the road!"

"He doesn't know. He's only a dog."

The vet turns to Jennifer. "Why don't you wait outside?"

Jennifer goes and sits in the dark waiting room amongst the rawhide chews and catnip mice. She tastes something foul—excrement, blood and something else, her own sweat—and looks around for something to drink but there isn't anything, not even a toilet where she can wash her hands, so she waits in the dimly-lit silence studying rows of flea treatment packs and birdseed bells and tries not to read anything into the fact there's nothing but total silence coming from the examination room.

It's nearly an hour before they emerge.

"We'll watch him closely overnight, Lenise, and call you in the morning."

The dog is still alive. Jennifer allows herself to breathe.

"Thank you, doctor," says the woman flatly.

The vet pats her shoulder and asks Jennifer to take her home.

Lenise does not sit in the front, but in the back, and stares out the window in silence.

"I don't know where you live," says Jennifer, starting the engine.

"Thirty-four Pine Ridge Road."

"Really? The Jacksons' old place? That's right across the road from me. I must have missed you moving in. They've been trying to rent it for ages."

The woman says nothing so Jennifer just drives and steals looks in the rearview at the hooked-nose profile and thin-lipped mouth and hand stroking the empty space where the dog had been.

When they pull up at number thirty-four Jennifer turns around. "Lenise? Is that your name? I'm Jennifer. I just wanted to say how sorry I am about all of this, truly sorry."

Lenise pauses, her fingers coiled round the door handle. "I know you've been drinking," she says. "I can smell it."

Then she gets out of the car and walks swiftly, with purpose, up the path and into her house.

3

Lenise Jameson can't sleep. The temperature seems wildly out of control and she flips between blankets on, blankets off, blankets on, blankets off until she finally gives up and tosses them aside and lies there in the center of the bed curled up like a whorl on a fingertip. She can't get the image of him out of her head, hurt, those sweet, soulful eyes pleading for help.

When he was a puppy she'd started out so strict, determined he would not become one of those weak dogs, the ones that suffer separation anxiety the moment they lose sight of their master. Such neediness was pathetic. Any animal she owned would be independent and resilient so on the very first day she brought him home she made him sleep in another part of the house. But she hadn't been prepared for the heart-wrenching peal of his lonesome and bewildered cries, night after night, as if he was lost and afraid of the dark. On the third night Lenise gave in. She let him into her room then onto her bed, where he became a permanent, warm, heart-beating lump curled up in the arch of her back.

And now look at what had happened. All because of that drunken TRESemmé-haired bitch from across the road, Baby may never come home.

Downstairs she hears the key clatter in the lock and the front door open and close. She looks at the bedside clock, 3.30 a.m. She gets up and goes to the kitchen. Cody is there, elbows on the bench, finger-scooping out brown goop from a jar of Nutella.

"Don't start," he says, without turning around.

"I wasn't going to."

He looks up.

"What then?"

She begins to cry. He looks shocked because he has never seen her cry before, especially not like this, with the rolling, breath-robbing sobs and complete lack of restraint.

"Baby was in an accident."

"You're joking."

She shakes her head and can't get the words out.

"What happened?" he says.

"Over the road, the neighbor. She hit him with her car, he's at the vet. I don't think he's going to make it."

Cody stands there, arms by his side, looking useless.

"He'll be okay."

"He won't."

She wipes her nose and pauses.

"Cody, there's something else."

"What?"

"I noticed money missing again."

He stares at her, then turns to walk up the stairs and she knows she has lost him.

"I already told you I'm looking for a job," he says.

"I'm just asking because I'm going to need it for the vet."

"Make the neighbor pay. It's her responsibility."

"I wouldn't take a penny from that woman," she spits.

"You're always on my back. It's not easy out there."

"We've all had to adjust. Cody, please, don't walk away when I'm trying to talk to you, it isn't polite."

"I'm not three, Mother," he says.

He shuts his bedroom door, leaving Lenise to stand alone in the hallway. She doesn't go in because once the door is shut, that's it, their unspoken rule is in force—if he's in his room she will not disturb him. After all, he's a young man, twenty-four-years-old, and needs his privacy. But tonight Lenise wants to heave the door open and force him speak to her, make him understand their already bad financial situation is made worse by him. She is doing all that is humanely possible to support them but he needs to realize she isn't invincible and, by the way, doesn't he know she's given him the best years, the very best years of her life, so perhaps he could show a little more gratitude. Sometimes he is so much like his father she can't actually bear to look at him but she forces herself to anyway, because he is her son and that's what you do for people you love. All she wants is for him not to take, no, *steal* from her. That isn't too much to ask after all she has done for him.

But Lenise says none of those things. Instead she pulls her robe tight and goes back to bed.

The next day she feels no better and wishes she could stay in her room but someone has to pay the bills. She looks in the mirror and clenches her teeth as she pulls the comb through the rough and unruly hair she has cursed everyday of her life. At a bar once some wanna-be rapper type told her she looked like the serial killer Aileen Wuornos, only with ginger hair. She had laughed and Tupac had looked surprised because he hadn't meant it as a compliment. But Lenise had been called far worse. Her former husband had frequently referred to her as "pig" or "dog" so at least Aileen Wuornos was the right kind of species. And Wuornos was a woman of course, a strong, dangerous woman, who didn't take bullshit from anyone.

"You better watch out then, P Diddly," Lenise had said, inching close to his gold-hooped ear lobe. "Because I may have more in common with Ms. Wuornos than just looks."

Then she had clicked off a round with her finger and thumb, and just for a moment, the guy's eyes opened a touch too wide.

"Crazy bitch," he had said, walking off.

Lenise couldn't care less if she never looked in another mirror again and wouldn't even bother with make-up if it wasn't for the job, but in America it was expected you look "your best" or "professional" and for a woman that meant mascara and lipstick. She leans into her reflection and applies a layer of amber nights and thinks about how her teeth are in dire need of attention but that with her bank balance a trip to the dentist was not going to happen anytime soon.

Once she's done with the make-up, Lenise slips on her Brook River Real Estate blazer and, as always, experiences a tiny burst of pride. Yes, she had to tell a few white lies to get the job, mainly about holding similar roles back in South Africa, but that's what a person had to do in order to get ahead in life. It was called being resourceful. Not that the job had been an out and out success, and truth be told, some days it truly felt like she was getting nowhere. It had already been two years and she was hardly raking it in. Nevertheless, it was a vast improvement on handing out fries to slobs at Cheetos Burritos and she was certain her luck would turn any day now. It was only a matter of time before a prime listing or referral would come her way.

She walks past Cody's bedroom. He isn't up yet and she fights the urge to slam her fist into the door, at the fact she is sure he is at it again, even though he'd promised her a million times he would stop, but the money didn't grow legs and walk out of the house, did it? Lenise will have to deal with that later. Right now, there were more important things to think about, like Baby, alone and frightened in some steel cage.

The vet still hasn't called but the open home is at 10 a.m. and she has to leave so she puts her cell in her pocket, shoves the Brook River sign in the back of the station wagon and heads to Fitchburg.

When Lenise arrives at the four-bedroom colonial she's annoyed to see no one has cut the grass. The empty house was another mortgagee sale and had been in a general state of disrepair since the bank kicked the owner out nine months ago. She forces the sign into the hard earth, and goes inside to open a few windows to air the place out and prays someone will show. She needs this sale because last week she had to withdraw money from her credit card for groceries.

Lenise is considering a quick cigarette round the back when a blue SUV pulls up. Mike and Missy are from Texas and seem particularly interested.

"Great natural light. Lots of storage," says Lenise.

"Where y'all from?" asks Missy, noting the accent.

"Jo'Burg."

"Come again?"

"South Africa."

"No kidding."

Lenise hears a loud male voice downstairs she recognizes instantly. Bert Radley. A sanctimonious shyster who would sell his own mother if he thought there was a buck in it. The breathtaking audacity of it—to bring a client to view a house during *her* open home.

"If you'll excuse me for a moment," she says to Mike and Missy.

Lenise finds Bert Radley in the kitchen with a Korean couple.

"May I have a word?" she says.

"Certainly."

They leave the couple to inspect the size of the pantry and go into the hallway.

"This is highly inappropriate, Radley."

"They asked to see it, what could I do?"

"I'm going to lay a complaint."

"This isn't personal, Lenise."

"You owe me."

"I don't owe you anything."

"I could've had your license revoked after your get together in the Clarkson property."

"I don't know what you're talking about."

"You were in the client's bed," she smiles. "I saw you."

A sheen develops on his forehead. He glances at the kitchen.

"So that's the way you're going to play it?" he says.

Then he pauses and looks past her shoulder.

"Dirty business, this real estate," he says, walking off.

Lenise turns. The Texan couple stares at her from the doorway.

"It's not what you think," she says. "He slept with a prostitute."

But they won't listen and get into their trendy SUV and drive away, along with her commission.

Lenise waits out the rest of the hour but no one else shows. As she's returning the sign to the trunk, her cellphone rings. She looks at the phone, buzzing in her hand like an electric razor, but can't bring herself to answer it. Five more pulses and the hum stops. She gets in her car and stares out the windscreen. On the road, a black-backed gull plucks at the smashed carcass of a hedgehog. Lenise starts the engine and heads to the clinic.

4

It's difficult to concentrate and Jennifer's hoping Mrs. M won't notice she's distracted. Her mind is on last night's disaster. Was it three or four, the number of drinks she'd had? Jennifer can't recall. And just when she's settled on the idea it was three, doubt creeps back in and it's more like four, maybe even five. The fact she can't remember without struggling is probably a good sign it's five. But even if that's the case, they were weak, hardly any tequila all. More sugar than tequila, in fact.

Jennifer keeps telling herself it could've happened to anyone. It was dark, the dog was dark. How was she meant to see? That's what she plans on telling police. She's been waiting for them. It feels like she's been holding her breath since last night. But so far, nothing, which was almost worse. Then again maybe it wasn't so bad, because the more time that passed, the more chance the liquor would dilute in her bloodstream, the more difficult it would be to test. She can't believe she's thinking like this. A criminal. A shirker of responsibility. And what if the dog hadn't made it? God.

Now she's got the pitiful state of the dog inside her head as she tells Mrs. M to lean into the chin rest of the ophthalmoscope. The woman's a trooper because she has a small roll of Cert mints tucked inside her fist, and she's been sucking on two at a time because she doesn't want her breath to stink for Jennifer.

"That's it, just relax," says Jennifer, directing the pin point of light into Mrs. Mendoza's left eye.

Jennifer tries not to yawn because Mrs. M will think she's bored when it's actually due to lack of sleep. After she got in from the accident, Hank was not waiting up as expected. She had braced herself for an argument, the slamming of doors, recriminations, but he was in bed, asleep. She slipped in next to him, which was probably a mistake, because she was so wired and it must have shown because Hank murmured, "Jen, you're shaking, what's wrong?" and she said, "nothing, just cold" and then he held her, engulfing her in his arms, until she stopped the post-traumatic shudder thing.

"Sometimes I love you so much it scares me," he said.

She was going to tell him then, pour it all out, about the dog, even the reckless kiss, that she was sorry for ignoring him lately and all this crazy midlife shit, but she couldn't bring herself to do it.

And this morning he asked, "Where did you get to last night?"

She avoided his eyes and said, "It was Rosemary's birthday and we went for a drink. I lost track of time."

"I thought something had happened to you, Jen." He paused. "No more fighting, okay? And I'm going to try harder about the food thing with McKenzie, too."

Then he handed her a cup of coffee just how she liked it, hot enough to burn your nose, and she'd forgotten how good he could be and she wanted to hug him and hold on but that would be strange given their recent difficulties so she kept her hands to herself and watched him get dressed then depart to chase up another possible lead on a job.

After he left, she put on her clothes and went down to the kitchen where McKenzie was about to dump a full box of Chocolate Crunch Cereal into her bowl.

"Dad said I could."

Jennifer swiped it out of her hands. "You may have your father wrapped around your little finger, madam, but not me. And would you take off that silly cap."

Jennifer flinched. She hadn't meant to sound so critical.

"This is just as good," she said, placing the *Light and Low Bran* in front of McKenzie.

And there was that sullen face again, but Jennifer ignored it, and pulled up the blinds and looked out the kitchen window at the house across the road and saw no sign of the strange, woolly-haired woman, but her heart began to beat fast just the same.

"Did you know we have new neighbors?"

"They moved in last week."

"I didn't notice."

"You never notice anything," said McKenzie, getting up.

"They might have kids."

"You don't need to find friends for me, Mom."

Jennifer looked at that plump moon face and limp strawberry-blonde hair so different from her own. She used to think she'd taken the wrong baby home from the hospital until Hank assured her that he had an elderly Aunt that looked exactly like McKenzie.

"That's not what I meant," said Jennifer.

"Can I have some lunch money?"

"Over there," Jennifer pointing to a salad wrap and apple on the bench.

"Apples hurt my teeth."

Jennifer had heard this countless times before and it sparked the memory of the mandarins she'd stopped to buy last night from the all-nighter grocery store on the way home from the club because she'd wanted to avoid hearing the apples hurt my teeth excuse the next day.

"Wait there," said Jennifer.

She went into the garage to retrieve the mandarins and was nearly sick when she saw the blood on the fender. She got a rag and wiped off the mess and told herself she wasn't trying to hide anything, but who wants to drive around with blood on their car? She returned to the kitchen and gave McKenzie three mandarins and told her she better get off to school and then rang the garage and asked if they could fit her in.

And as she drove to the repair shop all she could think about was how the incident was one of those "brick moments" Oprah talked about. A wake-up call. Get-your-act-together type of thing because next time the wall comes down on top of your head and knocks you clean out. It could've been a kid, although a dog was bad enough. It was a sure sign Jennifer needed to shape up and change her ways.

Jennifer peers into the scope. She's close enough to see the pores in Mrs. Mendonza's cheek and smell peppermint and garlic and something Jennifer doesn't recognize, tomatoes maybe. She never gets used to the closeness. It seems like an invasion, like she has somehow taken the place of a lover. Mrs. M's iris is a beach shell worn down by the surf—gluey and swollen. The fibers of the optic nerve splay out brilliantly like dozens of tiny red-inked tributaries on a gas station map. Not good.

"You can sit back now," says Jennifer.

The older lady peels a mint from the silver foil and places it in her mouth while Jennifer makes notes.

"That your daughter?" asks Mrs. M, nodding at the photograph on Jennifer's desk.

It was taken on a day hike at Oak Valley, Jennifer's attempt to encourage McKenzie to be more active. McKenzie is crimson-cheeked and sweaty, her chubby twelve-year-old face half-hidden by that ridiculous Cleveland Indians baseball cap. McKenzie had never played baseball in her life. She'd never even watched a game.

"Her father gave her that cap," says Jennifer. "We've never even been to Cleveland."

"She's very pretty."

"What about you? Do you have kids?"

"A son. He lives in Texas."

Mrs. Mendoza offers Jennifer a mint.

"I'm good," says Jennifer.

Jennifer closes her folder and pauses. This was the part she hated. This was why she would not choose the human eye if she could begin again.

"Have you heard of macular degeneration, Mrs. Mendoza?"

"Dios Mio! You're telling me I'm going blind?"

Jennifer looks at her pretty olive skin and nicely fixed curly black hair and beach shell eyes that will soon close off the world around her.

"Vision impaired."

"Blind."

"Legally blind. There's a difference. You'll still have some sight."

"I don't believe it." Mrs. Mendoza looks at her hands. "Are you sure? How can you know for certain?"

Jennifer says nothing, gives it a few seconds to sink in.

"You must have had trouble with your sight for some time. If you'd come sooner, we could have done more—medication, surgery. We still can try some of those things but I want to be frank, your condition is highly advanced. Significant nerve damage has already occurred and there's cell loss."

"English please."

"It's bad."

"How long?

"It's difficult to say."

"Try."

"It varies. I know that's not helpful but I really can't be any more specific than that."

"You know I'm just going to Google it."

"Five years, maybe, before it gets really poor."

Mrs. Mendoza stares numbly at some midpoint in the distance. Outside a truck passes and rattles the windows.

"I was going to travel."

Jennifer reaches for Mrs. Mendoza's hand, still balled in a fist, mints at its center.

"There's time."

Mrs. Mendoza lifts her head and looks past Jennifer, out the small picture window.

"Sometimes I think the morning light could be butter."

"There are courses you can take to prepare," says Jennifer. "Arrange for a helper dog."

"I hate dogs."

Jennifer pauses.

"Is there someone I can call? Your son?"

"I'll be alright."

Jennifer gives her a tissue and Mrs. Mendoza wipes roughly at each eye. Jennifer wonders about the last thing they will ever see.

"Mrs. M?"

"Yes."

"Can I give you a hug?"

After Mrs. M there were two cases of eye ulcers, a new pair of reading glasses, subcapsular cataracts and a thirteen-year-old girl called Georgia whose special effect contact lenses had fused to her sclera, but no police. The neighbor, Lenise, hadn't said anything after all. Jennifer glances at the phone, thinks about calling the vet and her stomach contracts in a spasm. What if the dog hadn't made it? But death wasn't inevitable, was it? After all, it may have only been a badly fractured leg and dogs weren't like horses that had to be put down because of broken limbs. Even a three-legged dog wasn't an impossibility these days.

She picks up her car and on her way home calls into *Treasure Trove* and buys the most expensive gift box she can find. It is more hamper than box, filled with luxury food items like handmade Swiss chocolates, sugared almonds, preserved Turkish lemons and goose liver pate, all done up in cellophane and an enormous golden bow. Then she walks the block to Pet Smart and purchases a rubber chicken chew toy, a bag of beef bones and a brand-new leather collar.

It's a little after six when she pulls into her driveway and there's no movement at Lenise's house but a beat-up station wagon is parked haphazardly outside. Jennifer takes two belly-deep breaths and gets out of the car, hugging the gift boxes, one under each arm, and crosses the road.

She faces the hardwood door and the large brass pigeon knocker and puts down the box of dog treats to extend a trembling hand and raps the beak against its round, medal-sized counterpart.

A man of about twenty answers. Like Lenise, there's a mop of dark ginger hair. The family resemblance is striking.

"I'm Jen from across the road."

He glances at the packages. "I know who you are."

"Is Lenise here?"

He looks over his shoulder into the house.

"She loved that dog," he says.

Jennifer's stomach sinks.

"Oh God," she says. "He died."

"And guess whose fault that is."

Jennifer doesn't know what to say. "It was an accident. It was dark, he was on the road, I couldn't see."

"My father used to say there's no such thing as accidents, just carelessness."

"I'm sorry."

"You should be."

He slams the door in her face. The brass pigeon barely misses the tip of her nose.

Later, just as Jennifer, Hank and McKenzie are finishing dinner, there's banging on the front door.

"I'll go," says Jennifer, rising out of her chair.

It's Lenise, her face wild with grief.

"You think you can buy me off with trinkets?"

Jennifer is mortified. "Buy you off? God no, I was just trying to say I'm sorry."

"They had to cut off his leg!"

"Oh Jesus."

Jennifer hears Hank behind her, and he shoulders his way to the front.

"Who the hell are you and why are you screaming at my wife?" he demands.

Jennifer touches his arm. "Hank it's okay. She's our neighbor."

"They cut off his leg and he bled to death!" yells Lenise.

"What is she talking about, whose leg got cut off?" says Hank.

"Your sweet innocent wife killed my dog," says Lenise.

"*What?*" says Hank.

"It was an accident."

"She was drunk," says Lenise.

Hank looks at Jennifer. "Is that true?"

"Of course not."

"Oh, so you're a drunk and a liar," says Lenise.

"Listen to me you nutcase," says Hank, getting close to Lenise, "you better get off my property before I call the police."

"You'd like me to leave?" she says.

"You heard."

"Go right now?"

"Get out."

Hank tries pushing the door closed but Lenise stops it with her foot, and for one terrible moment Jennifer thinks the woman might pull a gun.

"Stay away from me and my son," says Lenise, eyes widening briefly as if to punctuate the sentence.

She throws them a parting, icy stare and strides back to her house, but not before she kicks over their trash can.

"Why didn't you tell me?" says Hank.

"Just don't," says Jennifer, pushing past him to gather the trash.

5

In the week since Baby died Lenise has managed to avoid the neighbors. Sometimes she sees the woman, Jennifer, go to work in the morning, dressed in those expensive clothes, sipping coffee from a reusable Starbucks mug, pretty face framed by the windscreen. Lenise wonders where she works and pictures an Art gallery or magazine editor's office or maybe a trendy boutique.

The husband, with his thick neck and receder so fashionably shaved, comes and goes at all hours in his oversized pickup truck. He has an overbearing sense of entitlement about him and Lenise suspects he is the type who likes to slam cupboard doors and thump walls when he doesn't get his own way.

She imagines them at night, in their fancy, pocket-sprung bed, whispering about her, the crazy neighbor, his arm protectively curled around Jennifer's midriff and him murmuring that he'll keep her safe from that nutcase with the dead dog while he hitches up Jennifer's nightgown and kneels behind her, searching out her waxy petals, readying himself to mount.

She knows they must think she has it in for them after losing control like that. But she was grief-stricken, who could blame her? On any account, it wouldn't hurt for them to be a little fearful. There ought to be some consequence for Baby's tragic demise. Let them think the worst. Let them worry themselves to sleep. It was the very least they deserved.

Lenise crosses her legs and smooths down the front of her dress. She does not wish to waste any more time thinking about them and pulls her thoughts back to herself, back to the unpleasant and immovable fact that not only is she without her beloved dog but that today is also her birthday.

She's come to hate birthdays. They are a reminder of everything she has never achieved, like the failure of her childhood dream to become a gemologist and travel the globe and source the world's most beautiful gems, quantifying and cataloguing, and make her mark and become a highly regarded expert in her field. But she never finished high school and was married and pregnant with Cody by the time she was eighteen and tonight, as she sits alone in her darkening kitchen, Lenise tells herself she is probably lucky to have that.

Headlights arc across the living room wall and her heart leaps hopefully then dies just as quickly when the car carries on up the road. This morning Cody told her to put on her best dress because he was taking her out for her birthday. She knew dinner was his way to make up for what happened. The entire sorry incident had been unfortunate, but Lenise couldn't abide by Cody's behavior and she had told him in as many words when she saw the two females, half undressed, messing about in his bedroom.

"This isn't a brothel, you stupid boy, get them out!"

Cody didn't take too kindly to being told what to do by his mother in front of his floosies, puffing out his chest and growling at Lenise to mind her own business. *Mind her own business?* Who the hell did he think he was? It was her bloody house. Lenise had spit out every hateful thing she could think of, every minor annoyance, every grievance, every little insult he had inflicted upon her since his birth. Then she began on the things his son-of-a bitch father had done, like the time he had driven down a dusty, weed-infested back road and pushed her over the bonnet of their car and raped her with his gun. You are no better than him, she yelled at Cody, jabbing a finger into his chest.

The girls had quickly strapped into their bras and Cody tried to gather his things but she didn't let up and trailed him around the room until she got in his way and he pushed her, which made her madder than hell, so she came at him and he shoved her off and his elbow connected with the bone of her right eye.

"You asshole!" she screamed, holding her eye, but he was already out the door and gunning it down the driveway.

She hadn't heard from him for three days, until this morning, when he turns up with an unsigned Hallmark card and the promise of dinner.

Lenise checks her watch again and drains her glass and accepts the fact he isn't coming. Delving into her handbag, she locates the fuchsia pearl lipstick roaming loose amongst the tampons and grocery receipts, applies a generous smear then leaves.

The bar is crowded, which is good because if anyone asks she can point to the dance floor and say she is here with a friend. She takes a seat and orders a Bloody Mary. By the looks of it, they are having a Hawaiian-themed night. Coconuts hang in bunches from the overhead racks and the bartender is wearing a multi-colored plastic lei and a stiff grass skirt over his regular clothes.

A man sits down on the stool next to her. "Ever been there?" he says.

"Where?"

"The great Aloha State."

He is at least twenty years her senior and Lenise can tell he rates himself. He is wearing a cowboy style shirt, open-necked, and has too much chest hair. He extends his hand.

"Ray."

"Tania."

"That an accent?"

"South Africa."

"Well, nice to meet you South Africa."

His eyes drop to her cleavage. She looks away as he roams the rest of her body. She drains her glass and orders another.

"Knocking those back," says Ray.

"It's my birthday."

"No kidding."

"I wouldn't kid about a thing like that."

"Nothing wrong with a more mature woman."

His hand lands on her thigh.

"Who you calling mature, Grandpa."

She means it as an insult but he simply laughs.

"Ain't no substitute for experience, darling."

The hand slides further up and makes its way under the hem of her dress.

"So what are you into, Tania?" he says, rolling his tongue behind his lower lip.

Lenise doesn't know why she does it, but she goes with him to the car park, behind the green WM dumpster and drops to her knees and takes him in her mouth. He is as hard as a bone.

"Oh yeah, darling, that's the sweet spot right there."

His cold fingers cup the back of her head and he jack-hammers against her. Her knees hurt from the ragged concrete, but she continues on, propelled by some perverse sense of duty to finish what she has started.

"Holy Jesus!" he gasps.

Her mouth fills with salt and sweat. Then, just as quickly, he steps back and zips up his fly.

"Thanks for obliging, darling."

He peels two twenties from his money bill and tucks it down the front of her bra.

"Happy Birthday," he says.

When she gets home, Cody still isn't there. She leaves off the lights and climbs the stairs. Whatever alcohol-induced pleasure she has managed to gain over the course of the night has left and a headache now drums at the base of her skull.

The bedroom curtains are open and she sits down and stares at the moon. Beyond the houses, Pine Ridge Forest is a dark unchartered wilderness. Looking at it now, she thinks of home and the great African Savannah.

Across the road something catches her eye. Movement in the upstairs window at the neighbor's house. The girl's room. There's a faint amber glow as if a child's night light has been left on. Lenise can barely see a thing, just shapeless shadows moving about. Then a man steps into a strip of moonlight, the husband, then the daughter, and her blood runs cold.

6

A car door slams and Lenise stirs. Morning. Too fresh and bright. At first, she's mystified as to why she is in her bedroom facing the window, slumped in this rattan chair, left forearm indented with the braid of the wicker. Thoughts are loose stones jiggling round in her head. She thinks of a man, his smell and feel, and glances at the slight graze on her right knee. Over her shoulder, the bed covers are still in place, corners tucked tight.

She raises her head and looks across the road and realizes her mistake. Not here, but there.

The window to the girl's room is black because light hits it the wrong way. Lenise rakes her memory but everything is too vague and unreachable. She forces her brain to engage, trying to needle the images to click into place. Then something. A smile, delivered with such sincerity that at first you could be fooled into believing it was not the act of treachery that it was, and a flash of white skin as the father lifts his chin to the ceiling.

Lenise becomes aware of the chill pricking her skin. Could she be making it up? Was she putting things together that weren't meant to fit?

She remembers her phone. It had slipped beneath her thigh in the night and she retrieves it, fumbling with the apps, until she gets to the camera, the gallery, the photos. Baby, panting happily, looks back at her. Lenise swipes at it furiously. Images flashes past. Paws. Ears. Baby on his back in the grass. Her accidental feet. Then she realizes it's the wrong app and she has to go all the way back to the start until she locates the movie camera icon. She touches it and the screen comes to life—mostly just the sound of her own breath, but there are moving images too. The jarred, hazy impressions of two figures. Grey ghosts. Not much to anyone else but irrefutable confirmation to her.

The garage door shudders upward and the woman called Jennifer backs out the drive. Lenise glimpses that attractive, Starbuck-sipping face. If only she knew what was going on beneath that pretty nose. The front door opens and Lenise leans back from view. It's the daughter, back pack across her shoulder, iPod on, traipsing down the pavement to school. Lenise fights the urge to open the window and call out. But what would she say?

Lenise turns back to the house and the husband emerges. He springs up and down on the front step, gives his quads a stretch, shakes out his hands like he's a real pro. Lenise watches as he takes off, his feet striking the ground at a decent pace, chest out like he's a big somebody. But he can think what he likes, she knows what he is.

Long after he's gone, Lenise just sits here, picking at a loose curl on the arm of the chair. There are important decisions to make.

In the end, she decides to wait. Watch and wait. For three days and four nights she observes their comings and goings, the ebb and flow of their domestic life—groceries on Tuesday, taking out the trash on Wednesday, mowing the grass on Thursday. Lenise has some necessary duties for work to attend to, and of course there are personal ablutions, but apart from that she is parked on the chair, flask of sweet tea, an ashtray and packet of cigarettes by her side.

It is hum drum and boring but she has to be sure: she can't accuse anyone of anything unless she is sure.

She doesn't like to spy. In fact, like any good South African citizen, she has been raised to look the other way. Over there, other people's business was never your concern, no matter how many broken noses you saw or bribes you witnessed. The golden rule was: do not tell tales. The one time she had, when she was ten and saw Nathan De Kock cheat on a mathematics test, her father had slapped her backside and she could not sit down for a week.

The girl's bedroom with its pop star posters was, of course, her primary focus, especially at night. Sometimes the curtains would be pulled, other times not. Sometimes the girl would be on her bed reading or brushing her hair or tidying her room. Other times she would sing into a bejeweled microphone and perform some sort of synchronized dance—two steps forward, arm above the head, two steps back, side turn—as if she is a one of those tweeny stars with one million followers and a bank account big enough to support Nigeria. And sometimes the girl would come right up close to the window, lean her elbows on the sill and stare mutely at the stars. Lenise had never seen a human being look so alone.

But the father, the false protector and taker of innocence, never goes into the room again, and Lenise begins to doubt herself because she can't be sure she really remembers anything and thinks that maybe it was all just a result of the drink or stress or a vivid imagination, and the more time that passes what she does remember seems to fade and become more fiction than fact.

She replays that clip over and over, zooming in and out, trying to make the picture sharper, brighter, but it doesn't do any good. She knows an objective person would not see anything. It's too dark and amorphous. You can't even tell there are two human beings. Fed up and bone tired, she nearly throws in the towel.

Then on Friday night it happens again.

Her stomach turns at the sight.

Even so, Lenise allows herself a brief smile, not because she is happy he is at it once more, but because she was right.

Now that she's certain, Lenise accepts she owes a responsibility, a duty of care toward the girl. The only question is how to proceed. Once again she had filmed "the activity" with her phone, but disappointingly, just like before, the phone wasn't up to the task of a night time shoot. Therefore, it was not a simple matter of anonymously slipping a copy to the appropriate authorities. There was really no evidence apart from her say-so. Unfortunately she will have to go in person.

She's here now, driving around the block for the fourth time. There are plenty of parking spaces, she just keeps changing her mind. She wants to help the girl, she truly does, but the police and she are not natural companions. Finally, when the gas runs dangerously low she bites the bullet and pulls into a parking space outside the station.

When she gets inside there's a man with frayed gloves and soiled jeans at the vending machine checking the dispenser for coins. When he sees her staring, he withdraws his grubby hand and gives her the finger.

"What you looking at," he barks, sloping out the doors.

"Never mind, Angus," says the policewoman behind the counter. "He's a pussy cat really."

Lenise studies the uniform, the blueness of it, the shiny buttons and starched collar.

"Need help?"

Lenise looks up. "Pardon?"

"Do you want to lodge a complaint?" The policewoman announces each word as if Lenise is deaf.

"No, report a crime."

"Same difference."

"Oh."

The policewoman slips some sort of form on a clipboard and passes it over.

"Fill this out."

Lenise takes a seat and stares at the form. Incident Report is written in big black typescript across the top. Other headings call for a description of the offence, date, time, place, contact details of the complainant. For the first time, Lenise realizes she will have to put her name to something and be on record in the United States Justice system as an informant.

She understands now how stupid she's been. She thought she would just come and say, *I saw something bad over the road, a father messing about with his daughter, I think you should check it out.* But this was America, with a Constitution, amendment rights, chains of command, processes and procedures. Cops need clear evidence before they will look into anything. It isn't like back home, where they would just take dad out back and give him a thrashing he would never forget.

She stares at the spot where her name was supposed to go. And what good would it do? The father will just deny it. Most likely the daughter, too (shame will do that to a person). Both will say she is making it up and she'll end up being the one in trouble.

Lenise gets to her feet and returns the clipboard to policewoman.

"I made a mistake," she says and turns around and walks out the door.

When Lenise gets home she sees the filthy bastard leave the house. She could swear he is whistling as he gets into his truck and drives off.

After he's gone, she reaches into the back seat to retrieve her groceries and spots the girl, returning from school. The child is in her own world, or pretending to be, and walks along the pavement with head bent, face barely visible beneath that strange-looking cap. Lenise watches her walk up the steps and put the key in the front door.

Lenise calls out, "Hey there!"

The girl turns round and Lenise half-jogs across the road.

"I'm looking for my cat," says Lenise, breathless. "Have you seen him?"

The girl peers up from underneath the peak of her cap and shakes her head.

"You sure?" says Lenise.

The girl pauses. "What does he look like?"

That throws Lenise. "Ginger and white."

"Ginger?"

"Like my hair."

"Oh, you mean red."

"Yes, red, that's correct."

"I haven't seen any cat," says the girl.

"Shouldn't you be in school?"

"It's four o'clock."

"Is your mother home?"

The girl looks concerned. "She's sorry about the dog."

"I know."

Lenise hesitates. What is she supposed to say? I saw you in your room. I saw everything.

"Tell your mother."

"Tell Mom what?"

Lenise looks at the girl.

"Your father, what he does to you."

The girl's lips part in shock.

"That's all," says Lenise, turning and walking back to her house.

7

The change is barely perceptible, but Jennifer notices. The first to go is the light, a little less in the morning, then at night. The days are cooler, too. It won't be long before she needs slippers to warm her feet. Jennifer thinks about this as she cleans her equipment. The suffocating man-made heat of winter. The mud that will get trampled into the house. The dog that won't be chasing squirrels in the icy dark.

She never knew she could feel this bad about someone else's pet. After the trash kicking incident, Jennifer thought she might be in for neighbors at war. But all had been quiet, eerily quiet, in fact, almost as if no one lived at number thirty-four. Jennifer knew Lenise was still there only because of the occasional flash of red hair in the downstairs window, or glimpse of that gaudy mustard-yellow Brook River blazer as the station wagon chugged off down Pine Ridge Road.

Hank seemed hell bent on not letting Jennifer live the thing down. He bought it up every chance he could, like last night, just as she was falling asleep, he said out of the blue, "Not only do I have a fucking nutcase living next door to me, my own wife won't even tell me when she's in a car accident."

"Not again, Hank."

"You could have been seriously hurt."

"Go to sleep."

She felt him tense. "I don't like it when you hide things from me."

"We're not joined at the hip. I don't have to tell you everything."

That made him angry and he sat up and turned on the light.

"Now see, it's that type of comment that gets me worried."

She groaned. "Please turn off the light."

"That type of comment makes me think you're keeping secrets."

She sighed. "There's no one else, Hank."

He pulled the covers away from her head and pointed a finger in her face.

"So help me God, I don't know what I'd do if there was."

She didn't say anything and he seemed to relax.

"I'm sorry," she said finally. "I should have told you."

"Am I really being unreasonable?" he said.

"No," she said. "I was ashamed. It wasn't exactly my finest hour."

He paused.

"I don't know what I'd do if I ever lost you," he said.

She looked at him and saw the little boy standing next to his mother's grave with a bunch of broken daisies.

"You and McKenzie mean everything to me," he said.

"I know."

He leant over and kissed her cheek.

"Get some sleep," he said.

Then he lay back down and turned off the light.

Jennifer finishes wiping down the slit lamp with isopropanol solution and picks up the applanation tonometer and gives each component a careful rub, leaving the prism until last, which she lowers into a tiny bath of hydrogen peroxide to sit for at least fifteen minutes.

By the time the autoclave clicks off, it's nearly three. She catches Rosemary looking at want ads on the internet, but pretends not to notice, calling over her shoulder on the way out of the clinic that she's off to pick up McKenzie to take her to her monthly appointment with the nutritionist.

It's dead on three twenty when Jennifer pulls up outside the red-bricked building. Kids pour from the large green doors and Jennifer keeps a look out for the familiar yellow back pack and, of course, that dreadful cap. The flood soon turns to a trickle and McKenzie is nowhere to be seen. Jennifer waits, eyes fixed to the entrance.

At ten to four Jennifer gets out of the car, crosses the road and goes inside. The hallways are empty. Her heart begins to skip. Jennifer digs for her phone and calls McKenzie's cell. Straight to voice mail. She punches in Hank's number.

"I can't find McKenzie."

"What?"

"I'm at the school."

"She's here with me," he says.

Jennifer exhales. "Jesus, Hank."

"She wasn't feeling well at lunchtime and tried leaving the school grounds to walk home but a teacher stopped her. They called me to come get her."

"Well thanks for telling me." Jennifer looks down at her hand and sees a clenched fist.

"McKenzie never said you guys had plans," he says.

"She had an appointment with the nutritionist."

"How was I supposed to know?"

"Not your fault, I get it," snaps Jennifer. "Is she okay?"

"Stomach ache, growing pains, who knows? She seems fine now."

Jennifer rings off, pissed at him even though he wasn't really to blame.

On the way home, she stops at the grocery store and buys grapes and a pouch of organic chicken noodle soup, but when she gets home she sees Hank has beaten her to it by the looks of the wrappers of Little Debbie snack cakes and smear of frosting on McKenzie's upper lip.

"Where's Dad?" says Jennifer.

McKenzie shrugs without taking her eyes from the home renovation show playing on the TV.

"Shower, I guess."

Jennifer sits down. "How are you feeling?"

"Okay," says McKenzie, swatting sponge crumbs from the front of her Katy Perry t-shirt.

"I bought soup."

"I'm not hungry."

"Why didn't you call me to come get you?"

"You were at work."

"I know, but if you need my help, it's okay to call. You shouldn't be leaving the school grounds on your own."

McKenzie tugs her t-shirt over her belly. There's a pale strawberry splodge on Katy Perry's eye.

"I don't like that lady," she says.

"What lady?"

"The neighbor. She gives me the creeps."

Jennifer frowns. "You mean Lenise?"

"Can't you make her move away?"

"Is that what this is about? When she flipped out about the dog? Did that scare you?"

"You should get a restraining order or something."

"She's a hothead, that's for sure, but I don't think she's dangerous. She was upset about losing her dog, which is understandable."

"Well, I don't like her," says McKenzie.

"I'm sure she won't be bothering us again, I'm not exactly flavor of the month."

McKenzie looks at her. "Why do you have to be right all the time?"

Jennifer feels a sting. "What to do you mean?"

"You never want to hear anything I've got to say. It's like my opinion doesn't count."

"That's not true."

"See?" says McKenzie, voice rising. "You're not even willing to think that what I'm saying might be true. You just ignore it right off the bat. I mean, why should I bother saying anything at all."

Jennifer looks at McKenzie. "Why would you think that? I try and talk with you all the time."

McKenzie crosses her arms. "You mean talk *at* me."

"Well, I'm sorry if you think that."

McKenzie turns away and here comes that sullen face again.

"We can talk now," says Jennifer.

McKenzie gets to her feet and walks to the door and looks back at Jennifer.

"You think you know everything but you don't know anything at all."

8

Cody catches her staring out the window.

"You've been standing there for nearly an hour."

"No, I haven't."

"Yeah, you have."

Even though she denies it, what Cody says is true: she's barely taken her eyes off the house across the road these last three days. She's waiting for a sign, any sign to indicate the girl has told her mother, some change in routine or late-night departure, the father rushing from the house with a hastily assembled bag, some yelling or wailing or slamming of doors. But all Lenise sees is business as usual—Jennifer leaving for work in her fine clothes, the daughter going to school, the husband cutting the grass.

She has seen the girl, though, twice, both times at night staring out her bedroom window right into Lenise's room, backlit like some kind of strange angel in a baseball cap and blue pajamas. Lenise can't tell if it's some sort of challenge or plea for silence. Nonetheless, it's unnerving, both of them knowing what has gone on but neither of them saying a word.

She knows it's stupid, but Lenise is beginning to feel like the tormented one, like she alone has the power to change the course of history for this girl and her mother, whether she stays silent or sings like a bird.

"I've got a job interview," says Cody.

"Oh."

"As a ranch hand."

"Sounds nice."

"Are you even listening to me?"

"Where?" says Lenise, eyes still fixed to the window.

"Minnesota."

"You're leaving?"

"I'll visit."

"No, you won't."

"What's got into you? Is this about the dinner, because I already told you I was sorry."

She turns to look at him.

"This may surprise you, Cody, but the world doesn't revolve around you."

He throws down the TV guide.

"I'm sick of this shit," he says.

He thumps upstairs like a four-year-old, slamming his bedroom door. He doesn't understand, of course. Why would he? She hasn't breathed a word to anyone about the incident. It's none of his concern and he would most likely tell her to mind her own business and focus on her own problems and obligations, like her seemingly never-ending obligations to him.

Well, she has news for Cody. Right now there are more important things to think about than his childish needs and unlikely job prospects, especially today because Lenise knows on Saturdays the father takes the girl out somewhere, some morning sports thing by the looks of the baseball bat that always accompanies them. And just like clockwork, the garage door opens dot on ten and out they drive, the two of them sitting in front, normal as apple pie. No one would suspect a thing for they look like any other father and daughter pair, heading out for some weekend fun, maybe stopping for fries and a soda on the way home. That's what disturbs Lenise the most, the ordinariness of this entire sorry thing.

She watches the pick-up drive away down the road and a shudder runs through her. Who knows where they are really going? What if there was no sports thing after all, just some isolated playground or backwoods hut or public restroom where he can get his fill.

Not long after they leave, Jennifer appears in the front yard, a bright purple scarf looped around her neck, grey hoodie tied roughly at her waist. She shakes open a large black plastic waste bag, slips on a pair of gardening gloves and starts raking the fallen leaves.

Lenise knows she has only a small window of opportunity to act, but as she watches Jennifer go about her mundane gardening duties, Lenise can't move. Once she crosses the road, there's no going back, she will have to tell. But the implications are just so grave.

She turns from the window, goes into the kitchen, fills the kettle and puts it on the stove. She stares at her warped reflection in the stainless steel and thinks about all the times she wished someone had helped her escape her bastard husband but didn't. The jug whistles and she turns off the stove.

Slipping on her winter coat and pushing her feet into her shoes, she opens the door, walks down the path and pretends to check the mail. Jennifer glances up, offers a tight nod of acknowledgement then returns to pushing leaves into the bag one fistful at a time. Lenise takes a breath and crosses the road.

"It's a shit job," she says.

"Yeah, well, if I don't do it, nobody else will."

"Men are useless."

"You'll get no argument here."

Lenise looks at the sky. "The days are getting colder."

"I hate winter," says Jennifer.

"It's my favorite time of year," says Lenise.

Jennifer stands, wraps the tie tight around the neck of the bag. "Is this a truce? It would be good if it was because to tell you the truth all this fighting is not good for my daughter."

Lenise stares at Jennifer.

"She told you?"

"Told me what?"

"That we spoke the other day."

Jennifer looks perplexed. "No."

"She didn't mention it at all?"

Suddenly Jennifer seems angry.

"What are you up to? Because if this is about the dog, you know I'm sorry about that, really sorry and if I could take it back in a heartbeat I would."

Lenise pauses. "I just wanted to say hello. She looked lonely."

"Lonely?"

"Yes."

Jennifer stares at the weathered tips of her gardening gloves. "It's sad you should think that," she says. "Would you like to come in for coffee?"

Lenise drags her eyes from the safe haven of her own house.

"Tea," says Lenise, looking at Jennifer.

"Sorry?"

"I only drink tea."

"Tea it is."

Lenise follows Jennifer up the steps and into the hallway where shoes are neatly lined up against the wall. Pink slippers. Sneakers. A muddy pair of men's running shoes. Jackets and coats of different sizes hang from ornate copper hooks. A teal umbrella with white polka dots is slumped in the corner.

Jennifer takes off her shoes, places them next to a pair of men's steel-capped work boots and puts on the slippers. Lenise knows she should probably do the same, and reluctantly unties the laces on her four-year-old Skechers and curses herself for not throwing her socks out sooner.

Lenise trails Jennifer down the hallway. Photographs line the walls. A toddler that's most likely McKenzie is running through a sun-filled meadow. The baby-toothed smile of a first day at school. A formal family portrait, just the three of them, a unit, complete and magazine perfect.

When they enter the kitchen, Lenise is hit with the smell of baking and Jennifer nods at the cake cooling on the bench.

"It's gluten free carrot cake. I'm not sure how it will taste. I used dates instead of sugar."

Jennifer makes the tea and retrieves a bread knife from a knife block next to the toaster and cuts a slice of cake. It's still raw in the middle.

"Darn."

"Put icing on it, no one will notice," says Lenise.

"I should stick to the Oreos." Jennifer pushes the cake away and pours the tea. "Would you mind getting the milk?"

Lenise gets down from her stool. On the fridge there's a snapshot in a magnetic frame with daises on it—the girl and her father, his arm slung around her shoulder, sharing a joke.

Jennifer glances at the photo. "They're very close."

"Are they," says Lenise, passing over the milk.

"And is it just you and your son? Cody is it?"

"We're like two peas in a pod."

"That's nice."

"He's a shit."

Jennifer laughs and Lenise sips her tea.

"You're a real estate agent, aren't you?" says Jennifer.

"It comes and goes."

"How long have you been in the States?"

"For some time."

"You must miss home."

"I want to talk to you."

Jennifer frowns. "Okay."

"Something serious."

Jennifer laughs uneasily. "You're making me nervous."

Lenise looks at Jennifer's anxious face. "Your husband."

"What about my husband?"

Then Lenise doesn't know what else to say. It just seems too dark a thing to tell a mother.

"Lenise, what about my husband?" There's an edge in Jennifer's voice now.

Lenise stands up. "Never mind."

But Jennifer grabs Lenise's wrist and the mug of tea goes flying and hot liquid spills over Jennifer's freckled forearm.

"You can't just say never mind and leave it at that," says Jennifer.

"You've burnt yourself."

Lenise leads Jennifer to the kitchen sink and runs cold water over her arm. A red welt is beginning to form.

"*Tell me*," insists Jennifer. "Did you see him with someone? Another woman?"

Lenise stares at the running water, the way it courses over Jennifer's forearm like a fallen log in a stream.

She turns and takes Jennifer by the shoulders. "Your daughter."

Jennifer's face crumples. It's like watching a building implode, all the layers collapsing and falling in on themselves.

"I'm sorry," says Lenise.

She is sure Jennifer has stopped breathing.

"Are you okay?"

Jennifer's spine hardens. "What a vicious thing to say."

"I saw them upstairs, in her bedroom."

"Leave." Jennifer pushes Lenise down the hall and shoves her outside.

"Go on, just get out."

Lenise turns. "You need to stop him."

But the door has already been slammed in her face.

9

Jennifer can't move. Lenise's departing footsteps are a fading crunch on the limestone chip. She stares at the back of the door, with its tiny splits, fingermarks, the peephole never used, the dust atop the hinges and screws. She is two selves. The one who thinks it cannot possibly be true, the other who can't be sure it isn't.

Finally, she raises a leaden hand and turns the lock and goes back to the kitchen where water streams from the faucet, and the mug, upturned and broken, leaks amber broth all over the bench. She shuts off the faucet and lifts her head and looks at Lenise's house.

It was all just a lie, a vicious, vicious lie. It had to be. A perverse punishment for the dog, the stupid dog who should not have been out in the first place, riffling through the neighborhood trash, in the dark where no normal person could see it. Any other responsible pet owner would have apologized for not keeping watch and accepted the blame, but not that woman, with her mistrusting raw blue eyes and wheat-dead complexion. There was no doubt Lenise was disturbed. There was no other explanation for it. What kind of sicko would come into someone's house, their private space, their *sanctuary* for God's sake, where a family cooked and ate and bonded, and say a thing like that?

Jennifer looks at the phone. She should call the police. Lenise's behavior constituted some sort of harassment, surely. The woman couldn't just go round spreading lies that could destroy innocent lives. But maybe that's just what Lenise wanted—a feud. Some people got off on that, didn't they? A vendetta, with its imagined rights and wrongs, gave an empty life purpose, someone to hate and blame.

Jennifer turns from the window and sees the mess. Hank and McKenzie would be home soon. She does not want questions she can't answer. So she hurries, doing her best to ignore the throbbing red welt on her arm, gathering newspaper and wrapping the broken mug and tossing it in the trash, along with the gummy cake, which she must pry from the plate with a spatula because the gluten free disaster has stuck like glue, and she rinses the spoons and other mug and puts them away, then picks up the milk and reaches for the fridge handle, stopping when she sees the photograph. McKenzie and Hank. Two peas in a pod. A thought forms, one that has never really surfaced before but has always been there, deep in her gut, unacknowledged, the fact she has always felt like an outsider, that there were times when she was envious of their tight little duo. She had even called them that—the dynamic duo. Mulder and Scully. Donny and Marie. Dorothy and Toto.

The garage door rumbles and she looks over her shoulder. She's not ready. She needs more time to think.

"Hey, Mom," says McKenzie. "We lost."

And there she is. Jennifer's precious little girl, shy and polite and always so eager to please, looking at her with those expressive green eyes.

Next comes Hank, slapping the car keys down on the counter, giving her a quick peck on the cheek and going to the fridge to gulp down some juice right from the spout and he's so quick with this kiss that she doesn't have time to react so she just lets it happen and she wonders what McKenzie thinks, seeing him kiss her like that.

"Jesus, what happened to your arm?" says Hank.

She thinks she's answered him but she can't have because he asks her the same thing again.

"I spilt some tea," she says too loudly.

"That looks serious," says Hank. "Let's get you to a doctor."

"I'm fine."

"Who do you think you're kidding? Mac, get your Mom's jacket and purse and meet me in the car."

Jennifer looks at him and tries not to imagine the worst.

"What?" he says.

"I just thought…"

She falls silent.

He looks at her. "Thought what, Jen?"

"Nothing," she says. "Let's go, my arm is killing me."

That weekend she watches them. Takes notes inside her head, weighing up that hug or ruffle of the hair or gentle teasing. As far as she can tell, McKenzie is her usual quiet self, not wildly happy but not unhappy either. Then it occurs to Jennifer—what if this isn't the real McKenzie at all? What if she was actually a gregarious girl but this had been suppressed because of, well…*that*? And what if it has been going on for years?

Impossible. She would know. There would have been some sign.

And Hank? She just can't believe it of him. They had shared a bed for seventeen years. Sure, sometimes there were divisions, little hurts, annoyances, but by and large it was a normal marriage and he was a normal man.

But just as she firmly tells herself to forget what Lenise said, there is that voice, telling her to look again, look closer.

Jennifer glances at Hank, who's mixing ground turkey and onions and eggs in a bowl. He scoops out a handful and tosses it from one palm to the other.

"Better watch it," he says, nodding to the pile of carrot.

She looks down. She's on to the inedible green cap and her knuckles are next. Tilting the chopping board over the sink, she sweeps the orange and green mound into the waste disposal and asks McKenzie to set the table.

"We're out of ketchup," says McKenzie, looking in the fridge.

"I'll go to the store," says Hank. "Mac, you want to come for a ride?"

Jennifer's head swings up. "*No.*"

"I want to go, Mom. I've finished the table."

"I need you here."

"For what?"

"Just this once, McKenzie, do as I say," Jennifer snaps.

Hank stares at her. "Jen, what's got into you?"

"Nothing."

"It doesn't seem like nothing," he says.

Jennifer throws up her hands. "There you go again, undermining my authority."

"Give me a break."

"Just go get the stupid ketchup."

She turns on the faucet and pours herself a glass of water and his eyes burn holes into her back.

That night sleep doesn't come easily. Hank is a formless shadow beside her, light snores rattling through his open mouth. Perhaps he is pretending, waiting for her to fall asleep so he can get to work.

"Hey," Hank whispers. "You awake?"

"Yeah."

His arm snakes around her waist.

"You want to talk about it?"

"I'm okay."

He kisses her neck and draws closer and she knows what's coming next and part of her wants to, just to see if there is anything that gives him away but when his hand slides up her back and he pulls her toward him, she can't help it, she goes as rigid as a corpse. He stops and looks at her in the grey darkness.

"What is it?"

"Nothing."

"Just say if you don't want to."

"I don't want to."

There is a sharp outtake of exasperated breath.

"Unbelievable," he says, rolling onto his side.

She lies on her back and stares at the ceiling and all she can hear is McKenzie's voice.

"You think you know everything when you know nothing at all."

10

Her first thought when she opens her eyes is that she must search the house. If there's any proof, it will be here. She feels a rush of guilt. She does not want to play detective. She is not a snoop. But if there are any answers she needs to find them.

She rolls over and looks at the empty swirl of sheets beside her, at the petty way he has cast the blankets aside, so her bare back will get cold. Downstairs they are moving about and she listens, trying to decipher what they are saying, but it's only a murmur, a thready pulse, slipping away then coming back to life.

She closes her eyes and longs for the escape of sleep but knows there's no getting round things so she gets up, puts on some clothes and goes to the bathroom. She wipes the mirror and doesn't recognize the face. Drawn and pale, it could belong to someone else. She looks closer. Acne has appeared on her chin.

She goes downstairs and finds them in the kitchen.

"Aren't you going to be late for your meeting with Chip?"

There's a note in her voice, an octave higher than usual, and she smiles through it.

"Shoot," says Hank when he realizes it's after eight.

"Have you seen my house keys?" He chugs down the last of his coffee.

"By the fruit bowl."

He picks them up.

"See you Mac," he says, planting a kiss on top of her head.

Then there's one for Jennifer too, his lips briefly skating over her cheek. He gives them a half-wave and is out the door, getting into his truck like it's any other day.

After he leaves, McKenzie says, "Why are you acting so weird?"

Jennifer looks at her. "What do you mean?"

"You keep staring at me, like I've done something wrong."

Jennifer's chest hurts. "Do I?"

"Yeah."

Jennifer takes the seat opposite. "You know you can talk to me, don't you?"

McKenzie pushes her cereal away. "Not this again."

"Is there?" says Jennifer.

"Is there what?"

"Anything you want to tell me?"

McKenzie picks up her bowl, rinses it in the sink and places it in the dishwasher.

"McKenzie?"

"I'm going to be late," she says, grabbing her school bag.

A minute later Jennifer sees her cutting across the lawn, thumb hooked beneath the shoulder strap, cap pulled down low. Jennifer waits for her to turn around, maybe wave goodbye, but she never looks back. Why would she? Why would she look back at a mother she thought was a clueless, useless, waste of space?

Jennifer stands there for the longest time, the house stony quiet, the cottonwood tree molting leaves, knowing she should move, set to it, focus on the task at hand, but she can't.

Instead she's overwhelmed with a sudden potent fear. The same fear you get when a spider appears out of nowhere, when you first think it's only a scrap of loose thread or a stone chip or dead fly on its back but then it turns into an eight-legged frightener, bounding over the twill cut-pile toward you as if it can smell your blood, and the breath locks in your throat and your skin pricks and you have to fight the urge to run. God how she wishes she could run now, right out the door, down the road and into another life.

But somehow she moves, forcing one foot in front of the other, and climbs the stairs to her bedroom.

She doesn't know what she expects to find amongst the socks and boxers and t-shirts but looks anyway, unfolding every item, examining it carefully then returning it to its proper place. She combs through the wardrobe, his nightstand, the old suitcase he'd kept from college. Nothing out of the ordinary.

The laptop is on the chair by the bed and she flips it open, punches in the password. Internet history shows job websites, recruitment agencies and a recent search on investing retirement savings in Palm Oil plantations in Sumatra. She clicks randomly on months. December. February. July. But the history and files and downloads show nothing.

Her cellphone rings. It will be Rosemary trying to make sense of the garbled message Jennifer left this morning. Jennifer lets it pass to voicemail and delves back into the wardrobe but the only thing she finds is a long forgotten A-line skirt wedged behind some shoe boxes, a dirty sock covered in dust and a Planters mixed nuts can full of old buttons. She sits back on her heels and feels a tiny burst of hope. But it quickly dies. She's only fooling herself. It has never been about what she would find in this room.

When she opens McKenzie's door she catches a whiff of something that could be cinnamon rolls. The room is a space in transition—from girlhood to teen. In a corner there's a cardboard box stuffed full of My Little Ponies collecting dust. McKenzie's beloved set of Harry Potter books takes pride of place, along the top shelf in the pinewood book case. A One Direction poster is fixed to the wall. The bed is perfectly made, the violet eiderdown crease-free, with precise hotel tucks, a matching pillow, plumped up, at the top end, placed just so. All so very ordinary.

Jennifer expects to feel something, some sixth sense to kick in, where her skin shrinks or the hairs on the back of her neck stand up, anything, but she can't summon any images. It's as if there is a mental block, a wall, a line she cannot cross.

She steps toward the window and looks out. Across the road is the quaint sash window she had always coveted. What could Lenise have possibly observed from that far away? And at night? The whole thing was farcical. Even if Lenise had seen Hank in here with McKenzie who's to say it wasn't an innocent hug misinterpreted as something more sinister?

Perhaps that's what this entire thing had been all about. Connections made that weren't meant to be made, conclusions jumped to then seized upon, a simple mistake.

"I don't know what you think you saw but it wasn't that," says Jennifer.

And suddenly she is angry, not at Lenise, but at herself, for being so easily led, for being so willing to think Hank could do such a thing. She's strides across the room and is at the door before she knows it, fully intending to forget this entire thing and go to work, carry on with her very normal and ordinary life. But she wavers.

She glances over her shoulder. For the avoidance of doubt, to put the matter to rest once and for all, she should take a look, but that's all it was, not agreement with Lenise, not even "a just in case," but a look so she can put her hand on heart and say I checked.

So she begins to search, starting from the right side of the room and working her way round the circumference, looking behind the dresser, in the drawers and everywhere in between. She hunts in the wardrobe, checking the pockets of jackets, hoodies and jeans, then pulls down a box from the shelf above that's filled with old school exercise books and flips through each one looking for secret notes or scribbles in the margins or something that might resemble a diary but there isn't anything.

She spots the old toy chest at the back of the wardrobe and digs through the mountain of Lego, three different sets of bead collections, card making kits, half a dozen Bratz dolls and an old portable CD player, then moves on to the nightstand where she finds a bag of empty candy bar wrappers and a plastic money box in the shape of a basketball.

She closes the cupboard and gets up.

So that was that. Nothing unusual. Nothing to indicate a troubled girl. It could be any other twelve-year old's room in North America.

She pauses to switch off the night light plugged into the socket at the base of the wall. In almost an afterthought she decides to check under the bed. She lifts up the pretty violet eiderdown, crouching down to take a better look. That's when she sees the sleeping bag and the pillow.

Then she hears the footsteps coming up the stairs.

11

"What are you doing?"

She sees Hank there, in the doorway, his expression unreadable.

"Answer me, Jen."

"Don't pretend," she says.

"What's that supposed to mean."

She feels like she might be sick. "Oh, God."

Jennifer steps backward until she hits the wall. She wants to howl but she can't seem to make a single noise. He moves closer.

"Come downstairs."

"Don't make me say it," she says.

He locks eyes. "I don't know what you're talking about."

"The neighbor saw."

"I wouldn't believe anything that bitch says."

"She saw what you did to McKenzie."

Jennifer feels a crack across her cheek. "Wash out your God damn mouth," he says, showing teeth.

He stomps to the door then turns and thrusts a finger in her face. "You're out of your fucking mind."

"Say it, Hank."

"Screws loose in the head," he says, knocking her forehead. "Is it time for the doctor again?"

"How long?"

He looks at her as if he's found something disgusting on his shoe.

"Stop talking," he says. "Just stop talking now."

He begins pacing. "This is bullshit. I'm her fucking father."

"*Tell me*," she says.

"Fed her, clothed her, read her stories, saved her from you, her own mother. Who are you to accuse me of something like this?"

"When did it start, Hank?"

"Her own mother and you nearly let her drown in that bath tub. She was just a God damn baby. What kind of mother are you?"

"Tell me."

"I never touched her."

"Since she was a toddler? Before that?"

He rushes for Jennifer and grabs her by the shoulders and shakes hard.

"I would never hurt her," says Hank. "You've got to believe that."

He lets go and starts to cry.

"She can't even sleep in her own bed," says Jennifer.

"Oh, don't," he sputters and covers his face with his hand.

She launches at him.

"Get out!" she screams. "Get out, get out, get out!"

He pushes her off and she falls to the floor. When she looks up to tell him she hates him, he's already gone.

She lies there for hours, on the violet eiderdown, the sunlight shifting from wall to wall, caressing the top of her head. Her cellphone rings and rings and she finally picks up and tells Rosemary that she's been sick and must have fallen asleep and yes she was feeling better and no she was not pregnant and yes she would be in tomorrow and no there was nothing she needed and yes her clients would get over it because these things happen. Four times she tries to get to her feet and four times she fails. Her body is stone and it's all she can do to roll over and face the wall. She shuts her eyes, just for a moment, to gather her energy, so she can get to the bathroom to wash her sticky, tear-stained face before McKenzie gets home, but before she can...

"What are you doing?" McKenzie drops her school bag to the floor.

"Sweetheart," says Jennifer.

"Get out of my room."

"It's over McKenzie. He's gone."

"What?"

Jennifer reaches for her. "Sit down."

McKenzie pulls away. "No."

"I know he hurt you," says Jennifer.

"That's crazy."

Jennifer can't hold back the tears. "Oh God, I'm so sorry, hon."

"This is stupid. You're being stupid. Please get out of my room."

"If I'd known I would have done something, truly I would have."

"I'm not talking about this, I have homework to do," McKenzie unzips her school bag and starts digging through it, "an assignment on the big melt in Antarctica."

"Hon, please."

McKenzie ignores her and continues to hunt, pulling out a book, her tablet, pens. "Polar bears are starving because there's nothing to eat," she thrusts her arm inside her bag and feels around as if she's missing something, "because people use too much electricity." She tips the contents out on her bed and fans through the debris, "because of stupid, shitty, greedy people like us the polar bears are dying." She can't find what's she's looking for and shakes the bag. Out fall crumbs, candy wrappers, a blackened banana. "They never hurt anyone. They just want to get on with their lives."

"Please. Stop this."

McKenzie swings around to face Jennifer. "You don't understand. They're dying!"

"Let me help you," says Jennifer, choking on sobs.

"Leave."

Jennifer doesn't move. McKenzie picks up the tablet and throws it against the wall.

"I said leave me alone!"

"Alright," Jennifer says, finally. "You know where I am when you're ready to talk."

12

Lenise drops back into third gear and pulls out into the slow morning traffic. She's going to be late for her meeting with holier-than-thou office manager, Camille de Silva, but Lenise doesn't care. Camille and her trivial sales targets can take a flying leap because nothing can shake the feeling of accomplishment Lenise is basking in right now. Even the bread truck in front of her belching clouds from its filthy exhaust can't dampen her mood.

That's because she's thinking of yesterday and how that no good poor excuse for a father had rushed from the house and lurched down the driveway in that stupid truck of his. The look on his face said it all. Bleached white and wide-eyed, as if he'd witnessed a fatal accident. Of course, he would only be feeling sorry for himself, thinking of his own losses, not the pain and suffering he'd caused others. But the fact that he'd been exposed was a triumph.

God knows it had taken long enough. Lenise had been worried Jennifer would not have the guts to confront him. At the very least, she would have expected Jennifer to move out of the house with McKenzie and when that didn't occur Lenise began to have doubts that Jennifer would do anything at all. In fact, Lenise had made up her mind that if nothing had happened by the end of the week, she would put in an anonymous call to Child Protective Services. Then, finally, yesterday, there he was, careening from the house like a man on fire.

It was true that Lenise felt just a tiny bit of satisfaction at his undoing, knowing she was the one who had uncovered it—the good, if not reluctant, Samaritan. She'd half expected a knock on the door from Jennifer, some show of gratitude. After all, it wasn't easy to tell a mother her child was being molested. A lesser person would have walked away. Whatever way you looked at it Lenise had done the woman a favor, and a thank you or some small form of acknowledgement wouldn't have gone astray. But what Lenise got instead was a frosty silence as if the entire matter had somehow been all her fault.

By the time Lenise arrives at the office, her mood has soured. Camille—she of the Mikimoto pearls and substantial referral list—is on the phone and gestures in an off-hand way for Lenise to take a seat on the Laura Ashley wing chair. Ten minutes later Camille finally rings off and turns her attention to Lenise.

"We're going to have to let you go."

It's a punch to the heart.

"You're joking."

"There's been a complaint of misconduct."

"Misconduct?"

"Theft."

"But I haven't stolen anything."

"A very valuable time piece was misappropriated from a client's house. The Roxburgh Street property. You're familiar with the residence?"

"I've done a viewing there, but I don't know anything about any clock."

Camille places the small lead crystal clock on the desk.

"I've never seen that before," says Lenise.

"It was found yesterday morning, in your drawer. This is very bad for the agency. I won't involve the police if you leave today."

"This was Radley, wasn't it?

"That's irrelevant."

Lenise bites her lip and tastes pepper.

"He's had it out for me since day one. You know I saw him in a client's bed with a prostitute, don't you?"

"That will be all," says Camille.

"I'm telling you, he's the one who should be fired."

"Would you please leave now, Lenise."

Lenise gets to her feet. "This isn't over."

She fights the urge to do an arm-swipe across that impossibly orderly desk and slams the door on the way out instead. She takes a moment to catch her breath then launches herself into the agents' room. A startled Radley looks up from his paperwork.

"You snake. You think you can set me up!"

Lenise picks up his laptop and slams it down on his desk. Keys fly like woodchips. The letter P lands on Radley's thigh and he glances from that to the screen hanging from its split hinge.

"You're out of your mind," he says. "That's a thousand-dollar computer."

She feels an arm hook around her chest.

"Don't worry, I'm going," she tells the security guard.

When she looks back, Radley is on his knees, plucking the alphabet from the carpet.

The lights of the slot machine flash. A soundtrack reminiscent of a big top circus hones down from an undisclosed speaker somewhere above Lenise's head. Over to the left, near the entrance to the slots alcove, a large electronic banner displays the rising jackpot, like a clock calculating the debt of some third world economy.

Hours ago she'd handed over her last two hundred bills to the cashier for coins. When she did this part of her screamed, *Wait! What the hell are you doing!* But it was as if she was on autopilot, and when she saw just how many cardboard cylinders of quarters made up two hundred dollars, for a second there she had felt quite rich.

But she knew full well she would lose, that the machine would eat her last dollar and she would go home broke. She did it anyway. It was almost like admitting defeat. Here you go world, have it all. You would've taken it anyway.

So when she puts the final coin into the silver slot, she gets exactly what she expects. Nothing. She stares at the two cherries and the lemon and wonders how in the hell Cody could be duped like this so many times.

"You finished?" a black lady stares at her, holding a full cup of quarters.

"Go for your life," she says.

Lenise steps outside and blinks into the daylight. Morning has happened. Somewhere along the line she has lost an entire night.

There's no hurry, she has no job, no-one to return home to. She thinks of Cody working on some farm in Minnesota. It wouldn't kill him to give her a call sometime. Oh, he would be back, that was more certain than taxes. But still, a simple phone call just to check in and see how she was getting on wasn't too much to ask.

She wonders how her life has come to this. Unemployed, house she owes three weeks rent on, her dead dog's ashes in an old Famous Dave's pickle jar in the bottom drawer of the bathroom cupboard.

She looks at her watch. A quarter after two.

She walks the short distance to the Go Figure Finance office, which is hard to miss given the human-sized placard outside. It's the same sports guy on the ads, stupid grin planted on his dial, making the okay sign with his forefinger and thumb. Inside, mothers hold crying babies and grey-skinned addicts bite off the last of their fingernails. Lenise takes a number and a seat. An hour later she's called by an older woman with a Justin Bieber haircut and too much blue eye shadow and in less than five minutes Lenise has a new credit card.

"First payment due in fourteen days," says the Bieber woman.

"Understood," says Lenise.

She immediately walks to the cash machine around the corner and withdraws five hundred dollars. She stares at the money. Maybe she should just take off, leave this shit hole behind, cross the border into Canada to become a waitress in a good time bar. But she slips the money into her pocket. That wasn't for her. She was tired of moving, of fresh starts that turned out to be a step backwards not forwards. She would work this out. She was a smart, resourceful woman. She had done it before and would do it again.

When Lenise turns the corner, she's surprised to see Jennifer. She's up ahead by the deli dressed as usual in smart business attire, burnt orange leather bag hooked over her elegant shoulder, texting on her late model phone. Lenise imagines the girls' lunches, the shopping for designer clothes, the adoring daughter, the sense of accomplishment that comes with being an educated woman.

But when Jennifer looks up, Lenise glimpses the ashen skin and the nights without sleep and doesn't feel quite so envious anymore.

"Hello Jenny," she says.

13

Jennifer lifts her head. Lenise is standing in front of her, patting down her crinkled skirt, wild mane bushed out all over the place. Jennifer's first instinct is to turn around and walk the other way.

"You've seen better days," says Lenise.

"I suppose I have."

"He admitted it then," says Lenise.

Jennifer can't look Lenise in the eye so fixes her gaze on the hydrant just left of Lenise's shoulder.

"It's been hell."

"Well, it would be."

Jennifer looks down at her hands. "I knew nothing about it."

"I know that."

Jennifer feels a sudden rush of gratitude. It's overwhelming and unexpected and she begins to cry.

"I can't believe I didn't know. I feel so stupid."

She blinks through her tears. People stare and Lenise scowls. "Mind your own fucking business."

She takes Jennifer's arm. "Come on," she says, steering her into a nearby café. "Wait here."

Lenise walks to the counter and Jennifer takes a seat in the corner and bats away the tears. She tells herself to get a grip. She hates all this, making a scene, like she's some sort of fragile little girl. There's a painting of a buffalo on the wall above the counter so she focuses on that, tries to think of a happy time. Lenise returns with two walnut brownies and a passionfruit cupcake.

"Eat something."

Jennifer's gut flips. "I'm not doing food right now."

"Suit yourself."

Lenise slips into the chair opposite and places the Go Figure finance envelope down by her ankle.

"I was fired," says Lenise. "Unfair dismal. I'm going to take them to court."

"Sorry to hear that."

"Yeah, well, life's a bitch and then you die."

The pot of tea arrives. Lenise looks inside and shuts the lid in disgust.

"*Tea bags*. This country's a basket case." Lenise rotates the pot exactly three times, pours two cups and pushes one across the table. "Go on. It will make you feel better."

Jennifer feels the steam on her chin. She takes a sip. It's hot enough to blister her lips.

"I keep waiting to wake up. It's worse than a nightmare. McKenzie won't talk to me." Then before Jennifer knows it, she's crying again and the paper napkin is sodden and disintegrating in her hands. "I just wish I could've done something. I feel so incredibly useless, like the worst mother in the world. All I can think about is what he must have done to her and for how long."

"You want to know what I saw," states Lenise.

Jennifer looks up. "No." Then, "Yes."

"It won't help."

"I want to understand what she's been through."

"You already do."

Jennifer stares into her tea. Milk has formed a film on the surface and breaks away like an island from the mainland.

"What will you do?" says Lenise.

Jennifer runs a hand over her face. "I'm on my way to police."

"Police?"

"Of course."

"There's bound to be uncomfortable questions."

"What are you getting at, Lenise?"

"Why you didn't know."

Jennifer sits back in her chair. "What a cruel thing to say."

Lenise dismisses her with a hand.

"Jenny, I believe you but that doesn't mean they will."

"What else do you expect me to do? He's got to pay for he's done."

Lenise watches Jennifer over the rim of her tea cup. "I might know someone."

Jennifer looks at her. "What are you talking about?"

"To send a message, a clear message, to let him know that what he's done is unacceptable."

"A thug? You're kidding?"

"I wouldn't joke about a thing like that."

"We don't do things that way in this country. We have the rule of law."

Lenise barks out a laugh. "Have you watched *Dateline*, lately?"

"I'm a mother, Lenise, not a vigilante and I'm hardly going to risk jail and leave McKenzie to fend for herself."

Lenise throws up her hands. "Just trying to help."

"It's a ridiculous suggestion and I don't need your help. This is a private family matter."

Jennifer gets to her feet.

"I see," says Lenise.

"Which has, quite frankly, got nothing to do with you."

"You would still be in the dark if it wasn't for me."

"Listen to me. You have no idea what I'm going through or how difficult this is. It's easy for you to sit on the sidelines like you're watching some episode of *Beverly Hills Housewives* but this is my awful, shitty life. Do you get that? My life is ruined and so is my daughter's so why don't you just worry about your own problems. It certainly looks like you've got enough of them."

Lenise smiles.

"So you do have a back bone."

Jennifer stares at her.

"You're a real piece of work," she says, grabbing her bag. "Goodbye."

"Don't coming running to me when this all goes pear-shaped," calls Lenise.

As if she would, thinks Jennifer.

14

Officer Petra Rosen could have been no more than thirty but wore the hard, world-weary look of someone who'd seen things she would rather forget. In the seat opposite, Jennifer watches the officer click open a file and take out a checklist and place it in front of her.

"Have you been the victim of a domestic assault?"

"No."

"Has your husband ever struck you?"

"No."

"Has your husband ever called you names and made you feel worthless?"

"Not really."

"Has your husband ever used sexual violence to intimidate you?"

"No."

"Does your husband own a firearm?"

"No."

"Okay."

Officer Rosen places the final tick in the box and returns the form to the file and pulls the legal pad toward her.

"Go ahead," she says, pen poised. "Tell me what happened."

Jennifer's yanks a stray hair from her mouth and realizes she's trembling.

"I don't know where to begin," she says.

Officer Rosen puts down the pen and reaches for a typed statement from the file.

"Let's start with your husband's version then."

Jennifer sits back in her chair. "He's been here?"

"I spoke to him this morning."

"I don't believe this," says Jennifer.

"He said allegations had been made. Molestation of a minor, your daughter." Officer Rosen lifts her eyes from the document. "He says he didn't do it."

"Well, I'm not making it up," says Jennifer.

"Divorce can be ugly."

"Don't let him fool you."

"I'm not stupid, Mrs. Blake. I didn't say I believed him." She pauses. "What does your daughter say happened?"

"McKenzie won't talk about it, but I know he did it, the neighbor saw him."

"And will this neighbor give a statement, testify if it ever gets that far?"

Jennifer hesitates, places her hands palm down on the table.

"I don't know."

"I need evidence, Mrs. Blake—dates, times, places, specifics of the actual acts. DNA from inside the child's body, on her underwear."

"I don't have any of those things."

"Then it's only your word against his."

"You can't just let him get away with it."

"Want me to call child services to come and talk with your daughter? They might take her."

"To foster care?"

Officer Rosen nods. "Or a group home, until the matter gets resolved and who knows how long that will be."

"No."

Officer Rosen looks down at the statement.

"There's something else," she says.

"What?"

"He says there was an incident when your daughter was less than a year old."

Jennifer can't believe he would stoop so low.

"You left the baby alone in the bath," continues Officer Rosen.

"It was a moment's inattention. I was tired, not thinking straight, that's all."

"And as a result treated in a psychiatric unit for post-partum depression."

"So now I'm a crazy woman making this whole thing up?"

"That's what he'll argue."

Officer Rosen shuts the file and gets to her feet.

"Get some evidence, Mrs. Blake, real evidence, then we can take the matter further."

Jennifer manages to make it to her car without falling apart. She starts the engine and tells herself to relax before she snaps the steering wheel right out of its column and McKenzie loses the one good parent she has left. Her mind spins. She thought the police would help, so now what? This was uncharted territory, with no point of reference, no just turn east and you'll hit land, no You Tube advice like there was for fixing a burred screw.

The Leeston Avenue sign appears and Jennifer turns left and tries to put a lid on her rage because she doesn't want McKenzie to pick up on the negative energy. She was already dealing with enough.

Jennifer had suggested that maybe it was better to take some time off school, let things settle for a bit, but

McKenzie had been unmoved. There was nothing more to talk about, she'd insisted, she was going to school whether Jennifer liked it or not.

So Jennifer had given in, but now, as she pulls up outside the entrance and sees McKenzie looking so upset, she knew that had been a mistake. McKenzie gets in the car and nods toward the enormous Sugar Maple near the school gymnasium.

"It's Dad," she says.

Jennifer follows her gaze. Hank is parked in his pick-up watching them. Her pulse begins to race.

"Ignore him," she says, pulling away from the curb.

"He's mad at me, isn't he?"

"McKenzie, you don't need to worry about his feelings."

Jennifer looks in the rearview, expecting him to follow, but he starts his car and goes the other way.

"Why did he do that?" says McKenzie.

"I don't know."

"This is your fault," says McKenzie.

Jennifer's phone rings. It's him. She answers on the second ring.

"You bastard, you won't get away with this."

"This is our family and this is our business and we take care of it."

Then he hangs up before she can reply.

15

This was like the time with Alice Jackson. Hank could be out there watching just like that guy in the park, the guy who sprang from the bushes and hissed "little Yankee sluts" and chased Alice and Jennifer with a knife when they were thirteen and drinking cider bought with Alice's fake id and taking a short cut to the 7-11. He had looked like a netherworld goblin and he was fast and wily and Jennifer and Alice tore up the pathway to get away from him but they were deep in the park and it was a long way to the exit and it took forever and Jennifer could hear him pounding behind them, growling like a wild goat, and Alice grabbed at Jennifer's sleeve, trying to keep up, gasping wait, don't, please, wait, but Jennifer shook her off and kept running, half aware Alice was falling behind, but Jennifer couldn't stop, propelled by naked fear, she just ran and ran, until she finally made it out the gates and onto the other side.

Jennifer looks out her bedroom window and wonders what Alice Jackson is doing now.

Alice Jackson with her black Doc Martins and trench coat purchased from an army surplus store with rips in the cuffs where she could put her thumbs through. Alice Jackson who didn't like to wash because her stepfather had taken off the door to the bathroom. Alice Jackson who had looked at Jennifer and said "You were going to leave me behind" to which Jennifer had lied and said "No, I wasn't" but they both knew it was true—how she would have thrown Alice to the wolves just to save herself.

As Jennifer surveys the streets and roads below, and over there, by the green and more green of the woods, she tells herself that was a lifetime ago. She's a different person now, a mother, with the fierce instinct to protect her own young and she would sacrifice her own life for McKenzie's if it ever came down to it.

Jennifer hears the scrape of furniture against the floor next door and goes to check. McKenzie is on her hands and knees, surrounded by every possible cleaning product they have in the house, wiping down the skirting boards.

"What are you doing?"

"Nothing," says McKenzie, dipping the cloth into a bucket of steaming water.

The furniture had been rearranged, too. The bed was now on the other side of the room against the wall, the book cases were lined up next to the wardrobe, the posters gone.

"What are those?" says Jennifer, pointing to two bulging trash bags.

"Stuff I don't need anymore."

Jennifer reaches inside one of the bags and withdrew a summer dress.

"But you love this."

McKenzie doesn't say anything and gets to her feet and begins cleaning the walls.

"You don't need to do that," says Jennifer.

"I want to."

Jennifer pauses and sits down on the bed.

"Listen, hon, I was thinking about arranging counseling."

"Why?"

McKenzie drags her bucket behind her and shifts to the next section.

"It's not good to bottle things up," says Jennifer.

"I'm not."

"I think it will help."

McKenzie plunges the cloth into the hot water then squeezes it out with her two red hands.

"You go, then," she says.

A general feeling of unease stalks Jennifer all the way to work and she finds herself watching the rearview more than the road and nearly collides with some senior in a polar fleece crossing the street with her Bichon Frise. There are black pickups everywhere, waiting round corners, idling at the lights, parked up in alleyways, pulling in behind her. But none are him. This makes Jennifer more nervous than if he'd actually been following her because by now he should have received the divorce papers and she would have expected something. A phone call. A visit. But the silence is deafening.

She reaches the clinic car park and there's no vehicles there except Rosemary's red Starlet so Jennifer locks her car and goes inside, forbidding herself to check over her shoulder. Mrs. Mendoza is already in the waiting room reading *Woman's Own* with a giant magnifying glass from a home shopping catalogue.

"I'll be with you in a minute, Mrs. M."

"No need to rush. I'm happy with my book."

Rosemary gives Jennifer an eyebrow raise.

"You okay, you look a bit frazzled," she whispers, handing over Jennifer's messages.

"I'm fine."

"You have toothpaste on your cheek."

"God," says Jennifer, rubbing her skin with her index finger.

"Other side."

Jennifer tries the left cheek. "Okay?"

"Roger that."

"It's been one of those mornings."

Jennifer hurries to her office, checks her email, inspects her face in the mirror for more toothpaste then returns to the reception.

"Mrs. M? I'm ready for you now."

Mrs. Mendoza looks up.

"I was just getting to the good part. The girl fell from an airplane for two miles into the Amazon rainforest still strapped to her seat."

"Tell you what—keep it."

"I couldn't."

"Bring it back the next time you come in."

"Well, thank you," she says, slipping the magazine into her hessian bag.

They retreat into Jennifer's office and Mrs. Mendoza sits down in the exam chair, her sensible navy loafers and mismatched socks peeking out from beneath her trouser cuffs.

Mrs. Mendoza stares at her. "You have that look about you."

"That look?"

"You know, the 'man trouble' look."

"Oh." Jennifer picks up the ophthalmoscope and directs the light into Mrs. Mendoza's right eye and moves slowly from left to right. "Maybe I'm menopausal."

"Don't kid a kidder, I've been there myself."

"How have the drops been working?"

"He was a big rig driver and having sex with underage girls at truck stops. I found photos on his phone."

"Any loss of peripheral vision?"

"Even with the photos he denied it."

"What about the dog?"

Mrs. Mendoza stops and looks at her. "What dog?"

"The helper dog."

Mrs. Mendoza laughs. "I thought you were talking about my ex-husband."

"Mrs. M, that's disgusting."

"I wouldn't put it past him."

Jennifer lowers the light and sits back.

"That must have been hard on you," says Jennifer.

"It was. At first. But after the divorce I realized it was the best thing that could've happened to me. Now I can do whatever I please. I only have to cook for myself and do my own laundry. It was like being set free from an awful burden I didn't know I was carrying."

"Your eyes look good. You must be using the drops diligently."

"You were worried because of the socks. I saw you looking. But I've been using the medicine every day like you said."

"Good."

Jennifer unlocks the cabinet and gives Mrs. Mendoza two more bottles.

"I'd like to see you in another six months, and even though you're doing well now, I think it's still a good idea if you did a course at the sight clinic to prepare."

"So I don't set fire to my arm when I'm cooking?"

"Something like that."

Mrs. Mendoza gets up and puts on her coat, retrieving a knitted peach-colored hat from the pocket. She pulls it down so it covers her ears.

"The photograph's gone," she says.

"Sorry?"

Mrs. Mendoza nods at Jennifer's desk. "The one with your daughter and husband."

She tucks curls of brown hair into the hat, first the right side then the left.

"Just goes to show, you never know," she says.

"Never know what?"

"When there's a snake in the grass."

That night Jennifer doesn't dream of snakes but of cats, one cat, its grey feather-soft pelt, the black tip of its tail, her arms encircling its warm cat body until it yields against her like an infant, heart pacing through its chest like footsteps. And she could be anywhere. But then he's here.

"I don't know what's wrong with me, Jen."

She opens her eyes. Hank is standing at the foot of her bed. Fear floods her bones and she scrambles backward to the other side of the mattress.

"I need help," he says, looking down at his gloved hands, cheeks glistening with tears.

Somehow she finds her voice. "Leave now."

"A divorce?" he says, pained.

"Hank, I don't want you here. Get out."

He begins to sob. "You're all I have."

She reaches for her cellphone but it's not there.

"God, I'm so disgusting." He hits his head with a closed fist. "I make myself sick."

Jennifer searches for an escape route, but any way she plays it, he can get her.

"This is the end for me," says Hank.

Jennifer's fear turns to anger. "Don't be a child."

"Without you and McKenzie, what's the point anymore?"

"Don't you dare leave McKenzie with that guilt."

"I'm begging you, Jen. I can't go on without you."

"If you love us so much, you'll leave us alone," she says.

He seems to calm himself and wipes each eye with his forearm. He takes two steps forward, bends down and drags his knuckles against her cheek.

"We'll see," he says.

16

The locksmith is late. He'd promised Jennifer to be here by 7 a.m., but it's nearly a quarter after. Normally fifteen minutes wouldn't matter, but right now, this morning, fifteen minutes seems like the difference between life and death.

She waits at the window, guzzling coffee, double strength and black, her third of the morning. The caffeine has lost its punch and tastes unpleasantly bitter, but it's better than nothing and gives her something to do with her trembling hands.

This can't be good for a person's heart, all this stress, the pulse doing circuits around her system like a cyclist in a velodrome. She can't stop thinking about how his face looked like him but didn't. It was as if someone else was occupying the suit of his skin. She's never seen that look before, that tortured but slack affect, like he was having some sort of turn or there was a tumor bearing down on his cerebral cortex.

It was hard to believe this same man had proposed to her on Bascom Hill all those years ago, near the Abe Lincoln statue, the alabaster dome of Capitol Building glowing like a second moon in the distance. He had told her she was the best thing that had ever happened to him then whispered something so quietly she had to ask him to repeat it, "Will you marry me," he said. And afterward, when Jennifer lay against his shoulder in bed, he told her he thought she would say no. Oh God how she wished she had said no.

Overhead she hears the shower still going. McKenzie has been in there for forty-five minutes. Finally, the water squeaks off and McKenzie comes down, skin glowing red, hair wet, smelling of antibacterial soap.

"We're out of hot water," she says.

"Terrific," says Jennifer.

McKenzie heads to the cupboard and retrieves a bowl for her cereal. "That's disgusting," she says, staring into it.

McKenzie takes out another and another. "They're all dirty. God, this whole place makes me cringe."

She takes the stack to the sink and runs the tap and starts cleaning.

Jennifer looks at McKenzie and a new fear develops. What if Hank tried to take her? What if they became one of those nightmare parental abduction cases when a former spouse absconds with a child across state lines? What if Jennifer wakes up one morning and McKenzie was gone?

"Maybe you should stay home from school today. It's been a tough couple of days," she says.

"But you have to go to work. I'll just be bored here on my own."

"You can come to the clinic with me."

"That's stupid," says McKenzie, squirting dishwashing liquid over the final two bowls. "I'm going to school."

A car door slams. They both look out the window. The locksmith's van is in the drive.

McKenzie turns to Jennifer. "You're changing the locks?"

"It's just a precaution."

"For what?"

Jennifer doesn't know what to say.

"Mom?"

"I want to keep us safe."

"Dad wouldn't hurt us, would he?" There's a knock on the front door. "Mom?"

"I better get that," says Jennifer.

The day passes in a blur. Jennifer is a mess of nerves, glancing out her clinic window every ten minutes, constantly checking her phone. Over the course of the day, Jennifer calls McKenzie four times to check she's okay and she is and it's a relief when it's closing time and Jennifer makes it back to the safety of their newly fortified home without incident.

It's dark by the time Jennifer remembers it's trash night. She tells herself to leave it but then gets angry. Now he's got her afraid to take out the garbage. Still, she feels better when she sees Lenise over the road, putting her own bin out. Lenise looks up and gives Jennifer a curt nod then turns to go back inside.

Jennifer jogs across the road. "Hey, Lenise"

Lenise just folds her arms and looks at her.

"I'm sorry," says Jennifer finally. "I shouldn't have gone off at you like that."

"No, you shouldn't have."

"You were only trying to help."

"That's right."

They fall silent then Lenise reaches into her pocket and takes out a pack of cigarettes.

"I could use one of those," says Jennifer.

"You smoke?"

"Not in years."

"Then you shouldn't start again."

"Please."

"Suit yourself."

Lenise gives her a cigarette then lights it for her. Jennifer sucks and her tongue burns, but God it feels good.

"You're shaking," says Lenise.

"It's the cold."

"I see."

"He broke into the house."

Lenise nods. "I saw the locksmith."

"I thought it would be best."

Jennifer takes another drag. "He could be watching us right now," she says.

Lenise steps forward and looks out into the night. "Asshole."

"I won't argue with that."

"You don't think he would do something stupid?"

"I got a restraining order," says Jennifer. "They went to serve him at work but he wasn't there. He's lost his job."

"I've seen this sort of thing before. Men who can't let go. They can be very dangerous when cornered."

"He's too weak for that."

"Don't be naive," snaps Lenise. "And don't think that restraining order will save you, either. A piece of paper will mean nothing to him and police can't be there 24/7. You know how the rest goes."

"I'm scared he might take McKenzie."

"Or worse."

They fall silent and look out at the woods.

"Do you have a gun?" says Lenise.

"What? Of course not."

"A gun in the hand of a woman is a great equalizer. In fact, women have the advantage because men never think a woman will have the guts to use it." Lenise looks at her watch. "I have to go."

"Wait," says Jennifer. "How would I get one?"

Lenise laughs. "This is America. There's a gun shop on every corner."

17

Jennifer enters Guns and More and the smell hits her like the fourth of July—raw grease and explosives. She had intended to browse quietly on her own but realizes that will be impossible when she sees the layout of the shop. Wall-to-wall guns. Big ones like they had in the military, on racks and mounted on the walls, price tags looped around their triggers.

Over to the left, a locked steel cage holds more guns. The sign above says *hard to find items*. The "more" in the "guns and more" was apparently fishing rods, intimidating-looking crossbows, and other hunting supplies. Apart from a bearded man browsing leather waders and the woman behind the counter, the store is empty.

"Need help?" The voice belongs to the woman. Sixties, grey-haired. There's an id badge pinned over her left bosom, her photo and her name—Leonie U.

"I'm looking for a hand gun."

The woman nods at the glass counter in front of her.

"Forget about that one," says Leonie U, pointing to a large silver gun. "That's a 44 magnum. Way too heavy and way too messy. You'll want a 22. It's lighter, easier to handle, not much kickback and the like."

Leonie U unlocks the cabinet with a set of keys from her neck chain and takes out a compact gun not much bigger than the palm of her chubby hand.

"Looks like a cigarette lighter don't it? Don't be fooled, though, this sweetheart can be just as effective as the Magnum if pointed in the right direction. Shoot and aim.

100

That's all there is to it. Men try and make out like it's rocket science or something but that's just to make themselves look better. Here."

She places the gun in Jennifer's hand. It's cold and heavy despite the size.

"It's just for show, really," says Jennifer.

"You want to scare someone?"

"If I need to."

"No ammo then?"

"Maybe a box."

Leonie U reaches into the cabinet, pulls out a red box of ammunition and puts in on the counter next to the gun.

"We got a firing range downstairs if you want to pop a few shots. Five dollars for thirty minutes, plus ammo."

"I'm okay."

The woman lifts her chin to a glass cabinet.

"What about a suppressor? I got a nice one there for a 22 that's user serviceable. Off the books, of course. They ain't strictly legal in Wisconsin."

"That won't be necessary."

"Driver's license."

Jennifer hands over her license and watches the Mickey Mouse clock on the wall behind the counter while Leonie U fills out the paperwork. When the woman finishes she hands Jennifer the carbon copy.

"Come back in forty-eight hours and you'll be good to go."

"I can't take it now?"

"The DoJ needs to run a check first. It's the law. You got no record then you got nothing to worry about."

"But I need it right away, for safety."

Leonie U must have heard the panic in Jennifer's voice, because she lowers hers and says, "You got a stalker or something?"

Jennifer nods.

"My husband."

Leonie U goes silent.

"Alright," she says finally. "Let's do it off the books, in the name of the sisterhood. But not this one."

She turns from the counter, disappears into a back room and emerges a few minutes later with a bundle in a yellow chamois. She starts to unwrap it, but changes her mind. She looks at Jennifer.

"You a cop?"

"What? No way. I'm an optometrist."

Leonie U nods. "Yeah, you don't look like a cop."

She unwraps the cloth to reveal a similar sized gun.

"It's much the same but unregistered. Cost you an extra fifty, though."

"I appreciate it."

"No problemo," says Leonie U, slipping the gun and ammunition into a paper bag. "Just remember, shoot and aim. For the head if possible. You don't want that son of a bitch getting back up again."

18

The father will never let Jennifer and the girl go just like that. Men were too full of their own self-importance to permit the woman to simply walk away. Lenise had seen it too many times before.

She'd been watching over them, acting as a guardian of sorts. But she never saw him. He was like a vampire, staying in the shadows. Oh, he was out there somewhere, she could sense his presence, watching and lying in wait, and it was only a matter time before he struck.

It felt good to have a purpose, given Cody was gone.

He called the other night, collect of course, and she immediately demanded to know what he wanted then instantly regretted sounding so harsh.

"Calm down, Ma. I just wanted to see how you are."

If she had told him once, she'd told him a hundred times—Don't call me *Ma*. It made her sound old and ruined by life. But tonight she didn't mind. It was just good to hear the sound of his voice.

"Do you want me to send the rest of your things?" she asked.

"Leave them. You never know when I might be back," he said and her heart had done a leap.

He sounded bright, and she wished she could be happy, but it made her feel sad. She nearly told him everything. How she lost her job after being set up by Radley. How she had to pawn the last of his grandmother's jewelry. How she was days away from having an upturned hat on the pavement begging for change. She even thought about asking him to send money but lied instead, and told him she was doing just fine.

"I'll visit when I can," he said.

And afterward, when she had returned the phone to the cradle, and heard the mindless chatter of her fake friends on the radio, she wished he had never called at all.

Lenise spends the day handing out her resume to retail outlets and gas stations and grocery stores, and, the lowest-of-the-low, fast food restaurants. It's a major step down but she's desperate. She tries not to think about what life will be like with her hair smelling of fried meat. She doesn't bother with real estate agencies because she knows she'll be blacklisted. For a second there she considers returning to the Brook River office and going postal but decides Radley and Camille are not worth the jail time.

Some of the halfwits she encounters have the nerve to tell her she's not experienced enough. Real estate is a professional role, she had insisted to the Burger King Manager, a spotty kid not much older than Cody, and when he had laughed and said *don't you mean parasites*, she could have punched him in the face.

After four hours of pavement pounding, Lenise decides she's done for the day and turns for home, walking back to save bus fare. She is thinking about whether it's worthwhile registering with a temp agency for cleaning work when she rounds the bend into Simeon Street and sees McKenzie duck into the Safeway.

Lenise isn't sure if it's the furtive way the girl had looked over her shoulder, or the way she slunk down into that oversized jacket of hers, but Lenise is intrigued enough to follow McKenzie inside.

She's careful to keep her distance as McKenzie browses the sunglasses stand, scans the shelves of pet food then moves to the laundry aisle. Lenise shoots to the next row, picks up a jar of apricot jam and feigns interest in the nutritional label, and keeps watch as McKenzie studies the feminine hygiene section. Then, before Lenise can blink, McKenzie reaches for a douche product and slips it into her bag, then just as quickly, hand sanitizer, antibacterial soap, a bottle of disinfectant, and a box of latex gloves.

McKenzie spins around and heads for the exit. Lenise follows at a clipped pace. But before McKenzie makes it to the door, a security guard steps in her path.

"Open your bag for me, miss."

McKenzie clutches the bag to her chest.

"Why?"

"We reserve the right to check," he says, jerking his thumb at the sign by the entrance doors.

Lenise hurries over.

"There you are," she says.

She looks at the security guard. "What's going on?"

"This your daughter?"

"Yes."

"I need to look in her bag."

"What, that? The reusable tote we use for shopping?" She looks at the guard and laughs. "Oh, I see, you thought she was stealing. We were just heading to the checkout to pay for our items."

She takes McKenzie by the arm. "Come on, child, stop bothering the busy man."

She feels his eyes on them as they head to the check out. He continues to hover as the groceries are scanned and bagged and Lenise pays for them with her last twenty dollars.

Once a safe distance from the store, Lenise turns to McKenzie and detects the faint whiff of disinfectant coming from the girl's clothes.

"You're not using that to wash with are you? It will burn."

McKenzie blushes madly. "It makes me feel better."

"You'll do damage if you're using it down there," says Lenise.

McKenzie nods at the bag.

"Can I have my stuff?"

Lenise hands it over. McKenzie starts to walk off then changes her mind.

"You won't tell Mom, will you?"

Lenise looks at her.

"Not if you don't want me to."

McKenzie pauses and looks her sneakers.

"I'll pay you back," she says.

Lenise thinks about how many meals that last twenty dollars could have bought.

"Call it a favor."

19

The day has been a long one. Jennifer sits in the lounge, as she has these past six nights, listening to the click of the portable heater switch on and off as if it can't make up its goddamn mind. Her woolen jersey is buttoned all the way to the top and she's yanked up the thermostat as far as it will go, but there's still a chill she can't shake. It never seems to leave. But it's too early in the season for a fire. Besides, that would mean going to the shed to gather wood and she does not want to be outside alone at night.

Security is her principal concern right now and she's developed a routine of sorts that at least allows her to get some rest each night. First, she checks the windows and locks twice. She's meticulous, making sure the window latches are down as far as they will go and fixed into place, putting the key into each and every lock, opening and closing them, inspecting the mechanism to be certain it's functioning properly. Second, she waits until McKenzie is in bed then inspects all possible entrances, including the front and back door, the ranch sliders, and the garage entrance. Third, she makes sure her cell is fully charged and in her pocket and that the landline is working. Fourth, she repeats steps one through three until she is satisfied that she's left no stone unturned.

Yesterday McKenzie caught her in the act.

"I'm being over-cautious, I know," Jennifer had said.

"You always think the worst."

And Jennifer had to look away then, because written all over her daughter's face was the clear indication that

McKenzie thought this entire mess was somehow all her fault.

Maybe they should just leave. Start over somewhere new, back in Chicago. But the thought doesn't bring Jennifer much solace. Sell her practice? Leave everything she had worked so hard for? Disrupt McKenzie's life even more? And why should they be the ones to go when Hank was the one to blame?

She stares at the cup of coffee long gone cold and thinks about slipping out to buy a pack of cigarettes now that she's had a taste. But she doesn't of course. She can't leave McKenzie alone in case he comes back. Instead she scratches at the loose thread on the sofa arm and looks at the dish towel, the quaintness of the green apple print strangely perverse given the cargo hiding beneath it. She thinks about how the gun feels in her hand, rigid and heavy, like a car part, and the bullets, cool and smooth, clinking like leaden marbles in the hollow of her palm. Pushing those tiny missiles into the chamber had left a smear of grease on her fingertip and she can smell it now, the smoky sap-like odor, and feels oddly comforted.

She grows sleepy and spreads out on the couch, pushing the damask cushion behind her head. God she's so tired. She shuts her eyes and tells herself to relax. Everything is secure. Everything locked tight. No-one can get in. She repeats this until her breath grows low and heavy and she fades into a dreamless sleep.

She wakes up with his hand over her mouth. He is behind her. She knows the sound of his breath.

"I just want to talk," he says.

Startled, she yells into his palm.

"Quiet," he warns.

She obeys and he lowers his hand and circles to face her. He looks lucid and together—freshly showered, cleanly shaven, hair neatly brushed, like he is going on a job interview or a date. She can even smell the Ultra Tide on his clothes.

"I had to do this. I knew you wouldn't let me in otherwise."

"You need to leave," she says.

He nods but sits down beside her.

"Let me make it right, Jen. I know I've got work to do, but with time we can be a family again."

He places his hand on hers but she throws it off and gets to her feet.

"I said get out!"

She makes a dash for her phone, fully expecting him to stop her, but instead he says, "Go on. Call them."

She hesitates as if it's some sort of trick.

"There's a reason you can't, Jen. In your heart you know we can work through this."

"Work through this? Are you completely dumb? You've been abusing our daughter for God knows how long then sleeping next to me like all is good in this world. Don't you know how sick that is?"

"No one feels worse about this than me."

She shakes her head, incredulous. "You don't have any idea what you've done, do you?"

He reaches to touch her. "Jen."

"Get your hands off me!"

His touch turns vice-like and his face hardens. "Give me a chance, Jen."

She tries to twist away, but he squeezes tighter, mashing muscle against bone. "Let go!"

Sweat breaks out on his upper lip. "You're not going to ruin our family, everything we've worked so hard for."

She struggles against him. He grips harder.

"Stop it!" she cries.

He slams her onto the couch. Oh God, the gun, she needs the gun. She tries to pivot for it but he pins her down with his right knee and the green apples remain hopelessly out of reach.

"Hank!"

He puts his hand across her mouth and she screams. But the sound goes no further and all she can think of is the gun, centimeters from her head, the gun that would stop him in his tracks. He pushes up her skirt and tugs at her underwear and Jennifer tries to bite but can't get traction. He unzips his pants and loosens his grip and Jennifer takes her chance and powers her knee into his groin, throwing him off. She grabs the gun and points.

"Get out."

Her hands are trembling.

"Really, Jen. A gun?" he says.

He lifts his chin and touches the space between his eyes. The gun rattles in her hand.

"You can't do it, can you?" he says.

She straightens her arms and cocks the trigger.

"I said get out."

Then he smiles and reaches over and takes the gun. She can't believe it. It's as if he's removing a dangerous object from the hands of a child.

"What's going on?" calls McKenzie from the top of the stairs.

"Hon, stay there," says Jennifer.

McKenzie's jaw drops. "Freaking hell, is that a gun?"

"Come down for a minute, Mac," he says.

"Don't listen to him," implores Jennifer. "Go to my bedroom and call the police."

But McKenzie runs down and turns to Hank.

"Dad what are you doing?"

"I want you know I'm sorry Mac," he says, "for all of it."

McKenzie's face softens. "I know."

"It's too early for forgiveness but I hope one day you can."

McKenzie doesn't answer.

"Mac?" he whispers.

"You hurt me."

He begins to cry. "Oh God, Mac. I know."

He looks at the ceiling and chokes back sobs and starts thumbing the safety catch. On. Off. On. Off. Jennifer feels weightless. Every little thing, every sound, movement, smell, is magnified.

"Dad?"

But he isn't listening and Jennifer's ears begin to ring— a high pitch flat line like a TV warming up.

"Hank, please," says Jennifer.

Her throat closes in on itself. They were going to be a page three newspaper story. Their bodies would lie here undiscovered for days.

"Give me the gun," she says.

He shakes his head.

"No."

He presses the barrel flush against his temple.

"Daddy!"

His eyes flip open and he turns the gun on McKenzie then on Jennifer.

"We go together," he says.

He reaches for McKenzie. "She goes first, so she doesn't have to see you die."

Then everything's a blur. Jennifer is running for him, knocking him to the ground, the gun skittering across the floor. He grunts and tries to throw her off.

"Run!" she yells.

"I don't want to leave you," cries McKenzie.

"Go!"

Then, mercifully, Jennifer hears the click of the front door and McKenzie is out. Hank reaches for the gun and Jennifer gets up and slams her foot down on the back of his neck. She makes a break for it, bracing herself for the shot but there's none. Outside McKenzie is nowhere to be seen. Then, across the road, two shadows. Lenise calls out, McKenzie by her side.

"Hurry!"

Jennifer looks over her shoulder. Hank is on his feet.

"*Quickly*," hisses Lenise.

Jennifer runs across the road and they hurry inside and lock the door.

"Is he coming?" says McKenzie.

They stand in the dark, back from the window.

"He's looking over here," says Lenise.

"Have you called the police?" says Jennifer.

Lenise doesn't answer and keeps watch. "I told you this would happen, didn't I? Men are loose cannons when crossed."

"Lenise, have you called 911?"

"No."

"Why not!"

Jennifer reaches for the phone.

"Wait. He's leaving," says Lenise.

They watch as he gets into his car and drives away.

"What if he comes back?" says McKenzie.

"He won't."

"How can you be so sure?" says Jennifer.

"You surprised him. He didn't expect you to fight so hard. He needs time to think about his next move."

She takes the phone from Jennifer's hand.

"What are you doing? We need to call the police."

Lenise places the phone back on the cradle. "I've got a better idea."

20

Lenise shows them to the spare room upstairs. "You can stay here tonight."

She disappears briefly and returns with pillows and blankets, then disappears again and comes back with a glass of milk for McKenzie.

"To help you sleep."

Lenise turns to Jennifer. "And when you're done here, I've got something stronger downstairs."

Lenise leaves them and they stare at the empty doorway, standing there like two stunned wretches forced to flee a fire in the night.

"Drink your milk," says Jennifer.

McKenzie nods numbly and drinks while Jennifer organizes the blankets and pillows. When she's done, McKenzie gets into bed and Jennifer tucks her in tight.

"He was going to kill us," whispers McKenzie.

Jennifer doesn't know what to say. She can't say it's all over now and everything's going to be A-okay. She can't say he didn't mean it and isn't a nutcase and wouldn't have really hurt us. She can't say one day we'll look back on this and laugh.

Suddenly McKenzie grabs her and holds on tight. Jennifer can't remember the last time they had hugged and it feels good.

"I was so sacred, Mom."

"He's gone. We're safe now."

"I thought you were so brave."

"You're the brave one," says Jennifer, kissing the top of McKenzie's head. "Get some sleep."

Jennifer leaves McKenzie and finds Lenise sitting in the half-light sipping amber liquid from a tumbler.

Lenise signals with her chin to a bottle of liquor and full glass on the coffee table. "That's for you."

Jennifer drops into the armchair and takes a pull. Bourbon. Spicy and numbing. She touches the ache on her face. Bruises. Swelling. She can't cry. But a second later she is, uncontrollably and noiselessly, tears splashing into the bourbon, stinging the cut on her lip. Then she remembers she isn't alone and looks up to see Lenise staring at her.

"Don't waste your tears on him." In the glow of the light, Lenise's face is softer than usual, although her coarse hair is sticking out all over the place. "He's an asshole of the highest order."

"Yes," says Jennifer. "Yes, he is."

Jennifer drains her glass and Lenise pours her another.

"In South Africa we have street justice."

"You mean lawlessness."

"No, you're quite wrong. There is law there, just a different type."

"If you say so."

Lenise leans in to make her point. "Don't be one of those cases were the cops arrive two minutes too late. What I'm talking about Jennifer is *effectiveness*."

Jennifer stares into her glass. "I'm not sure I like what you're getting at."

"You can't leave this situation in the hands of other people who don't have a true interest in your wellbeing, who see you as just another name on a complaint sheet, another task of a hundred more they have piling up in their in-trays." Lenise pauses. "I'm talking about dealing with this once and for all."

"I'm not a killer."

Lenise waves a hand. "No, no. Not that far. He needs a scare. He needs to know you will no longer tolerate him."

"Why would he take any notice of what I do?"

"Because he wants control of the situation. You have to make him think he's still in charge."

All of a sudden, it's too much, and the tears are back, more fiercely than before.

"Oh God, why is this happening?"

"Cut it out," snaps Lenise. "You can't be afraid. That's his weapon. He's just like any other terrorist. We have to beat him at his own game. Now I'm not going to lie to you, this is going to be dangerous. You need to be strong for yourself and that girl in there. But above all else, Jenny, from now on, you show no weakness."

Jennifer wakes on the couch beneath a multi-colored afghan. She blinks heavily. The glass tumblers and bottle of bourbon sit empty on the coffee table. Her tongue is sandpaper against the roof of her mouth. She sits up, bracing herself for the rush of blood to the head, and when it comes she's still not ready for it, the pressure forcing itself mercilessly against her skull like its own unique weather system.

She unfurls her limbs from the tangled blankets and goes into the kitchen where Lenise is making tea.

Lenise looks up. "Your face."

Jennifer touches her aching cheekbone. "Bad?"

"It'll heal."

"Where's McKenzie?"

Lenise lifts her eyes to the ceiling. There's the hiss of water through pipes.

"Oh God, again?" says Jennifer. "Her skin is beginning to crack."

"It's how she copes," Lenise pours Jennifer some tea. "There's no sign of him. I checked."

"Good," Jennifer gulps down a mouthful. "I've been thinking. I'm going to shut the business for a week, get my head together."

Lenise puts down her cup. "Carry on as normal. He has to believe you're not frightened."

"But what if he tries something while I'm there?"

"He won't. There's too many people around and when it comes down to it, he's a coward. Just make sure you stick to public places and don't go walking down any dark alleys."

"What about McKenzie? I can't send her to school."

Lenise nods. "I think you're right. He could snatch her. She can stay here with me."

"Are you sure?"

"I wouldn't offer if I wasn't." Lenise points to the clock. "You're going to be late. You should go. We'll talk tonight."

Jennifer says goodbye to McKenzie and returns to the house for clean clothes. At the front door, she hesitates, struck with the fear he was still here, lurking somewhere behind a curtain or in an upstairs wardrobe. She shakes it off and goes inside but wishes she hadn't because the house doesn't feel like home anymore. There was a hollowness to it now, like the place had been abandoned after some cataclysmic event.

She's expecting to see chaos, but nothing is out of order, even the chintz cushion is resting on the sofa arm exactly where she'd left it. And there on the side table, next to the cold cup of coffee and reading lamp, is the neatly folded apple print dish towel and the gun placed on top.

Jennifer wraps the gun and hides it in the hot water cupboard beneath a stack of double sheets then goes upstairs to change her clothes, forgoing a shower to get out of the house more quickly. But when she looks in the mirror, she knows she's got a problem. The bone under her eye is a deep, curdled black, her left cheek livid and swollen. She pulls out the tube of concealer from her makeup bag and does her best.

When she gets to work, Rosemary says, "Oh my Gosh, Jen, what happened to your face?"

Jennifer decides to keep as close to the truth as possible. "I had a fight with Hank."

"Hank did this to you?"

"I don't want to talk about. I'm okay now."

"But Jen, he hit you?" she says. "I just can't believe it."

"How's it looking for today? Are we busy?"

"Has this sort of thing happened before?"

Jennifer falters. "Rosie, please, just leave it."

She flees into her office and tries to calm down and nearly gets there until Rosemary buzzes. The first client of the day has arrived.

Jennifer feels the clients survey the damaged terrain, as if she's the one under examination not them, and before

118

they can ask what happened, she tells them it was a car accident, but when she offers her explanation she can feel the doubt, from the women mostly, who nod silently, but with sympathetic and skeptical faces. None of the men ask, but Jennifer doesn't care what they think, she's just relieved to get through the day.

She finishes just after five and heads for the grocery store, leaving a concerned-looking Rosemary to lock up. The store is busy and she encounters more stares and wishes she'd had the foresight to wear sunglasses. She can't believe she's doing something as mundane as shopping for groceries in the middle of all of this, but she can't expect Lenise to feed them. She'd done enough already. Jennifer does a quick circuit and gets what she needs and hands her bank card to the clerk and he zaps it through the machine.

"Declined," he says.

"What?"

"The card declined."

"But there should be enough money."

Hank had done this, she was sure of it, and Jennifer knew when she checked their online accounts, he would have drained them too. She fights back anger, digs around in her purse and hands over another card.

"Try this."

The guy puts it through the machine.

"Invalid."

The queue grows behind her. People crane to take a look at the beat-up woman with the bad credit.

"You got cash?" says the checkout guy.

She looks in her purse. Two twenties. Not enough. She grabs the milk, cereal, eggs and bread.

"Here."

She pays the money and wheels the cart to the side. The tub of frozen yoghurt drips onto the linoleum floor.

"Sorry," she says uselessly.

Jennifer hurries to the exit. Over the loud speaker Sophia is called to put the groceries away.

21

When Lenise opens the door Jennifer is hit by the smell of oven-baked vanilla.

"That was unnecessary," says Lenise, looking at the bag of groceries.

"You didn't ask for any of this."

Lenise waves a hand. "Forget about it."

In the kitchen Jennifer finds McKenzie peeling carrots, face scrubbed clean, wearing a blue hoodie and sweat pants Jennifer doesn't recognize. Her hair isn't wet so that was a start.

"How you holding up, hon?"

"Lenise made us dinner."

Lenise blushes. "It's only simple fare."

"Would you mind if I clean up first?" says Jennifer.

When Jennifer's done with the shower, she goes downstairs and finds Lenise in the living room.

"Dinner won't be long," says Lenise.

Jennifer takes a seat on the couch and picks up the book on the coffee table. *Precious Stones.*

"I was going to be a gemologist back in South Africa," says Lenise. "Things didn't work out."

"You still could."

"What? At my age? And then there's the cost. Education isn't cheap."

Jennifer puts down the book.

"Sounds like you gave up too soon."

Lenise flashes with anger. "What would you know?"

Jennifer shrugs. "Sometimes you've got to fight for what you want. The universe rewards action."

"Don't give me that new age bullshit."

McKenzie appears with a casserole pot.

"Dinner's ready," she says.

Jennifer picks her way through the meal, a beef stew of some kind, spiced with fennel seed and marjoram. It may have been good, Jennifer can't tell because she seems to have lost her ability to taste. McKenzie is bright and talkative and Jennifer wonders if she's experiencing some kind of post-traumatic stress thing. After they finish, McKenzie gets up to put the plates in the dishwasher but Lenise shoos her away.

"That thing leaks. Off you go, girl. Your mother and I will do them the old fashioned way."

"I don't mind," says McKenzie.

Lenise shakes her head. "I have a rule that whoever lends a hand with dinner doesn't do the dishes."

"But I like helping."

"It's okay, hon, Lenise and I need to talk," says Jennifer.

McKenzie looks like she's about to argue but finally leaves.

"She's has a forgiving heart," says Lenise, filling the sink and adding a squirt of dishwashing liquid. "Although that may not last forever." Lenise dunks a pot in the hot water and washes the inside in slow smooth circles. "Daughters are so much easier than sons. Oh, everyone says how easy boys are to raise, all they need is three meals a day and a bed. But that's a lie. Males are far more complex than that. You cannot take them at face value as they would have you believe. They have secrets. They're selfish. They drain you of emotion and give nothing in return. A girl, well, she takes the initiative. She'll do things for other people that she gets no personal benefit from. She will do things without being asked. A man you have to prod and cajole and nag. You have to make lists for them to follow. They can't think beyond themselves. But a girl, a girl is thoughtful."

Lenise looks at Jennifer. "I think I've found someone who will assist," she says.

Jennifer stares at her. "I don't want to involve anyone else in this mess."

"You didn't think we could do this by ourselves, did you, Jenny? Your husband needs to know you're serious. Outside help will show him you mean business."

"What exactly are we talking about here, Lenise?"

"Use your imagination."

"Beating him up?"

"If that's what it takes."

"What if things go too far?"

"They won't, Ron's a professional."

"Ron? I don't like the sound of this. I'm not a violent person."

"That's what Ron's for."

"What if something goes wrong and we get caught, we'd be accessories. I'll end up in jail and where would that leave McKenzie?"

"You want him gone from your life, don't you?" says Lenise.

"Yes."

"This is your only real option."

Jennifer drops into the chair. "I didn't ask for any of this."

"You need to keep it together, Jenny, for the girl's sake."

Jennifer looks at Lenise. "Can we trust this guy? Ron?"

"He won't let us down."

Jennifer runs a hand over her face. "God, I can't believe I'm even contemplating this."

"Effectiveness, Jenny, remember that."

"So you keep saying."

"His fee is ten thousand dollars."

"What!"

Lenise shrugs. "He's taking a risk. He needs to be well compensated."

Jennifer looks at Lenise and lowers her voice. "Hank has drained my accounts."

Lenise puts down the dish cloth. "Bastard. Without money this is going to be difficult. What about the business?"

Jennifer shakes her head. "I could be audited. I can't explain away a ten thousand dollar withdrawal."

Lenise places the final plate in the dish rack and drains the sink.

"Think of something. I need it by tomorrow."

The drain gurgles and the sink runs dry.

"Okay," says Jennifer, finally. "I'll find a way."

22

Lenise met Ron three years ago at a bar in Lebanon, Missouri. He was small but well-built, with the ropy biceps of a fulltime construction worker. And he liked to show them off. He was younger than her and when he first bought her a drink she was suspicious that it was some sort of set up, that perhaps he had friends hiding around a corner laughing their heads off as he bought some mature a drink on a dare.

But it wasn't a set up. He'd been alone and just passing through. He told her he moved around the country doing his thing, "freelancing" he called it. They had talked all night and then went back to his trailer and made love. Both of them knew it wouldn't last, but that was okay.

They met up every once in a while and he'd show off his latest bloody knuckles or bruised ribs and she would fuss over him and coo "poor baby" and they would polish off a bottle of Jack and end up between the sheets.

She hadn't spoken to him in over a year and was lucky he still had the same cell number.

"Hey Lenny, how you been keeping?" he says.

"Peachy."

He laughs. "Smartass as usual."

"I might have some business for you," she says.

"Yeah?"

"How does 10k sound?"

"Sounds mighty sweet to me."

She'd be a liar to say it hadn't occurred to her to pad out Ron's fee, take a commission. Lord knew she needed the money. But it wasn't right in the circumstances, given what that son of a bitch had done to the girl.

"It's for a friend of mine. Husband trouble."

"Better not on the phone, Lenny."

"Oh, yes. That was careless."

"Usual place?" he says.

"That would be good."

The usual was a diner on the outskirts of Madison. He is already there when Lenise arrives. She has taken extra special attention with her hair. She knows it's stupid, that this is purely a business transaction, but she can't help it. He smiles and gives her a hug. She feels his muscle contract beneath his plaid shirt. He had grown older, but in a good way, and Lenise wonders, not for the first time, why it was when men got older it was salt and pepper sexy but when a woman aged she was a washed out has been.

"You're a sight for sore eyes, Lenny."

"Liar."

"You get hitched yet?"

"Cut it out, Ron." But she loves the attention.

They order coffee and when they're alone, she pushes the envelope across the table.

"It's all there."

He takes a look, raises his eyebrows.

"The full amount?"

"I trust you."

They fall silent. Outside, over by the dumpster, a fat guy in a ketchup-stained chef's apron alternates between smoking and knocking back a diet coke.

"Any special requests?" says Ron.

"She wants him out of her life for good. You need to convince him of that."

He looks at her, curious. "Whatever's going on with your friend has had an effect on you too, Lenny."

"If it was up to me, I wouldn't just be scaring him."

"Fair enough."

The coffee arrives. Outside, the filthy cook stabs out his cigarette.

"You up for something stronger, Lenny? My motel's just around the corner."

She looks at him and aims for her best smile. "What took you so long to ask?"

When Lenise gets home the back door is open which is strange because Jennifer and McKenzie had returned to their house four nights ago. She calls out but there's no answer. She calls again and the kitchen door opens.

"Hey," says Cody.

"For God's sake, turn on some lights. I thought you were a rapist."

"Nice to see you too, Ma."

She pushes past him into the kitchen and he follows.

"What's all that?" he says, nodding at the scrabble board on the table.

"The girl from across the road comes over sometimes."

"The dog killer's kid?"

"What happened to Minnesota?"

"Didn't work out."

"And what's that got to do with me?"

He opens the fridge, whistles when he sees the home-made pizza and lemon-frosted chocolate cake.

"Having a party or something?"

He takes a long gulp from the pineapple Kool-Aid Lenise had made especially for McKenzie, then takes a slice of pizza, dropping crumbs all over the place.

"Watch what you're doing," she says, retrieving the dish cloth to clean up the mess.

"Hey, I bought you something," he says.

Cody digs around in his satchel and passes her a small box made of soap stone. An intricate Asiatic lily is carved into the lid.

"I got it from an old Indian guy. Eagle Feather, would you believe. He had a stall on the side of the highway with snake skins and other dream-catcher shit, but then I saw that. The dude said someone in his tribe made it. I thought you could use it for Baby."

Lenise traces a fingertip across a fluted petal.

"It's nice," she says.

"You're welcome."

She puts down the box. "Why are you here?"

"I told you. Things didn't work out. I had to leave the place I was staying at."

He turns back to the fridge and drinks more Kool-Aid. She takes it from his hands and returns it.

"Bad luck," she says.

"Yeah."

She knows what's coming next.

"I thought I would move back here."

She doesn't say anything.

"Just for awhile," he says. "Until I build up a bit of cash."

Lenise walks into the lounge, straightens the afghan across the back of the couch.

"That's not convenient, right now, Cody."

He stares at her. "What do you mean?"

"Just that."

"What am I supposed to do?"

She shrugs.

"You're a smart boy, you'll work it out."

"But I've got nowhere else to go."

She looks at him. For a moment she feels bad enough to relent but she won't be his door mat. There was also the small matter of tonight's planned event.

"I've got somewhere I'm meant to be," she says, looking at her watch.

"You're really going to do this? Turn away your own son?"

"Call me when you get settled," she says.

She returns to the kitchen and seconds later the front door slams. On the bench, she picks up the soap stone box and admires the detail of the delicate lily. She softens. It was truly the nicest thing he'd ever given her. Perhaps she'd been too rash, not letting him stay, forcing him out on the street. She turns the box over for a closer look at the lacework running the length of the bottom, and blinks at the tiny white sticker. *Made in Pakistan.*

23

Jennifer is certain she has developed a permanent tic. This morning she awoke to the feel of a recurring pinch on her upper left eyelid and when she looked in the mirror, she couldn't see a thing, but it was there, hidden somewhere inside the lithe tunnel of a blood vessel, twitching like a mini heart beat.

Part of the plan was to move back into the house and pretend like everything was normal, which she had done. There'd been no sign of Hank since he drained the accounts and she'd taken to watching from the kitchen window, waiting to catch the glint of a steel barrel in a shard of moonlight or a white-eyed blink from the darkness. But there had been nothing except for the slow stir of leaves and the occasional throaty hoot from an owl.

Jennifer hopes that when she tries his cell it will be disconnected or he will answer and say he's moved to Texas or Albuquerque or Maine.

But she's just playing games with herself. He hasn't left town. He was waiting for the right time to strike. For all she knew, he could be spying on the house right now.

She looks at the cordless phone resting on top of the closed toilet seat and thinks about what she has to say. Just act natural, Lenise had said, it's as simple as that. Simple when you're not the one doing it.

That damn tic is working overtime and Jennifer tries to rub it out. Oh God, this was never going to work. He's going to pick up on the thread of uncertainty in her voice. She should call the whole thing off.

"We need to talk," she says out loud. Then again. "Hank, we need to talk. *Tonight*."

"What are you doing?" says McKenzie, appearing in the bathroom doorway.

"Nothing."

"Who were you talking to?"

"Myself."

"Oh."

"I think I'm going nuts, hon."

"Great. Two crazy parents," says McKenzie.

Next week, when all this was over, Jennifer would need to think about their future.

"I'll be down in a sec."

She waits until McKenzie leaves, picks up the phone and dials the number.

He answers on the fifth ring, breathless and eager.

"Jen?"

He sounds so normal. She can't believe this is the same man who tried to kill her a week ago.

"I've arranged for me and McKenzie to be somewhere else tonight. The papers are on the table, Hank. *Sign them*. I've bagged up some of your things too. I'll leave the backdoor unlocked."

He says something, but the phone drops out as if he is walking into wind.

"I can't hear you," she says.

"I'm sorry."

"Just sign the papers and leave us alone."

When she gets off the phone she nearly throws up. She dials Lenise.

"I don't think he bought it."

"He'll come."

"I'm not sure I can go through with this. I mean, actually pull it off, seeing him face-to-face."

"You're stronger than you think."

"What if he figures it out?"

"He won't."

"There's got be another way."

"We've been through this already, Jenny, there isn't. We need to trust Ron."

Jennifer stares at the flagstone tiles on the bathroom floor. "Why are you doing this Lenise?"

There's a pause. "Your girl deserved better."

"Thank you."

"Just be ready."

24

When she was in college, Jennifer had trained for a marathon. Being a complete novice, she sought advice from a sports coach, a fifty-something bear of a man appropriately named Jack Fit. Jack Fit obliged her by designing a program for her to follow three months out from the race. He told her baby steps at first. Jog for one minute, rest for thirty seconds, then jog for two minutes, rest for twenty-five seconds and so on. "The point," he said leaning on bent knee with a paddle-thick forearm, "is to build upon what you have done before until you can take off the training wheels and soar from your Mama's nest". Jack Fit also liked to toss about his catchphrase, "you just gotta bury yourself in the process". He would say it every time they met, jabbing his finger into his palm for emphasis.

Jennifer followed his advice to the letter, never missing a training session no matter the weather or how tired or busy she got and in less than six weeks she could run thirteen miles in one hit. Jennifer even saw the college nutritionist and followed a strict diet of brown rice and boiled chicken and steamed broccoli. It was the most self-disciplined she had ever been. Come race day, when she gathered at the starting line, along with a few hundred other hopefuls, number forty-nine bib strapped to her chest, she felt like she truly deserved to be there.

It started out great. The first ten miles were fine, the next five a little harder. But she persevered, despite throwing up lime Gatorade all over herself, the brutal chafing between her thighs, and the continuous flatulence that threatened to become more.

But when she reached the seventeen mile mark, she hit a wall. Not physically, but mentally. Nothing in all of her dogged, by-the-book training had prepared her for the sheer boredom of it. The monotonous pounding, the 'are-we-there-yet' child's voice stuck on repeat in her head. Around the corner was just another corner. A flat line of unhappy never-endingness, where the logic of time became illogical.

And as her light-footedness abandoned her and each step became a leaden, swamp-sucking feat, it dawned on her that above everything else—the hamstring strength, the well-developed slow-twitch muscle fibers, the mastery of the exhale stress breathing technique—the most important requirement for a marathon runner was the ability to delay gratification. *Mental stamina. Endurance of the mind.* Two thirds of the way through, Jennifer realized she did not have that particular attribute and collapsed and couldn't get back up.

She knew that somewhere miles up ahead at the finishing line Jack Fit was waiting in his mirrored sunglasses with a slap on the back and a fresh bottle of water, and that she should get to her feet and carry on, but when some old lady in a purple tank top offered Jennifer a granola bar and a lift to the First Aid bay in her ancient green VW, Jennifer agreed.

Jennifer takes a heavy drag from the cigarette and thinks about that race. What had started out as a triumph based on good planning and determination ended in dismal failure. That marathon attempt, so long ago now, had been death by a thousand cuts. Much like tonight. The waiting. The need for all this to be over before she broke.

"Take this."

Lenise hands her a glass.

"I can't drink anything."

"You can and you will. You'll need another before he arrives."

Jennifer takes the tumbler, stamps out her cigarette and immediately lights another.

"It's chilly out here," says Lenise. "Let's go inside."

"The cold makes me feel better."

Jennifer drinks some more. The glass shakes in her hand.

"Everything will be okay if you just stick to the plan," says Lenise.

"I just want it over."

"You can do this, Jenny. Just think of McKenzie. By the way, she was asleep the last time I checked."

"She loves spending time at your house. Better than here," says Jennifer.

"Nonsense."

"Sometimes she looks at me like it's my fault."

"Don't go down that track. It won't do anyone any good, least of all yourself. Is everything done?"

Jennifer nods.

"Excellent."

They fall silent.

"Hear that?" says Jennifer.

"What?"

"There's a screech owl out there somewhere. I've heard it every night since I've been back. It makes me feel better just knowing it's there."

"A guardian angel."

"Something like that."

"Superstition is for dummies," says Lenise.

"You know," says Jennifer. "Sometimes you could try being a little less blunt."

"There's nothing wrong with honesty."

"All I'm saying is there's ways of putting things."

They fall silent. Lenise sips her drink.

"In South Africa hunters use a particular type of booby trap. They dig a hole, place a wire around the circumference, cover it with leaves then wait for the animal to walk by. When the thing falls in, the hunter tugs the wire and triggers a special type of slipknot that contracts around the animal's neck and strangles it. It's called The Devil's Wire."

"So we're doing the Devil's work now, terrific," says Jennifer.

"Sometimes the animal gets decapitated."

"Nice."

Lenise drains her glass and opens the door to go inside.

"Shit happens," she says.

25

She is in the kitchen, waiting, hands palm down on the countertop trying to calm her shuddering breath. Close by are the divorce papers, blue biro laid across the top, wine glass a quarter full next to an open bottle of Australian red. Her stomach rolls at the smell of tannins and she turns away to watch pearls slip from the faucet and thump into the sink.

It's not long before she hears fumbling at the backdoor and footsteps in the hallway.

"Jen, what are you doing here?"

He's genuinely surprised.

"Jen," he says again. "What's all this about?"

He regards her, wary, eyes scanning the room.

"There's no gun," she says.

"Okay."

She straightens her spine and picks up her wine glass.

"They know I'm here with you—my lawyer, the police— and they'll be here in seconds if you try anything."

"Brave," he says.

"I won't be scared in my own home, Hank."

He takes off his jacket and lays it across the dining room chair. There's a waft of Jovan Musk. She can feel herself shake, and tries it hide it, but decides it probably doesn't matter. He nods at the wine.

"May I?"

Without waiting for a reply, he retrieves a glass from the cupboard, pours himself a drink and takes a fulsome mouthful.

"You always did have good taste," he says, taking another sip and sitting.

"This isn't a party, Hank."

He looks at the dripping faucet. "I keep meaning to fix that."

She pushes the divorce papers toward him. "I wanted to make sure you signed these."

He glances down at the papers. "I can't believe it's come to this."

"Well, believe it."

He drains his glass and pours another.

"When did you become so cold?" he says. He waves a hand. "Oh, no I'm not talking about now, I mean before all this. You were cold long before now."

She can barely contain her outrage. "You're blaming me?"

"You've never been happy. I've never been good enough. Even with McKenzie, you—"

"Don't you dare."

"You always made her feel like a disappointment. Her weight, her school work."

"Stop it."

"All she ever wanted was for you to love her, accept her, *unconditionally*. You know what that word means Jen? Unconditional?"

She picks up the papers and slams them down in front of him. "Sign them and get out."

He looks at her. "I'm not signing anything."

"It's over, Hank, and there's nothing you can do about it."

He gets to his feet and points a finger in her face. "You are my fucking wife."

She takes a step backward. "I want you out of my life."

"Tear up those damn papers."

"You don't scare me, Hank."

"You're my wife and you'll do as you're fucking well told." He grabs the papers and shoves them in her face.

She pushes him away.

He looks at her then pauses. "That's the third time you've done that," he says.

"What?"

"Checked your watch. What's going on?"

He begins to waver on his feet. He looks at his wine glass on the countertop and picks it up, angles it under the light. He turns to her and smiles.

"Clever," he starts to laugh. "Oh, very clever. You put something in the wine."

"Don't be ridiculous."

He continues to laugh. Jennifer's temple pounds. It isn't working quickly enough. He should be flat on his back by now. He sways dramatically, catches himself and holds out the glass.

"Drink it."

"I'm not trying to poison you, Hank, if that's what you think."

He steps forward, the laughter now gone, and presses the glass to her lips.

"I said drink it."

She tries to push him away. "Let go of me."

"You stupid bitch."

139

He throws the glass, smashing it against the pantry door. He rushes for her and puts his hands around her throat.

"Stop it, Hank."

His hands grip her jugular, crushing the tiny bones in her larynx, and Jennifer begins to see grey snow. She tries to hold on. Lenise should be here any second.

Then his hold softens, slips away entirely and she scrambles backward until she collides with the wall, gasping and sucking in oxygen.

Hank squints at her and tries to say something but can't form the words. He gives his head two hard shakes and stumbles into the coffee table, tipping like a felled pine, crashing to the floor, flat on his back, final and silent.

Lenise appears.

"Oh God," says Jennifer. "He's dead."

"Don't be stupid. Can't you see him breathing."

"Where were you, he could've killed me."

"I had to wait, give it time to work."

Lenise disappears and comes back with a fitness bag. "We need to tie him up."

She rolls him onto his front.

"Help me."

Jen pulls his hands behind his back and Lenise does the zip ties and the gag.

"What's the time?" Lenise asks.

"Twenty to twelve."

"Ron will be here soon."

They sit down to wait.

26

The lump that is Jennifer's husband lies on the linoleum in front of them. The pose of the child, Lenise had once heard a yoga teacher call it. And right now it seems preposterous to see a grown man in such a state of vulnerability, preposterous and strangely gratifying.

His sleeping face is turned toward them in the half-light. He is snoring. The sound rattles Lenise's nerves and she fights the urge to strike him or roll him over or pinch his nose in order to stop it.

She glances at Jennifer who has remained quiet since they had bound his wrists. She has made a meal of her fingernails and is beginning on the quick. She had done well, though. Lenise hadn't been entirely sure Jennifer wouldn't crack.

"It's after midnight," says Jennifer, getting up to look out the window.

"Ron's a professional. He'll be here."

Jennifer folds her arms across her chest. "I don't like this."

"Be patient."

Jennifer continues to savage her digits. Another ten minutes passes. Then twenty. Still no sign of Ron. Lenise joins Jennifer and stares at the empty street.

"There'll be a good reason why he's late, I'm sure of it," says Lenise.

"Call him."

"Ron said not to, in case things could be traced back."

Jennifer nods toward Hank. "What if he wakes up?"

"He'll be out for another hour at least."

Jennifer looks at her watch. "It's twelve forty-five. I think you should call him."

"Alright. Don't get your knickers in a twist," snaps Lenise.

She pulls out her cellphone and dials Ron's number. Straight to voicemail. She clicks off.

"Something must be wrong," she says.

"Maybe he had an accident."

"Possibly."

Jennifer stares at Lenise. "He's not coming, is he?"

"For God's sake, will you cut it out."

Lenise tries his phone again. Leaves a curt message. *Call me.*

"He's taken the money and run," says Jennifer.

"Ron wouldn't do that."

"Why not? He'll beat someone up for cash but won't swindle a couple of stupid women? I bet he's laughing at us right now. We were easy pickings."

"You don't know what you're talking about."

"Take a look around you, Lenise. Where is this knight in shining armor?"

Hank groans.

"Oh God, he's waking up," says Jennifer.

"That's impossible."

"Well, I'm not imagining things, Lenise. You can see him as clearly as me."

"Did you put the entire amount in the wine?"

"Yes."

"You couldn't have."

"I did!"

"You must have made a mistake," says Lenise.

"Me? What about you? Did you work out the correct dosage for his weight and height?"

"There was enough to sink a ship."

"Apparently not," says Jennifer.

Hank moves his legs.

"We don't have long," says Lenise. "Where's the gun?"

"What!"

"We need it."

Jennifer shakes her head. "No."

Lenise pushes past her. "Stupid woman."

She opens the cutlery drawer and takes out the biggest knife.

"What are you doing?" cries Jennifer.

"We haven't got a choice. He's going to wake up and there's nothing we can do about it."

Lenise stands over the groaning Hank. Jennifer steps in front of her.

"We have to let him go," says Jennifer.

"Let him go? Are you crazy? You untie him, he kills us. Even if he doesn't do it now, he'll come back."

"I'll tell him he hit his head and passed out."

"That's ridiculous."

"I'll say I drugged him but I was an idiot for doing it."

Hank is raising himself off the floor like a punch-drunk fighter. Lenise holds out the knife to Jennifer.

"It will be self-defense," she says.

Jennifer takes a step back. "No way."

"Don't be weak."

"I won't do it."

He is on his feet, shakes his head thickly. He looks over his shoulder at his zip-tied wrists.

"What the fuck..." he slurs.

He looks at Lenise, confused to see her there. His eyes jump to the knife in her hand. Fear clouds his features, then rage. He growls and stumbles as if to grab the knife but forgets about his bound hands and loses balance and goes down, falling forward, straight into Lenise and the knife.

It feels, to Lenise, as if a sack of rocks has been leveled at her, and she lies trapped beneath the weight, unsure in that moment whether the knife has plunged into him or her. She can hear screaming. Stupid Jenny, she thinks, then realizes the noise is coming from inside her own head. She tries to shout but her mouth is pressed into the bone of his shoulder.

She feels release and sees light. He has somehow hauled himself up and is standing above her, the knife stuck in his ribs like some sort of ghoulish Halloween trick. He looks down at the knife in disbelief then lurches across the kitchen, bumping into the table, the cupboards, the fridge.

"What have you done!" yells Jennifer.

"Quick, help me up. I've hurt my arm," says Lenise.

Hank figure eights in an expanding pool of blood.

"Hank, you're hurt, you need to stop moving," implores Jennifer.

He tries to talk but it comes out as a whistle.

"Hank please do as I say."

His movements are slowing, becoming exaggerated, his breathing strangled and faint. Jennifer tries to go to him but Lenise holds her back.

"*Wait*," says Lenise.

"Let me go!" Jennifer struggles against Lenise. "We need help!"

"Just wait."

They watch color leach from his face and he stumbles and falls. He lies in the red mess on the floor still and silent, the knife in his side like a handle. They wait for him to get back up but he doesn't. Lenise kneels down and checks his pulse then stands up and looks at Jennifer.

"What a fucking disaster," she says.

27

It was an all-American house. A wagon wheel out front, stars and stripes flapping from a sixteen foot flag pole, a bespoke birdhouse, blue with white trim. If you looked in the distance behind the house, there was a church steeple too. Tuesdays and Wednesdays were Jennifer's days. She took the different bus route from school. Her mother insisted she not be in the house alone but come here to Mrs. Baker's instead.

At twelve, Mrs. Baker said Jennifer was old enough to look after the young ones so homework was left undone. Instead there were snotty noses to wipe and dirty diapers to change. Jennifer never told her mother what went on there, how they would be made to sit in the hard-backed chairs and listen to Mrs. Baker preach and thump the black leather bible as if it was the behind of one of the naughty boys.

And Jennifer never told her mother about the time when she got up from Mrs. Baker's prickly molasses sofa to warm a bottle for one of the under-twos and left a melon-sized starburst of red behind. Mrs Baker had called her back to look. "Sinner." She made Jennifer pray on her knees beneath the wooden crucifix on the back wall. "Louder, sinner." The other children did not even glance her way and continued to watch cartoons on the old television set that showed everything in a flickering green and yellow hue.

Afterward, Jennifer had run to the bathroom to check under her skirt and cried when she saw the bloody starfish that was her hand. She was certain she was dying from the inside out.

"*Hey.*"

And there was that smell, like rust.

"*Hey. Wake up.*"

And the sound of Mrs. Baker banging on the door, yelling for her to come and clean up her mess.

"*Jenny.*"

Jennifer opens her eyes. Lenise. Who has a red starfish of her own smack in the middle of her chest.

"You fainted."

"What?"

Then she smells it, the blood, and turns to look. Hank is an island in a sea of crimson.

"Oh God, it isn't true."

"Get up," says Lenise.

"I'm going to be sick," says Jennifer.

Hank has one eye open and it's looking directly at her.

"No, you're not. Get up."

Lenise hauls Jennifer to her feet and Jennifer runs to the sink but nothing comes out then suddenly waves hit her but amount to no more than two slippery strings of bile. She reaches for the tap and slaps water on her face. It is blessed and cold and bracing.

"You killed him," she says, turning to Lenise.

"He did it to himself."

Lenise's eyes are unnaturally bright.

"You got the knife," says Jennifer.

"He would have killed us."

"I'm calling the police."

"They won't believe anything you say when they find the medication in his system. They'll think you've planned everything."

"I'm not taking the blame for this," says Jennifer.

"I'll deny it and there's nothing to say otherwise," says Lenise. "I did you a favor."

"You're joking!"

"I did you a favor and that was not without risk to my own life."

"I didn't ask for any of this!" cries Jennifer.

"Neither did I. You saw what happened."

Jennifer buries her face in her hands. "How could I have been so stupid to go along with this?"

"You think this is easy for me? I was betrayed too."

They fall silent and stare at the body. Blood is beginning to tighten in places.

"We need to work together," says Lenise. "No fighting. It's the only way."

"Oh God, what are we going to do?"

Lenise sits down. "We have to get rid of the body."

"Lenise, we can't. This is beyond us."

"There's no other choice."

"I can't believe I'm hearing this."

"Well, believe it."

Jennifer shakes her head. "This is already way out of hand. We need to own up."

"Own up? Are you crazy? We're not talking about a Snickers bar you might have stolen at the corner store when you were eight. This is homicide. A felony. We know it was self-defense but they'll say it's murder. You think if you tell them the truth—that you didn't *mean* it—they're just going to let you off the hook? No way. There's jail time here anyway you look at it."

"I wasn't the one holding the knife."

Lenise leans in close. "You don't seem to get it, Jenny. You're in this as much as I am, whether you want to admit it or not. There's a highly illegal surgical grade sedative in his system because of you."

"I don't care," Jennifer gets to her feet and picks up the phone. "This insanity stops right now."

Lenise snatches the phone from her hand.

"You will spend the rest of your life in prison. McKenzie will have no one. Is that what you want?"

Jennifer feels faint again. "Of course not."

"Are you on board, then?"

"This isn't some real estate deal, Lenise," says Jennifer.

Lenise slams her hand into the pantry door. "You know what," she spits, "maybe I should walk away right now, leave you with this mess, because I could do that Jenny, I could do that right now and where would that leave you?"

Jennifer glances at Hank's body and swallows. "Don't," she says.

"Don't what?"

"Don't go. I'll do it."

"Good." Lenise calms down. "Like I said we need to work together."

She takes a glass from the cupboard, fills it with water and drinks the entire thing.

She turns to Jennifer. "We better get started."

28

At first Lenise suggests the backyard given the practical benefits: it's close, convenient and easily controllable. Dig a hole in the ground. Put him in it. Job done. But Jennifer vetoes the idea. A grave where they had once held fourth of July BBQs and made snowmen at Christmas was way too sinister. And there were also the associated risks. What if Jennifer sold the house and the new owners wanted to put in a pool or add an extension? Imagine their surprise when they unearthed the remains of an adult male, all traceable back to Jennifer.

Then Lenise suggests weighing him down in a lake or some other waterway. It's an attractive idea. But Jennifer says no. While in theory it seems viable, in practice, there's too much risk. Bodies stay submerged for a time but also have a habit of eventually rising to the surface.

Jennifer says no to a staged suicide, too. The stab wound meant an autopsy could reveal an unexplained knick to a rib bone or some other injury that would give them away.

"You can't just say no to everything," says Lenise.

"I'm not."

"Well, I don't hear any ideas."

"We're overthinking this. We need to get back to basics," says Jennifer. "A grave in the forest. Natural decomposition. Throw in some lime to speed things up. Jesus, I can't believe I'm saying this."

"We don't want to be caught on camera buying compost at 3 a.m.," says Lenise.

"There's lime in the garage."

"Good. Are we agreed then?"

Jennifer is silent.

"Jenny?"

"Yes."

From the garage, Lenise retrieves six large black polyurethane trash bags, a bottle of bleach, scissors and rags. When she returns, she throws Jennifer a pair of kitchen gloves, and puts on a pair herself.

"We've got to wash him down to get rid of our DNA, just in case they find him, which they won't, but it's best to be thorough."

First they needed to drag him out of that pool of blood.

"You push, I'll pull," says Lenise.

Lenise covers the blood puddle with trash bags and tucks her hands under his belt while Jennifer braces herself at the small of his back.

"Go!"

He is heavier than they could have ever imagined.

"You're not pushing hard enough!" says Lenise.

"You need to pull more."

They try again but he could be super-glued to the floor.

"No wonder they cut bodies up," says Lenise.

They make another attempt. Movement. Just a bit. They get a rhythm going, shifting him an inch at a time, slowly but surely.

"That's enough," says Lenise, breathless.

The body is about two feet clear of the blood, an ever-decreasing red smear rainbows out from the spot where he fell to where he is now.

"How are we going to get him out of the house?" says Jennifer.

"We'll think of something. Give me the scissors." Lenise cuts off his clothes and the zip ties and shoves them in a bag. "I'll burn these later."

Then she soaks two strips from an old towel in bleach and gives one to Jennifer.

"Start from the bottom, I'll work from the top."

But Jennifer can't bear to touch him. The nakedness under the harsh kitchen light is disarmingly explicit. The body is like a poorly filled human suit. It's Hank, but it isn't. An imitation of the real thing. Jennifer has stepped into a dual universe.

"I can't do this."

"Yes, you can." Lenise kneels down and gets ready to begin.

"Wait," says Jennifer.

She goes to the cupboard beneath the sink, lifts a clean dishtowel from the drawer and places it across Hank's face.

They work steadily and methodically. Big toe. Buttocks. Chin. Clavicle. Earlobe. Elbow. The harsh solvent stings their eyes but they continue on until they are sure to wipe every part of the body. When they are done, they roll him onto three clean trash bags sliced open like tarps and get ready to wrap him. But Jennifer stops Lenise with her hand.

"What about the knife?"

"That's a point," agrees Lenise. "Away you go, then."

"Me? I'm not doing it."

Lenise shakes her head. "Oh, for heaven's sake."

Lenise reaches over and grips the plastic handle and pulls out the knife leaving behind a tiny chasm and a stream of claret. Lenise puts the knife in the same bag as his clothes for later disposal and they wipe him down again then remove the dishtowel covering his face, and fold the plastic around him, tying it in place with Home Depot garden twine until he looks like a trussed side of beef.

"How are we going to move him?" says Jennifer. "He might as well be a half ton of cement."

"I've got an idea," says Lenise.

She disappears and returns with the Aztec rug from the living room.

"It's a trick I learnt when I had to move a refrigerator on my own."

She lines up the rug next to the body then looks over her shoulder at Jennifer.

"Well, don't just stand there," she says.

They roll the body onto the rug and lie it flat on its back.

"Now we pull," says Lenise.

They each grab a corner and are soon out of the kitchen, down the hallway and into the garage. Lenise opens the trunk of the car.

"He'll be way too heavy to lift," says Jennifer.

"For God's sake, Jenny, try and be a bit more constructive would you."

Lenise bends down and wraps the body up in the rug as tight as she can, and together they angle the package upright next to the lip of the trunk.

"Push," says Lenise.

They both shove and the cylinder tips inside the trunk cavity.

Jennifer wipes sweat from her eyes and looks at Lenise. "Now what?"

29

"I don't like leaving McKenzie alone like this," says Jennifer, reversing out of the garage. "What if she wakes up and finds nobody's there?"

"It's a risk we have to take. The sooner we go, the sooner we get back."

They drive in silence through empty streets and it's not too long before they reach the entrance to Pine Ridge Forest. Someone has thrown a clod of mud at the sign and grey muck has dripped down to look like a reverse exclamation mark. Multiple unsealed roads lead to different parts of the forest. Horseshoe Lake. Sweetheart's Peak. A rocky outcrop called the Crow's Nest. But there's one spot Jennifer remembers from the early days when she went on a trek with Hank, McKenzie in a baby-pack strapped to his back. She angles the car onto the narrow gravel road and turns left.

Jennifer follows the unsealed road and a canopy of trees fish-bones around them. It's like driving into a cave. Trees either side are impenetrable and the further in they go the more impossibly dark it becomes. The car is an icebox and Jennifer reaches over to turn on the heater, but Lenise shakes her head.

"I wouldn't. Heat and bodies don't mix."

That's right, thinks Jennifer, there's a body back there in the trunk, her husband's body, she had almost forgotten. She glances at Lenise who is staring straight ahead through the windscreen. There's a dark smear across her neck and over her t-shirt. Jennifer examines her own face in the rearview and sees blood on her chin. She reaches to wipe it.

"Leave it," says Lenise.

Jennifer returns her hand to the steering wheel.

"I can't believe this is happening," she says.

"Keep driving."

The windscreen begins to mist and Jennifer winds down her window to let in some air. It's frigid and vital and Jennifer sucks in four large mouthfuls but it will take more than fresh air to make this nightmare go away.

"Do you even know where you're going?" says Lenise.

"It was a long time ago now."

"Stop here. It's as good a place as any."

"A little further on."

Another mile on and thick woods give way to trees in rows, all of them the same type, large and ancient, their barren winter branches giant fan-shaped skeletons against the night sky.

"What is this place?"

"An orchard. At one time, anyway."

Jennifer turns right and takes a smaller trail into a more private area. She cuts the engine. Through a break in a stand of California Redwoods, Stickle Creek swimming hole shines like a beveled knife.

"There," she says, pointing through the windscreen.

Right in front of them is a magnificent Arizona cypress.

They step out of the car. Somewhere close by water rushes beneath ice.

"What's that smell?" says Lenise.

"Pears."

Jennifer clicks on the torch and a beam of light hits the trees. Fruit, rotten and brown and bird-pecked, lies forlornly in the undergrowth. A smatter of wasps hovers over the fallen bounty.

"I'm allergic," says Lenise.

"To pears?"

"Wasps."

Lenise reaches into the back seat and retrieves two shovels and gives one to Jennifer. She probes the ground for the weakest part, but it's hard all over, so she moves away from the rooty portion of the ground, about two feet from the tree, and traces a large rectangle with her shovel.

"This will do."

Progress is slow. There are layers of leaves and undergrowth and earth and rocks. Their shovels barely penetrate the surface. But they keep going, their bodies soon hot with effort and the two headlights aimed their way. *Kush, slap, kush, slap*. The sound of slicing and dumping seems too improbable and loud in such a lonely place. Occasionally too, the metal lip of the shovel pings off a flinty rock and sparks a tiny ginger flash.

An unbearable thirst grips Jennifer. It's as if her body is depleting its water stocks with every slice of the shovel. She tries swallowing but her mouth could be full of sand. How careless not to bring water or sensible shoes or a sweat towel or anything necessary to digging a coffin-size hole in the middle of nowhere. She bites down on her tongue to generate salvia and imagines something chilled and wet and quenching. It even crosses her mind to eat one of those worm-ridden pears.

She wipes her sticky forehead with an aching arm and stops to look at the pit. They have barely touched the surface. "This is going to take forever."

"Stop moaning and get on with it. It's not going to dig itself."

On and on it goes. Wasps buzz and the forest creaks and the sweet-sour decay of fruit saturates their pores. Jennifer's upper back burns and her wrists scream but she keeps up with Lenise's frenetic pace, matching her shovel for shovel until, finally, the pile of dirt has grown to a large mound and there's a box-shaped hole.

Jennifer squints at the sky. "How much deeper?"

"We need to make it as big as possible," says Lenise, continuing to dig.

"There isn't time."

"Just a bit more."

"No!" Jennifer snatches Lenise's shovel away. "We need to get him in there before daybreak."

Lenise looks at her, eyes glossed with exhaustion, and wipes her nose with her knuckles.

"Who died and made you president," she says.

Jennifer backs the car as close to the opening as possible then joins Lenise at the trunk, and once again they face the mission of trying to move their leaden freight, by now growing stiff with rigor. They tug and pull and press and push but he's too heavy to lift over the lip of the trunk. Jennifer hears a sniff. Angry tears are running down Lenise's dirt-streaked face.

"Hold it," says Lenise. "We need to stop rushing, do a bit at a time like before."

They do and it works and they maneuver the body until it is a see-saw plank across the ridge of the trunk then tip it into the grave like a bag of bricks.

Lenise jumps into the hole and removes the rug and unties the string and unfolds the plastic. Jennifer sucks in a breath because it's a shock to see Hank's pale-skinned corpse, gleaming and translucent and too human, slouching there in that humus pit.

"Get the lime," says Lenise.

Jennifer does and they shake it over the body and begin to fill the grave.

"What about his truck?" says Jennifer.

"Give me the address where's he's staying and I'll drop it off once we're done here."

The process of putting the dirt back is quicker than removing it, but it's still hard work. They soldier on and it isn't long before they are on the homeward stretch. When they are nearly there Jennifer stops and stares at the hole.

"Jesus, Lenise. What are we doing?"

"Don't think about it."

"I'm burying my husband."

"I said don't think about."

Jennifer doesn't move.

"Hurry up," says Lenise. "We need to get back to McKenzie before sunrise."

Trying to ignore the blisters on the bridge of her hands, Jennifer forces her shovel into the earth and dumps the contents into the pit then does it all over again.

Soon the quality of the sky alters and the forest stirs and they are done. They change quickly into fresh clothes and bag up the ones they've been wearing for later disposal.

The mound looks too fresh so they cover it with branches and stones and armfuls of cracker-stiff leaves. But it still looks like a grave.

"Over time it will blend in," says Lenise.

"If nobody finds it before then."

"They won't."

They stand under the canopy of the Cypress and stare at the mound.

"We should say a prayer or something."

"He was a bad man, Jenny."

"Not always."

"He was. You just didn't see it."

30

The shower is hot and Lenise stands there for a long time, dirt and blood and grime pooling at her feet. She brushes away torn stamps of winter-blown leaves that have hitched a ride home on her calves, then reaches to pick a blood-encrusted seed from between her toes and lets it slip into the water and down the plug hole. Everything is evidence now. All of it. Even what she says.

She closes her eyes and pushes her face into the torrent, her hands two fists at her side. It was remarkable how easily his skin had yielded to the blade. A single slip between his ribcage and it was done.

No suitable word could describe how Lenise feels. Not sadness. Not shame. Not happiness or triumph. If anything, all she feels is the absence of regret. A court of law, she thinks, would probably call it lack of remorse. Well, it wasn't as if she'd had a fight with a loved one and things had got out of hand. He was a stranger. Much less emotionally complicated.

She had come close before. God only knew how many times she'd been angry with Cody and how easily a shove could have meant the back of a head crashing on a hardwood corner or concrete step. And how could she forget that awful incident when he was three or four, when she shook him until he turned blue because he would not eat his brussel sprouts. It was easier than anyone could ever imagine—accidental death that wasn't really accidental because you were there with a knife or a bad attitude or a temper you could not control.

She shuts off the faucet and gets out.

First light punches through the patterned glass. A lone bird trumpets from atop a TV aerial. McKenzie will soon be awake. The child was safe now, at least. She would never have to face her father in a court or be subjected to McDonald's visits on Saturday afternoons or his fake apologies or the uncertainty of whether he would try it on again. She could grow into everything that she was ever meant to be, everything that Lenise never was. Yes, perhaps last night had been a blessing after all.

Lenise wraps a towel around the dripping tendrils of her hair and puts on some fresh clothes and goes to her bedroom and closes the door. She pushes the bed away from the wall and pries the loosened floorboard to access the hiding place where she kept valuables from Cody. Just enough space for a bag of bloody clothes, a bunch of stinking rags and a freshly used carving knife.

Then she combs her hair and goes downstairs. She will make pancakes—all-American—with maple syrup and bacon, and some of that stuff they called potato hash. Everything her special guest could want.

31

The plan is to keep everything as normal as possible. But Jennifer doesn't feel normal, far from it. In the dark hours before dawn she jerks awake to find herself lying in a wet patch of sweat, a nightmare just beyond her reach. The single open eye. The stiff crab of a hand. The plum-colored bottom lip.

And there's a refrain, stuck on a loop inside her head. Hank is dead, Hank is dead, Hank is dead.

She's never felt so exposed. What if someone finds out what she's been a part of, what she did, burying him like that to cover her own tracks? What if someone finds out she is a coward of the worst kind? Because that's how she feels, like a coward, sick to her stomach, disgusted that she ever agreed to any of it.

On the third day she begins to clean. Every inch of the house. The skirting boards and window sills and door handles and light switches and refrigerator and oven and bathtub. She scrubs the kitchen floor so many times the blue and black polka dots begin to crack. Jennifer cleans all morning and afternoon and well into the night and into the next day and the day after that. She cleans until the chrome shines and mirrors wink and tiles gleam.

On Friday she decides to get rid of his clothes. She calls Rosemary to reschedule her morning clients and waits until McKenzie leaves for school then retrieves some trash bags and goes to the wardrobe and puts everything in them. The second skins hanging in the wardrobe, gone. The well-worn brown leather loafers and laceless Reeboks, gone. The birthday boxer briefs and cotton socks and faded t-shirts and woolen sweaters, gone. His toothbrush and Abraham Lincoln soap on a rope and Remington shaver, gone. All of it, tied up neatly into six trash bags, ready to go to a good home or a bad one, she doesn't care which. She just wants the stuff out, like the memory of that shovel in her hand.

Jennifer takes the bags to the Goodwill and the lady in the Elvis Presley jumper gives her a free fridge magnet and a ten percent discount on anything in the store. Jennifer discards the more personal items in a dumpster behind a Lebanese takeaway then goes to work.

But when she gets back home that night and sees the empty section of the wardrobe, she doesn't feel any better.

"Where are Dad's clothes?" McKenzie walks past Jennifer and reaches down to pick up a man's charcoal dress sock on the bottom of the wardrobe floor. "Mom, where are his things?"

Jennifer's mouth goes dry. "I was going to tell you."

"Tell me what?"

"I spoke to him last night. He's decided to move away."

"What? Where to?"

"I didn't ask."

McKenzie sits down on the bed. "Will I see him before he goes?"

"He already left. He came today and got his things while we were out."

"Oh."

"It could be for the best, hon."

McKenzie stares at the sock in her hand. "He doesn't care about me, does he?"

"That's not true."

Jennifer puts her hand on McKenzie's arm.

"I'm nothing to him," says McKenzie, blinking back tears.

"He knows he hurt you," says Jennifer.

"Don't defend him."

"Oh God, McKenzie I'm not, but I really believe he's sorry for what he did."

"He's a piece of shit."

"Hey, since when do we talk like that?"

"Since I found out my father was a piece of shit."

"You sound like Lenise."

"So what if I do? At least she's real about things."

"What's that supposed to mean?"

"She doesn't pretend everything's alright when it's not." McKenzie lifts a forefinger to brush away her tears. "He shouldn't have left without telling me, I'm not a little kid."

"Hon, we've got each other, you and me, that's not so bad, is it?"

McKenzie looks at Jennifer. Her eyes flash with something Jennifer can't place.

"Mac?" says Jennifer.

"Don't call me that."

Then she walks away.

32

On Saturday Jennifer can't get out of bed. Her head feels like yeast and her joints ache too. She isn't sure she's slept, really slept, and she doesn't mean just closing her eyes, but going right under into that merciful blackness. It could be why her body feels this way, heavy and drained and shackled, her mind too. It's hard to form thoughts, even when she concentrates, which is too bad because she really needs to think her way out of this mess, like whether she should speak to her lawyer or just go right ahead and confess to police. She's gotten as far as nine and one but can't go all the way, slipping the phone back on its cradle before pressing that final digit. What's stopping her is the image of McKenzie sitting at a beige Formica table and the voice on the loud speaker announcing visiting hours are over.

"Are you going to stay in bed all day?"

McKenzie appears in the doorway of Jennifer's room, dressed in a shapeless sweatshirt and pants, looking more boy than girl.

"Sorry, hon, I'm under the weather."

"We're out of detergent and bleach. We need paper towels too. Get the jumbo-sized ones. And shampoo and soap, don't forget that."

Jennifer glances at McKenzie's raw, cracked hands.

"Maybe it's time to cut back on the showers."

"I can go if you want, if you're not feeling well."

Jennifer gets up. "No, it's alright,"

"And Mom, make sure you get the 100% stuff."

The ground shifts like sand beneath her and she grips the cart to help stabilize her clumsy legs. The grocery store is busy given it's a Saturday and she's having problems keeping out of people's way. She usually comes armed with a list and a menu for the week ahead but that was asking too much of herself today, so she wings it, tossing whatever into her cart and hoping for the best.

After passing through the bottleneck in the vegetable section, she makes it to the meat aisle and sees a fresh whole chicken and decides to get one. She will roast it tonight. She and McKenzie will sit at the table and have a regular meal together and pretend to be normal. Jennifer even buys a chocolate tart.

"Ma'am, you alright?"

"Yes, why?"

"That's my cart."

She looks down and sees shaving cream and a six pack of Bud light. "Oh God, sorry."

She quickly removes her items and puts them in her own cart.

"You'll need this too."

The man hands over the knife Jennifer has just selected from the hardware section. She goes cold at the sight of it.

"It's for the chicken," she says.

When Jennifer gets home she hears laughter burst from the lounge.

"Lenise bought pizza," says McKenzie, biting into a cheese-laden triangle. "Did you remember the soap?"

"And something for the grown-ups," says Lenise, holding up a bottle of Bourbon.

Jennifer hasn't seen Lenise since that night. They had agreed to keep their distance but here she was now, sitting on Jennifer's sofa, like a long-lost friend of the family.

"Hello, Lenise."

Lenise nods at the grocery bag hanging from Jennifer's hand. "Did you have other plans?"

"It's fine."

"Good because there's enough pizza to feed a rugby team. You're dripping."

"What?"

"Your bag."

Jennifer looks down to see chicken blood seep from the corner.

"Perfect."

Jennifer hurries to the kitchen and dumps the bag in the sink and removes the items.

"You don't want me here."

Jennifer looks over her shoulder. Lenise is standing in the doorway.

"I thought we agreed to keep our distance," says Jennifer, placing the chicken in a dish and putting it in the fridge.

"I understand," says Lenise. "These are difficult circumstances."

Jennifer stops and looks at Lenise. "You've heard something."

"No. And why should I? He's not going to be found. We were very thorough."

Lenise reaches into the cupboard for two glasses and pours some liquor in each.

"You look tired. Have you slept?" she says.

"I feel like I'm swimming in a vat of molasses," says Jennifer.

Lenise studies Jennifer over the rim of her glass.

"Relax. He's vanishing as we speak."

"It's not as easy as that, Lenise," says Jennifer. "I can't just forget about it."

"Listen Jenny, you need to learn to let go. Stress is not good for the soul." She hands Jennifer a glass. "McKenzie told me her father moved away."

"Yes."

"You did the right thing, telling her that."

"I lied to her."

"Stop looking back, focus on the future," Lenise sits down. "Actually, I have a job interview next week. It's a good opportunity. In fact, I was wondering if you had something I could borrow? A nice suit jacket or dress?"

Jennifer stares into her glass. A stray hair skirts across the surface.

"I don't know if I have anything suitable."

"My clothes are a little dated," says Lenise.

"I'm not sure we're the same size."

"You'll find something."

And before Jennifer can say anything else, McKenzie is calling out. The pizza is getting cold.

33

The ivory blouse is a perfect fit and Lenise can hardly believe she's actually wearing something so nice. She's never been lucky enough to own such a thing of beauty and, at first, she's worried she won't have anything to match it. But after hunting through her wardrobe, she finds a simple black skirt and pair of navy sandals. She would have preferred the black pumps but the heels are worn down to the plastic bone and she doesn't want to make a bad first impression.

She looks in the floor length mirror on the back of the wardrobe door and smiles. Yes, a true professional. Elegant and feminine. And the color was really lovely. It brought out the best in her hair. The harsh ginger she thought she was stuck with for life had transformed into much lovelier hues of henna and copper.

The feel of the silk was wonderful, too. The way it floated like a caress across her skin. There's a faint trace of Jenny's sweat and perfume, like a tester strip left too long in your handbag, but Lenise doesn't mind. If she was honest, it makes her feel closer to Jenny, in a sisterly way, of course.

Yes, she likes that, *sisters*.

To avoid dirtying the blouse, Lenise lays a towel on the driver's seat and heads for her interview over on Barlett Road. When she gets there, she's twenty minutes early so she circles the block and parks under a tree to think through some answers.

She wants a cigarette. But this time she's determined to quit. It's expensive and trashy and since she's turning over a new leaf, there's really no place in her life for such bad habits. Lenise fears she's been a bad influence on Jenny in terms of the smoking. But those had been special circumstances. Well, not any more. All that was behind them now. Mind over matter, she would tell Jennifer, together they were stronger than that.

Thankfully, Lenise has overcome the small problem of not being able to mention her last six months of work history. She was going to tell them about Camille de Silva falsely accusing her of a crime she didn't commit, but then came up with a better idea. She'd stated on her resume she had worked as a receptionist in Jenny's clinic.

"If you could just say I worked here for six months."

"You want me to lie?"

"They probably won't even call."

In the end, after some pretty intensive cajoling, Jennifer had reluctantly agreed. It was irritating that it took so much to convince her, especially in light of how Lenise had gone out of her way to help Jenny in her hour of need.

Lenise unwinds the window for some fresh air and thinks about how she will cope with the big question. *Tell us about yourself.* A person could get lost in the wastelands with that one but she was fully prepared, had this whole spiel about being a fighter in life, and how even though many times everything seemed to go against her, she'd persevere, and how even though life or God or whatever seemed to take great pleasure in knocking her down, she would simply dust herself off and get back up again. Lenise's eyes begin to well. They'd be fools not to give her the job.

The grocery store manager was one of those bitter, older women, who seemed resentful about life. For most of the interview, she sat with her hands laced across her fat stomach looking disinterested in what Lenise had to say. At one point, she even had the nerve to ask Lenise to repeat something because she couldn't understand her accent. You should listen more carefully, lard-arse, Lenise had wanted to say. She had even called the woman Ma'am several times and lardy seemed to like that very much. In the end, there was nothing to worry about because Lenise got the job on the spot. Things were looking up. Her life had turned a corner. She would call Jenny and share the good news.

34

Jennifer sits on the bench in Redmont Park, a green space close to the clinic. It's too cold to be outside but she needs the oxygen because she can barely lift her head. She had to flee that stuffy clinic because everything seemed worse there, with those stainless-steel instruments and unflinching eyes looking back at her, right into her soul.

She picks up the limp roast beef sandwich trapped in its triangle plastic capsule, and the meat flaps there like a tongue. She can't bring herself to eat it. Her mouth tastes like a sewer and her throat burns so she tosses the sandwich into the grass where it becomes fodder for the gulls.

She casts aside her coat and the chill finds her tacky skin. Better. She squints at the dwindling triangle of sun and listens to the dull scratch of leaves across the stones.

Up until the point she had buried Hank in the woods, Jennifer's worst crime had been to steal a collection box for the Blind Foundation with Alice Jackson when they were both thirteen. Jennifer's role was to distract the grocery clerk while Alice swiped the box from the countertop and hid it under her trench coat and walked out the door. Afterward they went to Hanson Park and smashed it apart with a brick and filled their pockets with nickels and quarters and pennies and boldly went back the store where they stole it from and spent the entire $23.25 on chocolate milkshakes, Hershey kisses, peanut M&Ms and their very first pack of Marlboro lights.

Jennifer hears voices and looks up. A couple in matching woolen scarves amble along the pathway, a toddler skipping between them. The girl waves at Jennifer but Jennifer doesn't wave back. Instead, she hauls herself up and leaves.

Rather than return to work like she's supposed to, Jennifer goes to the cinemaplex, and asks for a ticket. The guy with the Walter White goatee points at the display board above his head.

"To what?" he says.

She looks up. The electronic letters blur into a meaningless smear. She blinks at him. Her eyelids feel like sandpaper.

"I don't care," she says.

The guy shrugs, gives her a ticket and tells her cinema five. She follows the carpet-cocooned hallway until she finds the cinema and takes a seat but soon a woman with a crew cut enters and uses the light from her cellphone to scan the seat numbers then stops abruptly when she reaches Jennifer and demands she move because Jennifer is sitting in her spot, even though there are only two other people in the entire place. Too bone-tired to argue, Jennifer lugs herself out of the seat and into another row.

Her head feels like a balloon and she blots her brow with her forearm. It's too hot in here. Someone should turn the thermostat down. But there's no attendant to ask.

A man three rows ahead glances over his shoulder and gives Jennifer a look. At first, she thinks she must have said the thing about the heat out loud but then realizes the man is giving her a "I want to hook up" look, and she wonders if the guy at the counter was pranking her and sold her a ticket to a porn or something and do they even have those sorts of theatres anymore since the internet but then the lights go down and the titles roll and she sees the movie is a rom com. But the guy looks over his shoulder again and she stares back and thinks about fucking him in this spongy, velveteen upholstered chair, her legs in a V, heels in the cup holder circles, underwear round her ankle, him pounding into her, grunting and breathless, making her think of something else, taking her away from that cadaver stench and single milky eye.

When she wakes up her hair is a curtain over her face. She's drooling like an addict, bent forward in her seat. It hurts too much to swallow and she wipes the saliva on the back of her sleeve. Close by, a cleaner with a vacuum strapped to her back is sucking up popcorn that looks too much like brain matter from the purple carpet.

Jennifer tries to stand but her head spins and she collapses back down. She's burning up. You could fry an egg on her forehead and she laughs a half laugh. *Huh.* Because that's something her mother would say—so hot out here you could fry an egg on your forehead. The cleaner stares at her, rolling the pearl of her gum around her tongue as if she's tying a knot in a cherry.

"You tripping or something?" says the cleaner.

That bad? I really look that bad? But Jennifer doesn't say it because there's a giant slug in her mouth. Her phone buzzes against her thigh, and she digs inside her pocket. She tries to say hello but it comes out only as a soft *haaaa* like her voice has run out of gas.

"Jenny is that you?"

"Uhuh," which is more like an air leak from a tire.

"What the hell is going on?"

"Uhuh."

Jennifer gives up and hands the cleaner the phone.

She is half aware of Lenise, arm hooking through hers, the overbearing citrusy smell of her perfume, walking Jennifer to the car, strapping her into the seat, pushing the nib of the water bottle into Jennifer's mouth which Jennifer bats away because it hurts too much to drink, and now there's a splash on Lenise's linen skirt, and they are driving on the road, then getting out and going through automatic doors to some sort of clinic that is not her own, she can smell the antiseptic and there are children donging Fisher Price toys and skating matchbox cars down a tiny plastic slide and women studying *People* magazines and an elderly man in a wheel chair with a colostomy bag peeking out from beneath a crocheted blanket. Two seats over, there's a boy on his mother's lap, leaning against her breast, staring at Jennifer with his cold little eyes.

Then she is sitting alone, like an outcast. Even Lenise is far away talking to someone at the counter, and no wants to come near because of the darkness, it encircles her like some sort of modern day plague.

She wishes this pain would go away. Maybe this was her punishment—disintegrating vocal cords and fire breath. She may never speak again.

She hears her name and looks up to find herself in a different office, the doctor coming at her with a tongue depressor. *Say Arghhh*. He tuts then declares *Strep throat. Maybe some infected tonsils thrown in for good measure. High dose antibiotics. Needs complete rest.* And Lenise nodding, *of course, doctor.*

Then she's home, being chauffeured past a frowning McKenzie, placed into her glorious bed, someone tugging at her shoes.

"I tried to drown my baby."

Then she falls asleep.

35

There's a helicopter in her room, the fan of its blade slicing and whirring above her head in great, heaving whooshes and she sees the President, half bent, holding on to his hat as he exits the Marine One aircraft. Or maybe it's just an opened window and squally wind and blinds batting against the wood, Jennifer can't be sure. Just like she can't be sure there isn't a silhouette framed in the doorway, watching her, like a warden or keeper.

Jennifer tries to ask the keeper's name and where the keeper is from and why the keeper is there but she gets no further than lifting her head from the pillow before she's pulled back under the rolling surf then tossed back out again.

She dreams her fingernails have fallen off and she is lost in the Australian outback and someone has sewn her mouth shut with black cotton. How thirsty she is. She calls for water but no one is there. She will die in this red sand desert.

Then she is in the ground in a grave with roots and stones and bark and pupa and earth-loving arthropods. She is nothing but a rack of ribs, a shoulder blade, an eye socket, home to albino insects that never see the light of day.

It begins to change, the heat in her bones. She can feel it slip away, sneaking out the side door like a lover. She almost wants it back. And when Jennifer finally opens her eyes by her bedside is a man—benevolent and competent—ministering to her. But when she looks again, it's Lenise, standing over her, sipping a coffee.

"You look like shit."

Jennifer blinks slowly and licks her lips. She tries to move but can't, she's tucked in tight like a newborn.

"I got the job," says Lenise. "Thanks for asking." Her eyes sparkle at her own joke. "I think it was your lucky blouse. I already told you but you probably forgot."

Jennifer sits up, breaking free from the taut covers.

"Where's McKenzie?" Jennifer's voice does not sound like her own.

Lenise picks up a glass on the nightstand and holds it out. "You should have something to drink."

"Where is she?"

"You worry too much. She's in school. I've been taking good care of her."

"How long have I been out?"

Lenise shrugs. "3-4 days."

Jennifer looks down. She's wearing a nightgown she doesn't recognize.

"I couldn't keep up," says Lenise. "You were sweating so much that you ran out of your own, so I lent you one of mine. It's at the dry-cleaners. I'll drop it off when it's done."

"My nightgown's at the dry cleaners?"

"Your blouse."

"Keep it," says Jennifer.

She puts her feet on the ground and gets ready to lift herself off the bed.

"Oh, no, you need to rest," says Lenise.

"I'm fine Lenise, you can go home now."

Jennifer feels lightheaded but there's no pain and she's hungry.

"You've been sicker than you realize," says Lenise. "I think you should get back into bed."

Jennifer pulls on her robe and goes to the bathroom. Lenise follows her.

"Really, Jenny, this will only set you back."

Jennifer turns around.

"I don't need a bathroom chaperone," she says, firmly closing the door.

Jennifer stays in the shower until the water runs cold. When she gets out, she feels better, weak but better. She goes to the kitchen and Lenise is there, putting dishes away in all the wrong places.

"You've lost weight. I'll make you something to eat. Scrambled eggs and sausage?"

"I'm fine."

Lenise fills the kettle with water and spoons coffee into the pot.

"McKenzie has been doing just fine." She looks at the clock. "In fact, she should be home soon."

"I know what time school finishes, Lenise," says Jennifer, putting the empty glass in the dishwasher.

"Why don't you relax in the lounge and I'll bring in the coffee."

Jennifer doesn't have the energy to fight and heads to the living room, stopping short when she reaches the doorway.

"You can't be serious."

"Do you like it?" says Lenise, coming up behind her.

"You rearranged my furniture?"

The sofa now looked out at the pond, the TV was in a different corner and the two bookcases had been switched to the other side of the room.

"A change is always good. Besides, you'll have more space this way."

On the sofa there's a pile of folded blankets, a Harlequin Romance on top of the lamp table beside it, a small overnight bag parked underneath.

"You've been sleeping here?"

"Who else was there to help you?"

Jennifer turns to Lenise. "You must be eager to get back to your own place."

"What are you saying?"

"I can take things from here."

"I see," Lenise looks at Jennifer. "If that's what you really want."

Without another word Lenise packs up her things, snaps the clasps on the bag shut and turns to Jennifer.

"I said I'm much better, Lenise."

"I know. I heard."

"Then what is it?"

"I promised McKenzie I would make everyone a nice dinner, when you got better, over at my house but I suppose that's too much to ask."

Jennifer remains silent.

"I knew you wouldn't be interested," says Lenise. "Well, maybe I've got better things to do."

Jennifer pauses.

"Okay," she says finally.

"Don't look so enthusiastic," says Lenise.

"I said I would come."

"Saturday at six o'clock. Don't be late."

Jennifer was considering whether she should put the furniture back to the way it was when she hears McKenzie arrive home and head straight upstairs to her bedroom. Jennifer follows and knocks on her door. When there's no answer, she opens it. McKenzie looks up and removes her headphones.

"You're awake," says McKenzie. "I was worried about you, Mom. You were really sick."

That's when Jennifer sees.

"Oh God, what have you done to your hair?"

It's gone. Hacked off. Like someone had been at it with a knife.

"I was sick of having it long," says McKenzie.

It's ugly and *Les Miserables* short and Jennifer can't help herself.

"But your beautiful hair."

McKenzie kicks off her shoes, lies down on her bed and faces the wall. "It's *my* hair."

"If you wanted a change, I would have booked you in at the mall."

"Please go away."

Jennifer sees the mirror, the towel covering it. "Talk to me, hon. What's going on?"

"I want to be alone."

"You can't not talk to me forever."

McKenzie pulls a blanket over her head. "You're such a drama queen," she whispers.

Later, when Jennifer opens the bathroom trash to throw away a toilet roll she sees the plastic grocery bag, the bush of hair stuffed inside it, like the corpse of a Pomeranian dog.

36

When Lenise opens the door to greet them, she's wearing a turquoise baby-doll dress that belongs on someone half her age. There's been a special effort with the hair too, Jennifer notes. The thick red mane has been brushed umpteen times and sits perched on Lenise's shoulders like two strips of plucked wool.

Jennifer catches the flash of disapproval from Lenise at Jennifer's choice of a GAP t-shirt and jeans but she isn't about to apologize. She's been railroaded into this and just wants to get it over with.

When they go inside, a strange scent assaults Jennifer's senses. Baking milk. Her stomach churns and she tries not to show it. Benign music that could be Spandau Ballet plays on the small compact disc player on top of the sideboard.

Lenise turns to McKenzie. "There's a soda in the fridge for you."

Jennifer watches McKenzie slope off to the kitchen as if she's carrying the weight of the world on her shoulders.

"What do you know about the hair?" says Jennifer.

"I had nothing to do what that," says Lenise. "She emerged one morning after the fact. Never said a word about it."

Jennifer isn't sure she believes her.

"The cleaning's worse too," says Jennifer. "Now she's washing her hands a thousand times a day and refuses to touch the faucet without a paper towel."

Lenise hands Jennifer one of the two pre-poured Chardonnays from the sideboard. "You exaggerate."

"I am not exaggerating, Lenise. She needs help."

"It will pass."

Jennifer sits down on the tweed couch. "Was there any mention in the papers when I was sick?"

Lenise looks at Jennifer as if she's being particularly slow. "Stop worrying. They will never find him."

"Maybe they're just not saying. They do that sometimes—impose a media blackout while they investigate behind the scenes. Yesterday I saw a cop. I thought he was tailing me."

"You're being paranoid."

Jennifer raises her glass and gives herself a mock cheers salute. "Hello, Jennifer, welcome to the rest of your life," she says. "Paranoia becomes you."

"It's normal to feel this way."

"Is that so."

"You need to put everything behind you now, think of the future."

"Oh yeah and what future's that?"

"Now you're just being facetious."

Jennifer looks at Lenise all dressed up with no place to go, eyeliner smudged in one corner of her eye, the hard effect of her face.

"What is it you want from life, Lenise?"

"The same as anyone else."

"Which is?"

"Security. Friendship."

Jennifer nods at the gemology book on the coffee table. "You should go do it."

Lenise waves her hand. "We've been through that before."

"What's stopping you?"

"There's more to life than a career."

"But you want to."

Lenise gets up and puts the book in a drawer.

"Believe what you want," she says. "I'm happy with what I've got."

McKenzie walks through from the kitchen. "The oven timer just went off."

Jennifer tries to make an effort, she really does, but the beef is tough and loaded with some spice she doesn't like, and she ends up pushing most of it around her plate and washing the little she can stomach down with more wine than is good for her. Lenise is talking about her life as a girl in South Africa, and how her mother taught her to make milk tart, the custardy mess Jennifer was now expected to consume.

She blinks and, to be polite, dips her spoon into the cinnamon-topped goop, brings it to her lips and swallows. She's about to take another spoonful, then pauses. All this strange tasting food. It would be so easy to do, wouldn't it? Slip something in undetected. Drain cleaner. Anti-freeze. Leftover sedative. Then Lenise would have McKenzie all to herself, she could wear every blouse Jennifer had in her closet, sleep in her bed every night. On the stereo Paul Simon sings about fifty ways to leave your lover and Jennifer does a self-audit, assessing limbs, head and abdomen. But she's experiencing no unusual twinges or dizzy spells, apart from the effects of too much wine.

"What's wrong with your meal?" says Lenise. "Not to your taste? Maybe you need the doctor again."

Jennifer stands up and looks at McKenzie.

"We should go."

"But you haven't finished your dessert."

"Yeah, Mom, it's early."

"Do as you're told, McKenzie."

"But you're being rude."

Lenise pats McKenzie's arm. "Listen to your mother. She's not feeling well."

McKenzie shoots Jennifer a look then pushes past her to the front door. When she's gone, Jennifer says, "I think we should take a break."

"I need money," says Lenise.

"What?"

"I got behind on the rent."

"But you have a job now," says Jennifer.

"It doesn't pay that well. I should soon be progressing to another level though. Just one thousand to tide me over."

"A thousand dollars? You know Hank took everything," says Jennifer.

"There's still the business account."

Jennifer stares at her.

"I know what you're thinking," says Lenise. "But I would never say a word."

"Wouldn't you."

"It's not easy to ask, you know."

"Tomorrow," says Jennifer.

"Tomorrow will be fine."

37

Jennifer shields the number pad with her hand and punches in the pin. Every stab of her finger is a jab into Lenise's chest. Get. Out. Of. My. Life. Lenise and her growing list of demands. Lenise and her stupid milk tart. Lenise and her out of control hair and poor taste in clothes. Lenise and the annoying way she said "tiliphone" instead of "telephone" or "blake" instead of "black".

"You done yet?"

Standing behind Jennifer is some guy in a Rastafarian knitted cap. She wants to tell him white guys with dreads are try-hard, that maybe he should just keep his mouth shut, that she can take as long as she damn well pleases.

"Knock yourself out," she says, taking her money.

She buries her hands in the pockets of her winter coat and walks up the street and is back to thinking about Lenise and how she's becoming a bad influence on McKenzie and how last night there had been another screaming match with McKenzie about some inconsequential thing and McKenzie had called Jennifer a bitch and screamed "Stay out of my life!" before slamming the door right in Jennifer's face.

Jennifer knew she should rise above it. McKenzie was just a kid caught in the middle, but Jennifer had felt slighted, angry even, at McKenzie for taking Lenise's side, like a friend who starts hanging round with another friend and casually drops you for the more popular girl. God, how high school, how unbelievably petty, how team Jennifer, how team Lenise. What in the world was she becoming?

She rounds the corner and nearly collides with an executive type holding a tray of coffees and the guy curses at her and tells her to watch what's she doing but Jennifer doesn't say sorry, choosing instead to give the suit a wide birth, and continues on up the block toward the clinic, eyes tracking the toes of her boots, trying to keep her mind from returning to Lenise and her sad little life.

Then Jennifer steps off the curb and straight into the path of an oncoming car.

Everything's in slow-mo, even the screech of tires and burning rubber smell and the car rolling toward her with its just-in-time braking and the way the bumper kisses her knees.

Then it's still and quiet and not quite real. The engine ticks. People stare. She is made of stone.

Jennifer's respiratory system begins working again. Blood floods back in to her veins. People walk on. The driver gets out.

"You okay?"

"Just give me a minute," she says, head between her knees.

"You need to take better care, Ma'am. That was close."

It's the word Ma'am that makes her look, really look. She glances at the car. Sees the siren and the black and white paintwork. Then his uniform.

"You stepped out right in front of me."

There's a flash of anger there, the look of fear at what might have been.

"I'm sorry, officer."

She's shaking. He puts a hand on her shoulder.

"What's your name, ma'am?"

She laughs half-heartedly.

"You going to give me a ticket or something?"

He shakes his head. "You've had a scare. Want to take a seat in the patrol car for a second?"

"I'm fine." She pushes out a smile. "Really. I need to get back to work, actually."

She thanks him and dashes over the road, being sure to look both ways, not trusting herself to glance back over her shoulder, in case he's still there watching, or worse yet, following. She hurries across the car park, up the clinic steps and inside.

Rosemary stands up when she sees her.

"Don't ask," says Jennifer, ducking into her office.

She slaps cold water on her cheeks and presses paper towels to her forehead and looks in the mirror and is confronted with her ashen face. There's a knock.

"I need a minute, Rosemary."

But it isn't Rosemary.

"What happened to you?" says Lenise, nodding at the mud spatter on Jennifer's trousers.

"Forget about it."

"I thought we could have lunch."

"Lunch? It's a quarter after two, besides I have clients."

"I can wait."

"You want the money, is that it?" says Jennifer, digging angrily inside her purse.

Lenise sits down in Jennifer's chair.

"You're always in such a hurry these days," she says.

Jennifer stares at her, parked there like she's the chairman of the board.

"Lenise, didn't you hear me? I've got clients."

189

Lenise spins around to look out the window. "I've been thinking about what you said. About studying gemology. You really think I could do it? That I'm smart enough and not too old? I mean that would be something if I could go back to school."

Jennifer pauses, sees an opportunity.

"I think it would be good for you."

"You really believe I can do it?"

"You're not an idiot, Lenise. In fact, you're probably one of the shrewdest people I know."

Lenise pivots to face Jennifer.

"That's the nicest thing anyone has ever said to me."

"I mean it."

"Well, thank you."

Lenise riffles through her bag and retrieves a print out. "There's a program in California. I would have to take a pre-course thing, but if I pass it would only be another year before I was qualified."

"You should go for it."

"It would mean moving away."

"I could help. With tuition. Give you something toward it."

"You'd do that?"

"Sure," says Jennifer.

The smile drops from Lenise's face. "You want to get rid of me."

"What? *No.* I'm trying to help you, like you helped me."

"I wasn't born yesterday, Jenny. It's written all over your face."

Lenise stands up, stuffs the pamphlet into her purse, takes the money from the desk.

"Forget I said anything," says Lenise, pausing at the door. "Besides why would I leave Wisconsin when I've got such a good friend in you."

38

Lenise slips off her shoes and rests her throbbing feet atop the ottoman. The shift at the grocery store was a long one and she smells like salami. She was better than this, better than being reduced to the Palgrave's Best Beef Jerky lady. It was an embarrassment. Needs must and all that, but for God's sake, handing out cubes of preserved meat in a supermarket was a bridge too far. There had to be a better life. She picks up the crumpled printouts on the gemology courses salvaged from the trash and thinks of Jennifer. No one had ever said they believed in her before.

There's a knock at the door and Lenise hauls her aching carcass out of the chair to answer it.

"Hey," says McKenzie.

Lenise looks past her shoulder. "Did your mother send you?"

"She's at work. The gallery, remember? You said you'd take me."

A street art exhibition. They had discussed it when Jennifer was sick.

"I completely forgot," says Lenise.

McKenzie shrugs. "It's okay if you don't want to."

Lenise thinks of her tender feet, the varicose vein throbbing on the back of her calf.

"I'll get my coat."

The gallery is located in a basement made up of painted white brick and exposed steel girders. Lenise pulls out her wallet to pay the guy with the lip ring but McKenzie stops her.

"Let me pay."

"What? No, I'll have none of that," says Lenise.

"Please. I want to do it, for bringing me here."

Lenise looks at her. "If you're sure."

"I am."

The exhibition is not to Lenise's tastes. It's all just graffiti to her. But it seems to mean something to McKenzie and the girl takes great care to study each and every work, going in close to scrutinize the detail and read the description then standing back to assess the overall impact. When they'd done the circuit twice, McKenzie pulls out her sketch paper and the pastels Lenise had bought her while Jennifer was sick.

"Would it be okay if I did a sketch?"

"Go ahead," says Lenise, taking a seat on the worn chaise lounge.

Lenise wakes up with a crick in her neck. Someone is shaking her. The guy with the lip ring.

"We're closing," he says.

It's dark outside and McKenzie is planted in front of a giant Andy Warhol type of thing, dozens of pages beside her. Lenise looks at her watch. It's after 7 p.m.

"Girl, why didn't you wake me? Look at the time."

McKenzie gathers her things.

"We need to hurry," says Lenise.

Lenise ushers McKenzie out of the building only to find her car's been clamped.

"For God's sake."

"Forget about her," says McKenzie. "She only cares about herself anyway."

"We'll have to catch the bus."

By the time they reach the bus stop, it's switched over to non-peak hours and it's thirty minutes before another one is due. McKenzie's phone buzzes.

"Is that her?" says Lenise.

McKenzie shrugs. "She keeps calling."

"You should answer."

"She'll only yell at me."

"At least send a message."

McKenzie types something.

"What did you say?"

"I told her to quit bugging me."

The phone buzzes again.

"What did she say now?" says Lenise.

"Nothing," says McKenzie, slipping the phone into her pocket.

They wait in silence, in the descending cold, until the bus arrives.

McKenzie selects a seat in the rear and stares out the window, the blissful expression she'd had in the gallery now gone. She touches the back of her neck, where her pretty hair has been hacked away, and Lenise tries to think of something profound to say.

"Have you ever seen *Fantasy Island*?"

McKenzie shakes her head.

"We used to get reruns in Jo'berg in the 80s. Saturdays at 6.30 p.m. Mr. Roarke and Tattoo. People would go to the island and pay Mr. Roarke thousands of dollars to make their fantasy come true, but there was always a lesson. Be careful what you wish for type of thing. It was a strange show but I liked it. I liked the justice behind it. How the person would see the error of their ways and leave the island a better human being, learn something about themselves. Life is full of lessons, some of them painful, and it's up to us not to let them break us but grow from them instead."

McKenzie turns away and looks out the window.

"Forget it," says Lenise. "It was rubbish, really. I think Tattoo ended up broke and alone."

"It's okay," says McKenzie. "I understand what you mean."

"Anytime you need someone to talk with, I'm here. Think of me as a friend, a confidant so to speak. You know what that means?"

"Yeah."

"What you tell me will stay between us. Your mother need never know."

The bus doesn't go all the way to Pine Ridge Road so they have to walk the last fifteen minutes in the dark. When they round the corner, Jennifer is standing on her front doorstep.

"Where have you been?" she demands, doing the whole hands on her hips act which, to Lenise, appears a touch dramatic.

"Don't get hysterical," says Lenise.

Jennifer's jaw hardens. "I come home and my daughter's not here and it's dark out and you don't expect me to be concerned?"

"Sarcasm won't help, either," says Lenise.

Jennifer shakes her head in amazement. "Who in the hell do you think you are?"

"You're blowing this out of proportion," sniffs Lenise.

"Don't blame Lenise, I made her go," says McKenzie. "We went to look at an art exhibition, that's all."

"Why didn't you ask me to take you?" says Jennifer.

"You wouldn't have gone."

"You didn't even ask!"

"Really, Jenny, there's no need to shout," says Lenise.

"Shut up, Lenise."

"Mom, I told you already, it's not her fault," implores McKenzie.

"Go to your room," says Jennifer.

"No."

"Do as I say."

"Stop trying to control my life!" McKenzie bursts into tears and runs up the stairs.

"Well, I hope you're happy," says Lenise. "You know the pressure she's been under."

"Why are you still here, Lenise?"

"Someone has to say something."

"I think I know what's best for my own daughter."

Lenise almost laughs. "Oh, do you?"

"Watch my lips, Lenise. Stay away from us, don't come anywhere near this house, or McKenzie's school or my clinic. Get on with your own life and stop trying to hijack mine."

Then Jennifer slams the door right in Lenise's face.

39

Jennifer turns to go upstairs to talk to McKenzie but the phone rings. Surely not.

"Jesus Christ, leave us alone."

"Whoa. Bad time?"

It's not Lenise, but a man.

"I thought you were someone else," says Jennifer.

"You don't know me," says the voice, "but I used to work with Hank."

She stops breathing. The world becomes a tight black light focused on her.

"Um, this is awkward because I know you guys were having issues but Hank was staying at my place while I was on vacation and I got back yesterday and he's not here. In fact, by the looks of what's growing in the fridge, he hasn't been here in a while." He pauses. "Jen, is it?"

"Yes."

"I'm not sure what to do."

Her throat constricts to the width of a soda straw and it's difficult to talk.

"Jen?"

"Yes, I'm here."

"Have you seen him?"

"He mentioned Seattle."

"Seattle?"

It's the first thing that pops into her head. Seattle, way across the other side of the country, about as far away you can get.

"Something about a job," she says.

"But why would he leave all his stuff behind?"

"I don't know."

"It doesn't make any sense."

"He probably just needs time by himself."

"You don't think he would go and do something stupid. I mean if he was really upset?"

She sees the lifeline. "It's true he hasn't been himself lately."

"Listen, Jen, I think we should call the cops."

"The police?" She does her best to keep her voice even.

"Well, this is like a missing person isn't it? We should report it."

"I'm sure he'll be in touch."

"And if he isn't? Then what?"

"What's your name?"

"Sorry?"

"Your name?"

"Patrick."

"Let's give it another week, Patrick. See if he turns up."

She hears his breath on the other end of the phone.

"Alright," he says finally. "One week but then we call the cops."

Oh God. It's over. She was going to prison. McKenzie was going into foster care. The game was up. Jennifer turns and faces the wall, rests her forehead against the cool brick, tries to get some air into her lungs. What a screw up. Of course someone would notice he was gone. No human being lived in a vacuum. She'd been stupid not to think of it before now, not to be ready with a plan. Soon there'd be more than just this Patrick guy to deal with, like Hank's brother from San Diego who had the habit of phoning up out of the blue and saying, "Hey guys, I'm in town and on my way over," or Hank's old college friends who liked to catch up every once in a while for beer and football or a guys' night out.

Jennifer tells herself to calm down. She lights a cigarette and stares at the pond, which at this time of year is green and gelatinous. It was Hank's job to put the cover on for winter but with everything that had happened, she'd forgotten to do it. Now two dead sparrows drift across the surface.

The chill of the night settles her some and she flicks the spent cigarette into the brackish water and returns to the kitchen and takes a seat at the table. She stays there all night, listening to the wind circle outside and whisper through the gaps. The night grows impossibly dark.

Somewhere along the line it clicks into place and daylight happens and the kitchen turns grey then blue then white. There's no other choice. It's risky, but the only plan she's got. So at precisely 7:30 a.m. Jennifer gets to her feet and picks up the phone.

40

He tells her his name is Detective Ethan North and shakes her hand briefly. When he does so, his eyes are not on Jennifer but elsewhere, just left of her shoulder, like he's practicing a public speaking technique to focus on some mid-point above the heads of the audience. He isn't much older than her and seems shy or distracted, she can't tell which. There's a continuous, serious frown too. As if he's sleep deprived or has too much on his plate, which makes sense given the splodge of baby food on his crumpled lapel. Jennifer also notes the dark hair spilling over his shirt collar and thinks that someone ought to tell Detective North he needs a haircut and shave.

The night before, she'd rehearsed the meeting over and over in her mind because there was no room for error. She had visualized letting the police in, offering coffee, beginning with the story she had developed, affecting just the right amount of concern and indifference.

But things don't happen that way.

For one thing, Detective North turns down the coffee and barely looks at her, choosing instead to scribble in that little black book of his.

"When was the last time you saw your husband?"

When he speaks it's almost a mumble, which draws attention to his mouth and the faint, silken scar of a hare lip that ran, at an angle, from the bottom left side of his nose to the outer edge of his top lip.

"Two or three weeks ago," she says. "We were meant to make arrangements about the house, that sort of thing."

Jennifer tries to remain calm and hopes the blotchy red neck won't give her away.

"And where was that?" he asks without looking up.

"Sorry?"

'Where did you see him?"

"Here."

"This house?"

"Yes."

And he writes that down, holding the pen so tightly, Jennifer thinks it might snap in two.

"You're divorced, is that correct?"

"Not yet. Separated, I suppose."

Detective North stops writing and looks at the daisy frame photograph on the fridge.

"That him?"

She nods.

"Who's the girl with him?"

"My daughter, McKenzie."

"How old is she?"

"Twelve." She tries for her best smile. "Do you have kids, Detective?"

He shakes his head and turns back to the notebook. "Never had the pleasure. He been in contact with her?"

Jennifer glances at the stain on his jacket and concludes it must be his own doing and begins to wonder whether he might be one of those dedicated, dogged, workaholic types married to the job, which would most definitely not be a good thing in the circumstances.

"Isn't it unusual for a detective to be involved so early in the process?"

He pauses and his frown grows deeper. "The county takes all missing persons seriously."

She catches it then, a hook of resentment in his voice.

"Still, you must have more serious matters to investigate."

He ignores her and turns back to his notebook and repeats the previous question. "Has your husband had any contact with your daughter?"

"None that I believe."

He points a knuckle at the photo. "Can I have it?'

"Go ahead, if it helps."

He slips the photograph into his folder.

"And your full name?" he asks, pen poised over his notebook.

"Jennifer Marie Blake."

"And his?"

"Hank Andrew Blake."

"His date of birth?"

"Twelfth of November 1972."

There's a beep and Detective North digs into his pocket for his phone with his free hand and thumbs in a password. His eyes narrow as he reads a text message. He returns the phone to his pocket and closes his notebook and lifts his eyes to look at Jennifer, but even then she can't be sure he isn't really glancing past her shoulder, off to the side.

"There's something else," she says.

"Okay."

"He was abusing my daughter."

His eyes finally land on her face.

"I went to police to lay a complaint," Jennifer continues. "I'm sure you'll find it when you run your checks. They said I needed more evidence. He wanted to work things out. Of course I said no."

Detective North opens his notebook again.

"He seem depressed to you?"

She paused.

"He threatened to kill himself but I didn't take it seriously. My primary concern at the time was for my daughter."

"What about in the past? He ever show any signs of depression?"

"He had a bad patch. He's a building contractor and the market's been tough. He was on Prozac for a while. Look, I don't know if it means anything, but he mentioned Seattle. Suicide may not be the only possibility."

"You think he might be in Seattle?" says Detective North, writing it all down.

"I'm just saying he mentioned it."

"What are his doctor's details?"

"His doctor?"

"Yes."

"Dr. Little over on Corbett Street."

He closes the notebook.

"I'll be in touch," he says.

He circles around looking for the way out.

"This way," says Jennifer.

He follows her down the hallway and Jennifer opens the front door. A rush of crisp, wet air hits them. He looks out into the street and over at the woods, seems to forget she's there.

"It's pretty," he says and she can't be sure he isn't speaking to himself.

Then he turns and walks down the path toward his unmarked patrol car. He looks back at Jennifer.

"Oh, and I'll need to speak to your daughter."

A fist materializes in her throat. "I didn't want to her involve in this. It will just upset her."

He scratches the inside of his ear and stares at a rose bush.

"Procedure," he says.

Then he gets into his dirty, dented car and drives away.

41

The next day Jennifer gets to the clinic early to beat Rosemary and opens up herself. She has trouble remembering the alarm code and nearly sets it off, but then recalls it's the same date she first opened for business. After stepping inside, she allows herself a moment in the stillness. This clinic had been her greatest accomplishment. It had signaled the transformation from ordinary working stiff to business owner. At the time, the sense of pride she had felt was enormous. They had celebrated with a cake in the shape of eyeballs. One green. One blue. The David Bowie cake Hank had called it.

It all seemed to mean nothing now. That person no longer exists. That life gone, too.

She leaves off the lights and walks through to her office and searches through the top drawer of her desk. Among the bull dog clips and boxes of staples she finds the black leather business card holder. She flips through the plastic sleeves until she locates the one she's looking for.

Amy Stein.

It had been three years since Jennifer last spoke to her old college friend. They had bumped into each other at the National Optometric conference in St Louis and spent the night in the hotel bar laughing about frat parties, caffeine-fueled all-nighters and the sense of freedom they missed. Funny, beautiful, smart Amy Stein who graduated and moved South to pursue a great career and had done exactly that, eventually creating her own successful eyewear manufacturing business. Amy Stein who slipped Jennifer her business card at the end of the night and said if you ever want a change of scene, I can always use an outstanding woman like yourself.

Jennifer had saved the card never giving it a second thought. Now that offer seemed like a life line. She picks up the phone and dials the number and hears the spritely hello.

"Amy?" she says. "It's Jennifer."

"But we don't know anything about Florida."

"We can learn."

"What about school?"

"There are schools in Florida."

McKenzie's tears fall freely down her cheeks and onto the knife and fork she had so diligently cleaned with the antiseptic wipes she had taken to carrying around in the front pouch of her black hoodie.

"Come on, hon, don't cry."

A waitress hovers nearby, wiping circles on a table, shooting them glances. Jennifer leans forward and lowers her voice. "Everything's going to be okay. You need to trust me on this one."

"What about Lenise? She's my friend. We can't just leave her behind, she'll be lonely, and Dad? He won't know where to find us."

"I know this is a big change but think of it as a fresh start. The offer's just too good to pass up."

And it was. The chief operating officer of the new Miami branch, a salary forty thousand dollars than she was earning now.

"But I don't want to go."

Then McKenzie begins to sob, big chest-heaving numbers, sucking in breath like she's been running a race. The few customers there were begin to stare. A heavy-set woman in a snug navy polo looks pointedly over the rim of her glasses.

"The boy okay?" she says to Jennifer.

"She's not a boy," snaps Jennifer.

"I'm just saying the child don't look fine to me."

McKenzie regains her composure and wipes her eyes with her sleeve.

"I'm okay," she says.

Satisfied, the woman turns back to her meal.

"Please don't make me go."

"It'll be good for us. I promise," says Jennifer.

McKenzie looks at her through watery eyes. "When?"

"A few weeks."

"That soon?"

"Amy needs me on the ground before December."

McKenzie blinks in a daze at the plastic gingham table cloth.

"There's one other thing," says Jennifer. "Let's keep this to ourselves for now."

"What do you mean?"

"Lenise. She might take it badly and I want to pick the right time to tell her."

McKenzie doesn't say anything.

"McKenzie, it's important."

"I heard."

42

Jennifer runs across the road to seek cover under the striped awning of Dewberry's Deli. She hasn't thought to bring a jacket or umbrella, and her blouse clings to her skin like a wet suit. Perfect. Any other point in history and she would have probably laughed. But being stuck here wasn't going to help with her ever-increasing to do list. There were books to prepare for the accountant, real estate agents to select, movers to contact, accommodation to arrange, schools to speak to.

Rain pounds the canvas and others squeeze in, shaking droplets from their coats.

"Jesus must be angry today," says a woman with a toddler.

"Jesus, Jesus, Jesus is a friend of mind," sing-songs the little boy, holding out his hand to catch the rain drops.

This morning the singing and the smell of Polish sausage is a nauseating combination and Jennifer's stomach rolls. She focuses on a jar of green chilies in the shop window and wills the weather to ease. And it does, enough for her to duck away from the growing menagerie outside the deli and make it back to the clinic before another torrent comes down.

She stops short of the door when she sees Ethan North at reception. He looks up so there's no avoiding him.

"It's bad out there," he says.

He still hasn't shaved but at least his lapel is clean.

"It is," she says, feeling wet hair lick her chin.

Rosemary hands her a paper towel. "Your mascara has run."

"Brilliant." Jennifer turns to Detective North. "Come through."

When they get inside he says, "I called. Left messages."

Three of them. Listened to and not returned.

"I know. Sorry." She doesn't offer further explanation.

He falls silent and glances around the office, taking in the equipment.

"Have you heard something?" she says, aiming for neutral.

"No."

He says nothing more and walks over to the phoroptor and stares at it, keeping his hands in his pockets.

"I don't know what else I can help you with," she says.

"Your receptionist mentioned bruises," he says, without looking back.

Jennifer feels a stab of betrayal. "Did she?"

"She's just looking out for you," he says.

"A run in with a car door."

"Okay."

Jennifer looks at the floor. A puddle has formed at her feet.

"I need to get changed," she says.

His phone rings and he looks at the screen, swipes it to divert.

"I would like to talk to your daughter," he says, turning around.

"That's not going to happen."

"I know you're scared, but I can help."

Her heart hammers in her chest.

"I'm not scared," she says.

"It might not be as bad as you think. Tell me what's on your mind and we'll go from there."

His phone rings again and he tries to ignore it but it keeps going.

"Excuse me," he says.

He answers and looks out the window while he listens. Jennifer can't hear what's being said but the voice on the other end is loud and male.

"I can't now," says Detective North. "Where's Leah? Pop, I said I can't. Listen, I'll be home soon."

He rings off and turns around. There's that frown again.

"Don't let me keep you," says Jennifer.

"McKenzie," he says.

She sighs and drops into her chair.

"She's too fragile," she says. "She never wanted me to go the police. She somehow thinks it's her fault."

"This is hard on you too I bet."

"Yes."

"But we still need to locate Hank."

"Maybe he doesn't want to be found."

He nods. "That can and does happen."

"I just want to put this behind us."

He turns to her. "I still need to talk to her."

"You don't believe me," says Jennifer.

He walks to the door and opens it. "Don't get up," he says.

She watches him through the rain-streaked window. He pauses to look at the sky and mumbles something, pulls up his collar and walks away.

43

It has been four days since the gallery incident and Lenise is still waiting for an apology. All those hurtful, malicious things. Words stung just as much as a fist, if not more. She didn't deserve such a tirade, not after everything she had done to help.

And now Jenny was punishing her with silence. Such pettiness. She was acting worse than a child. Oh, she was all smiles when she wanted something, but a cold fish when she didn't. Well next time Jennifer reached out, Lenise was going to have to exercise a tough love approach and not give in. Jenny needed to learn her manners.

There's a knock on the front door and Lenise has to laugh because, well, four days wasn't that long to hold out. But it's not Jennifer.

"Hey," says McKenzie.

"Does your mother know you're here?"

"I don't care what she thinks," says McKenzie, shooting an angry look back at her house. "Can I come in?"

"Of course."

McKenzie drops her backpack to the floor and follows Lenise to the kitchen.

"I wished I knew where he was," she says.

"Who? Your father?"

"Mom never tells me anything. But I know she knows where he is."

Lenise leans on the counter and crosses her arms.

"Why do you say that?"

"I can tell. Sometimes she looks at me like she's about to say something important but then just turns away. She thinks I'm a kid and can't handle stuff."

"Well, I wouldn't worry about your father, he can look after himself."

McKenzie stares into her drink. "I don't want him to think I hate him."

Lenise pauses. Even after he hurt her.

"It's time to put yourself first now, girl."

McKenzie gets to her feet. "I better go before she comes home from work. She'll have a bitch fit if she knows I'm here. She's been really psycho lately."

"I noticed."

McKenzie picks up her bag.

"Wait there a minute, would you," says Lenise.

Lenise dashes upstairs, returns a minute later.

"Here." She holds out a necklace, a peach-colored heart stone on a black string. "It's from South Africa. It's called a Morbue stone."

McKenzie's face lights up. "That's cool."

"Put it on."

McKenzie loops it around her neck.

"Perfect," says Lenise. "Listen, girl, I don't know what your mother's got against me at the moment but any time you want to come over, you can. I won't say a word. Now off you go before the witch of Pine Ridge Road turns you into a toad."

McKenzie doesn't move.

"What is it?" says Lenise.

"Do you really think Dad's okay?"

Lenise studies McKenzie's face and thinks about telling the child the son of a bitch got exactly what he deserved. "Yes, girl, I do."

McKenzie seems satisfied. Then, "There's something else."

Lenise frowns. "Oh, yes."

"I'm not supposed to say."

"What is it, girl?"

McKenzie looks at her. Tears are forming.

"Tell me," insists Lenise.

Suddenly she falls into Lenise's arms. "I don't want to move to Florida!" she wails.

Lenise pushes McKenzie away. "Florida? What do you mean, Florida?"

"I hate her!"

"You're leaving?"

"I want to stay here."

"When did this happen?"

"I don't know."

McKenzie is crying hard and Lenise can barely understand her. "Come on now girl, get a hold of yourself. Tell me what your mother said about Florida."

McKenzie steadies her tears and wipes her nose with the heel of her hand.

"We leave in a month."

Lenise is sick of this shit. She is sick of the smell of garlic and hickory and salt. She is sick of the fatty residue on her fingertips even though she wears gloves. She is sick of being cold because some half-wit had set up her Palgrave's Best Beef Jerky stand right outside the frozen meats section. She is sick of the sound of the butcher's grinder slicing through muscle, bone and skin. She is sick of the sore feet and aching knees. But most of all, Lenise is sick of the people who look at her like she is nothing. Even the shelf-fillers seemed to regard her at the lowest end of the supermarket pecking order, lower even than that of the cart wrangler, who was apparently afforded more respect than her because of his retardation.

She stands here most days, behind the little stand in her stupid fringed cowgirl's uniform with the American flag in her hand, and watches the customers ignore the plastic platters of diced jerky. Although to be fair, she can always count on the fatties who pass her by then secretly circle back and extend a pudgy hand for a cube (or two when they think she isn't looking). And there are also the pretend connoisseurs, who would stand there and chew in front of her, gazing up at the ceiling as if their delicate palate was trying to detect the nuances of flavor. But most just want something for free. Cheapskates who give not a second thought to how hard it was for a single woman to make a living these days, especially when her income depends on sales.

To make matters worse, when she gets here this morning she finds her stand has been shifted directly in front of the fish section, a spiteful move on the part of the store manager probably because she'd complained about being so cold. It fit with the usual downward trend of her miserable life of late, including the very bad news that Jenny and McKenzie where moving to Florida.

Lenise looks up. A man with a screaming infant and supermarket cart with a faulty rubber wheel careens around the corner. She turns her head, not wanting to encourage him and his noisy brat to head in her way. Too late.

"You want to try some, Sammy?" says the man.

The wailing child holds out his arm and moves his fingers back and forth in a grabby way.

"There's chili in it," says Lenise, raising her voice over the skull-rattling cries, "and this one has whiskey in it, so I wouldn't give him that."

"Sounds like a good idea to me."

Lenise doesn't return the man's smile and cuts a portion of the plainest flavored jerky she has and gives it to the brat.

"Here you go junior," she says.

The toddler throws it back in her face.

When Lenise gets home she sees Jennifer removing grocery bags from the trunk of her car.

"Jenny."

Jennifer's eyes drop to Lenise's cowgirl outfit and Lenise wishes she had the foresight to change.

"I apologize for the other day," she says. "For taking McKenzie to the gallery without your permission."

To Lenise's surprise Jenny says, "I could've handled things better myself."

Jenny looks worn out. Like she might be getting sick again. Then Lenise reminds herself why she's here.

"When where you going to tell me about Florida?"

Jennifer looks shocked. "McKenzie told you?"

Lenise pats down her hair and the fringe on her sleeve shimmies like a wind chime. "Don't get annoyed at her. She was upset and had nowhere to turn."

Jennifer stiffens and disappears into the trunk to retrieve the rest of her groceries. "I want a fresh start, Lenise. Is that so wrong after everything that's happened?"

"You're running away."

"I don't want to fight," says Jennifer.

"Running away never solves anything, I should know."

"Well, this isn't your decision, is it?"

Lenise pauses. "I think you and McKenzie should stay."

"Honestly, Lenise."

Lenise reaches out to touch Jennifer's arm. "Jenny, please don't go."

Then to her own revulsion, Lenise begins to cry. Big fat watery marbles slide down her cheeks and splash onto her suede boots and she wants to disappear. She's never shown such weakness in public and she might as well be naked. Then, unable to stop herself, she goes further.

"If it's the house—because of what happened here—you and McKenzie can come and stay with me."

Jennifer laughs.

Lensie stares at her. "*Heartless.*"

"Lenise."

"No," says Lenise. "You've made yourself clear."

Lenise returns across the road, hears those stupid spurs jingle-jangling with every stride.

"Lenise! Come on, I wasn't laughing at you! Lenise!"

But that was a lie. Jennifer had taken Lenise for a fool and maybe that's exactly what she was.

216

44

Jennifer pours a cup of coffee and cradles the warmth in her hands. It has rained overnight and remnants drip in fingers from the eaves. A curl of sunlit steam rises from the grass. It seems perverse, this beauty in such bleakness of spirit.

Overhead floorboards creak. McKenzie is up. When she comes downstairs, she doesn't say a word to Jennifer and heads for the cupboard and retrieves the special bowl and cutlery she has taken to keeping in the plastic bag that's for her use only.

"I made eggs," says Jennifer, pointing to the plate on the table.

McKenzie ignores them and reaches inside the pantry for a single serve of tuna and places the can next to her bowl then goes to the sink and proceeds to wash her hands, soaping up the front, the back, the sides, in between the fingers, like she's preparing for surgery. She rinses and soaps three times then dries off with paper towels. She sees Jennifer looking.

"Don't make a federal case out of it," she says, finally popping the ring on the tuna and sitting down to eat.

Jennifer points to the polished stone around McKenzie's neck. "What's that?"

"Nothing."

"Where did you get it?"

McKenzie turns away. "Forget about it."

Jennifer puts down her coffee. "Lenise gave it to you."

"I knew you'd be pissed."

"Hey. Enough with the sailor talk."

217

"Well, it's true. You hate everything I do."

Jennifer sits on the stool and rubs her face with her hands. "I don't want to talk about Lenise. There's something more important we need to discuss. The police. A detective. He wants to talk to you." She pauses. "McKenzie, I had to tell him."

Jennifer watches the realization dawn on McKenzie's face. "You had no right!"

"There was no other choice. I thought he would leave you alone if I told him, but he won't let it lie."

Jennifer places a hand on McKenzie's arm but she brushes it off.

"You can't make me do this."

"It's the police. We've got to do what they tell us."

McKenzie turns and stares at her mother. "What's going on? Where's Dad?"

Jennifer swallows. "What do you mean?"

"Something's wrong. He wouldn't just leave and now the police want to talk to me."

"I don't know what to tell you," says Jennifer.

"They think something bad's happened, don't they?"

"It's their job to ask questions, that's all."

"Mom, please don't make me talk to them," she pleads. "I just want to forget about what happened."

"It's not up to me."

McKenzie wipes away a tear. "It isn't fair," she says, barely audible.

"I know but you can do this, hon."

McKenzie gets to her feet. "I just want to be normal," she says. "I just want to be like everyone else."

The room has an orange sofa and a single hard-backed chair. A pine coffee table separates the two. On top of the coffee table sits a jug of water and two glasses and a small unobtrusive recorder. One side of the wall is made entirely of mirror, the two-way kind, and that's where Jennifer stands in the dimness, arms around her middle like a brace, watching McKenzie on the couch.

The woman in the restaurant was right. McKenzie could have been a boy. The dark, shapeless clothing, the short hair, those rounded shoulders. There was nothing feminine about her anymore. It was if she was trying to erase every part of her female self.

McKenzie had insisted on doing the interview without Jennifer and the state-mandated social worker in charge of child abuse disclosures. *Just him*, McKenzie had said nodding at Detective North, and at first the social worker refused, saying it was against policy, but McKenzie informed them point blank she wouldn't talk otherwise.

McKenzie and Jennifer nearly had a stand up fight in the waiting area but Jennifer had finally let it slide and watched unhappily as McKenzie was led away. After that, a female uniformed officer showed Jennifer to this room and said, "It's never easy for the mother" and left Jennifer and the social worker to stare unseen through the mirror at the stranger sitting on the orange couch who looks a lot like Jennifer's daughter.

She knows she ought to give McKenzie privacy and feels like a thief, taking something precious Jennifer has no right to, but she cannot tear herself away.

McKenzie tells Detective North everything. The nights. The days. Where. When. What. She leaves nothing out. It doesn't seem to matter to McKenzie that Detective North is a man, or maybe it's the very fact that he is a man that means she can talk so freely about what happened. For his part, Detective North sits in the chair, a quiet presence opposite her, listening gravely, asking one or two questions for clarification but otherwise giving her the room she needs to speak.

At one point McKenzie falters and tears up and it looks like he's about to offer a hand of comfort, but he thinks better of it, choosing instead to say "we're in no rush" and he waits, patient and concerned, until McKenzie collects herself. Eventually, she carries on, scratching her cracked over-washed palms as she speaks while behind the two-way glass, Jennifer listens and weeps silently into her tissue. And when McKenzie is finally done, Jennifer has never been so glad that Hank was dead.

Afterward, a spent McKenzie goes to wait in the car and Detective North turns to Jennifer.

"Son-of-a-bitch," he says.

"I didn't know."

"It never occurred to me you did."

He shifts his weight, tugs his ear lobe.

"Sometimes," he says, "sometimes people get the idea into their head that taking the law into their own hands might be an acceptable thing. In situations like this, when a child has been hurt bad, people's emotions run high. Things might happen that people might regret. What I'm saying is that in situations like these the truth is important, more important than ever, no matter what it is, because there have already been too many lies told, because at the end of the day the truth is all we have." He looks at her and pauses. "Now's the time to say."

"I don't know where he is."

She holds his gaze, and he breaks off first, eyes landing on the potted plant near the exit.

A uniformed officer emerges from a back office. "Ethan, your old man's on the line."

Ethan nods okay to the officer then turns to Jennifer.

"You have my number," he says.

45

Lenise stirs. She's in that loose, hazy space between waking and sleeping and tries to hold on to it. But it's futile. Something is dragging her into the world by her tongue. She's lying prone on the bare concrete floor. Her eyes water and she's not sure if it's from the stench or the stark fluorescent light. There's a puddle of vomit where someone has missed the toilet and more splashed on the door. Then she sees a person, a woman, sitting against the wall staring at her.

"Where am I?" says Lenise.

The woman ignores her and Lenise gets to her feet and promptly throws up.

"God damn it!" cries the woman, pushing herself into the wall. "You nearly got my feet that time!"

Lenise wipes her mouth and looks at the woman.

"Who are you?" she says.

"The virgin-friggin-Mary."

Lenise shuffles over to the mirror, which isn't actually a mirror but more like the reflective steel they have in gas station bathrooms. Leaves and sticks are tangled in her hair, her eyes are ringed with mascara, and on the right side of her face there's a long bloody scratch. She turns to the woman.

"This some white slavery kidnapping thing?" she says.

The woman lets out a loud sharp "Ha! You'd be so lucky. You're more loaded than I thought."

The woman, come to think of it, doesn't look much better than Lenise, and has a large black bruise on her left cheek.

"This is detox," says the woman.

"Detox?"

"That's what I said."

Lenise becomes aware of an ache in her chest and groans and sits down on a concrete slab.

"That'll be your ribs. From the fight," says the woman.

"Fight?"

The woman points a red talon at her own black eye. Then somewhere in the fog a sketchy memory of a cop saying, "You girls sort out your differences," and the sound of the steel door slamming behind them.

"What day is it?" says Lenise.

"Thursday."

She'd lost three bloody days. She blinks at the floor trying to remember. Jennifer laughing in her face. Some shithole dance bar. Drinking. A blubbering call to Cody that was met with a, "you're so disgusting when you're drunk". A park. Passing out. Coming too with someone riffling through her pockets.

"You tried to rob me," says Lenise.

The woman shrugs. "I thought you were dead."

Lenise stares at the single, humming florescent strip. Dark outlines of dead insects line the bottom.

"Got a smoke?" she says.

The woman shakes her head. "You talk in your sleep, you know that? Ghosts and some such shit."

"Any names?" says Lenise.

"Nuh."

Lenise lies on her back and closes her eyes. "Good."

They fall silent then Lenise says, "What's the worst thing you've ever done, virgin-friggin-Mary?"

"The absolute worst?"

"Yeah."

"I stole an old lady's rent money to get a fix. I ain't proud of it, but I own it now, you know? I think about that old lady from time to time. You?"

"I left my back door open and my dog got out and was hit by a car and died."

"Jeez."

"I know."

"That kind of shit would cut me up."

"Strange thing is I became friends with the person who did it. Helped her out with something big, but she let me down."

"That's a lot of the problem these days."

"What is?"

"Lack of gratitude."

"Yes," Lenise nods. "There's nothing I hate more than a lack of gratitude."

They are released just before noon. Lenise steps out into the sharp morning light and her cell mate waves a goodbye above her head and sashays off down the road in her white dagger heel boots. Lenise is about to flag down a cab when she looks in her wallet and finds it empty. No money. Not a dime. That bitch had taken everything she had.

She shoves the empty wallet back into her purse. What did it matter where it had gone and who took what and who didn't? No money, no ride. Her head pounds and her mouth is sore and her ribs ache and all she wants to do is crawl into bed but instead puts one leaden foot in front of the other and begins the long walk home.

Lenise has the key in her door and is about to go inside when she sees a car pull up. A dark-haired man steps from the vehicle, handsome in an unkempt sort of way. At first, she thinks he's some sort of debt collector.

"Ma'am," he says. "My name is Detective Ethan North. May I have a word?"

His eyes linger on her dirty clothes, the scratch on her face.

"Are you going to charge me with something?" she says.

He looks startled. "Why would I do that?"

"For the detox thing."

The detective jams his hands in his pockets and looks over his shoulder at Jennifer's house. "I don't know anything about that. I just want to ask you a few questions about your neighbors, the Blakes."

Lenise feels sick. "What about them?"

"If we could just go inside."

"I need a shower, can't we do this later?"

"It won't take long."

Lenise sighs and unlocks the door and he follows her inside and glances around. The sketch of a lion she had picked up at a Jo'Burg market seems to interest him and he goes close to study it.

"Africa?"

"Yes."

"I've always wanted to go."

"They have airplanes for that now. What's this about?"

From his pocket, he takes out a pen and a black notebook and flips through it.

"Jennifer Blake told me about that night. How you helped when he came after them," he says, eyes on his notes.

Lenise tries to maintain her composure. "What about it?"

"It was kind of you. Dangerous even," he says, without looking up.

"I couldn't exactly turn them away."

He flips through his notebook until he reaches a blank page. "You see him after that?"

"The husband?"

He nods.

"Once or twice, maybe. I can't remember. Who cares?"

"He's missing."

"Ha! More likely gone on to terrorize some other poor, unsuspecting woman."

Detective North pauses. "What do you think of the wife, Jennifer?"

She looks at him. "You really want to know the truth?"

"Sure."

"She's weak. She needed to open her eyes and see him for what he is a long time ago. If someone ever pulled a gun on me...well...let's just say there would be consequences." She looks at her watch. "Now will that be all?"

"You see anything funny?"

"Funny?"

"You know, out of the ordinary."

She shakes her head. "I don't think so."

"You don't think so?"

"No."

"Has she talked to you, Jennifer, since then, I mean?"

Lenise shrugs. "In passing. Neighbor stuff. Waving when I put out the trash etcetera."

He writes something down but she can't see what it is.

"I prefer to keep to myself," she says.

"You live alone?"

"My son recently moved out."

He looks at the scrabble board on the table.

"Okay," he says finally. "Here's my number." He gives her his card. "Call me if you think of anything else."

Before leaving, he stops at the lion sketch.

"I saw a documentary once, about the Serengeti or some such place. Mostly it's the females who do the hunting yet the males who eat first. Seems the battle of the sexes isn't just a human condition. But I tell you something else for free. Those females can be ruthless. I saw one bring down an impala and you know how she killed it? By holding its nose and mouth in her jaw and suffocating it. Held it down like that while it thrashed about from lack of oxygen. And that's the other thing about them. Patience. They got a ton of it. But then again, so do I. Thank you for your time."

He gives her a nod and heads out. When he reaches his car, he turns to look at the forest and stands there staring at it, in those crumpled chinos, for what seems to Lenise like the longest time, like a bear with its nose in the wind.

46

Jennifer rises from her desk and opens the office window. She breathes in. Across the lot, the lawnmower man shaves a perfect rectangle path through the grass. He's working his way inward in precise formation, like some strange game of Tetris.

Her door swings open, and Lenise stalks in, furious. "What in God's name are you playing at, Jenny?"

"He's been to see you," says Jennifer, crossing the room to close the door.

"You could have bloody well warned me."

"I had no choice," Jennifer replies evenly.

"What did you tell him?"

"I thought it better to stick as close to the truth as possible."

Lenise shakes her head as if Jennifer is the dumbest human in history. "You should've kept your mouth shut. You've made yourself the number one suspect, you know that, don't you? You put me at risk too."

Jennifer takes a seat, rubs her temple, tries to will the universe into making Lenise disappear but when she opens her eyes, she's still there.

"I had to tell him," says Jennifer. "Besides, sexually abusing your daughter and threatening to kill your family is a good reason to disappear."

"For heaven sakes Jenny, don't be so naive!"

Jennifer explodes and leaps to her feet.

"Who do you think you are, Lenise? We wouldn't be in this mess if it weren't for you!"

"Don't pull that shit on me. You know it was an accident. You're not laying everything at my door. You're up to something and I don't like it."

"You're being ridiculous."

"I'm not having a bar of it."

"Lenise, they've got nothing. You'll see. It will die down now. They'll make a half-hearted attempt to look for him, another big case will come along and they'll forget all about Hank Blake."

Lenise pauses. "Does this mean Florida's off?"

Jennifer meets Lenise with a level gaze. "Everything is still moving ahead as planned."

The door opens.

"Everything okay?" says Rosemary. "You guys were shouting."

"We're fine," says Jennifer.

"You sure?"

"I'm just leaving," says Lenise. She gives Jennifer a look. "If anything changes, call me."

"Whatever you say."

"I mean it, Jenny, don't leave me in the dark again."

As Jennifer pulls into Seener Road, her hope of making up lost time soon fades when she sees traffic backed up all the way to Cooper Street. She had wanted to collect some empty packing boxes from the moving company before peak hour traffic hit, but by the looks of the trail of red tail lights there wasn't much chance of that.

There's no avoiding it, so she pulls in behind a gold Lexus, and joins the wait, planning on breaking away and taking a left on Quincy Road when she reaches the intersection. Outside pedestrians are walking, chins down, jackets pulled tight at their throats. Then, to her right, Jennifer sees him. Ethan North.

She's startled at first, thinking perhaps she's caught him in the act of tailing her. But then her mind computes what she is actually witnessing—Ethan North on the sidewalk trying to wrangle an old man into his unmarked sedan. The man's being uncooperative and keeps shuffling to the left, pointing at something down the street, causing Ethan to circle around in an attempt to coax him back toward the car.

Initially, Jennifer concludes the man must be an intoxicated vagrant until Ethan kneels down to tie the lace on the old man's shoe. The man smiles and places his hand on top of Ethan's head, gently, father to son.

She's almost embarrassed because it feels like she's walked in on someone in their private space. Ethan and his father continue their back and forth rumba up and down the sidewalk until Ethan finally wins out and gets his father into the passenger side of the car, guiding him into the seat, then reaching over to click the safety belt it into place.

A car honks behind her. Traffic has begun moving again and she pulls away.

An hour later, when Jennifer returns home, the back seat filled with packing cartons, she nearly hits the fence when she sees Ethan North's empty sedan parked out front. Trying to quell her shaking hands, she angles the car into the garage and opens the internal door and finds McKenzie and Detective North in the kitchen.

"He says it's about Dad," says McKenzie.

"Oh, yes?" says Jennifer, heart pounding.

Ethan North gets to his feet. "You're moving away."

"That's right."

"You should have told me."

He seems harder now and she wonders where that tender shoe-lace-tying son went.

"I wouldn't have just left," she says.

"Oh?"

"Of course not. It's just with everything going on…"

"Florida?"

She laughs, uneasy. "You bugging my house?"

"McKenzie just told me."

"It's stupid and I don't want to go," McKenzie chimes in.

"I know how it must look," says Jennifer.

"How's that?"

"Husband disappears, wife leaves town," she tries for another laugh. "But McKenzie and I, we deserve this."

He pauses. "We're conducting a search."

He is watching her and she uses every inch of self-control to keep her face passive.

"A search?"

"In Pine Ridge Forest."

Jennifer feels a rush of blood to the head.

"Why there?" she says.

Detective North hesitates, glances at McKenzie. "It's better if we talk alone."

"Go upstairs, hon," says Jennifer.

"I want to stay."

"Please, McKenzie, do as I say."

"Stop treating me like a kid. I deserve to know what's going on too."

"Alright," says Jennifer, relenting. She nods at Ethan North to continue.

"Your husband's bank account hasn't been touched, which could mean a possibility of suicide."

"Dad wouldn't do that!" cries McKenzie.

"Hon."

"I know he wouldn't," McKenzie insists.

Ethan looks at his hands, and shoves them in his pockets.

"We have to rule out every possibility. Most research shows people don't stray too far from home to carry out the act, so the forest is a good guess."

"That's a big area. Where will you start?" says Jennifer.

He rubs a knuckle over his lip. "People tend to stick to the tracks and like to be close to water. Thinking time, I guess. Our focus will be on a small, targeted search in a ten mile radius."

"When?"

"Monday," he says. "If the weather holds up."

Two nights away.

"You're wasting your time," says McKenzie flatly. "You won't find him."

He looks at them both. "I just thought you should know."

"You won't," she says.

Afterward, Jennifer stands on the landing and hears McKenzie crying in her room. Jennifer has no tears though. She is thinking instead, about where they had put the body, somewhere not far from a walking track, close to water.

47

Jennifer paces. She needs to keep moving or she might fall apart. She picks up the cordless phone and takes it into the garage, keeping the lights turned off. She presses the glowing digits.

"We've got a problem," she whispers. "We have to move him."

"What do you mean move him?" demands Lenise.

"They're doing a search on Monday. Oh God, they're going to find him."

Silence.

"Lenise? Are you there?"

"This isn't really my problem anymore is it, Jenny?" Lenise replies coolly.

"What do you mean this isn't your problem?"

"I'm getting on with life and trying to put the incident behind me."

"What are you talking about? I'm in this mess because of you."

"If that bastard was still alive you would probably be dead by now, Jenny. You could show a little more gratitude."

"Gratitude? Are you crazy?"

"Now you're insulting me."

Jennifer pauses, tries to collect herself. "You can't be serious," she says. "You have to help me."

"And you haven't exactly been neighborly as of late."

Rain tap-dances across the roof.

"I was trying to get on with things, like you. Put it behind me," says Jennifer.

"It's not right to use people."

"I didn't use you."

"Then throw them away like they are nothing."

"God, Lenise, I'm sorry," Jennifer starts to cry. "I can't go to prison. What will happen to McKenzie?"

"Calm down. You're not doing yourself any favors by losing your rag."

"Please, Lenise. I've got no one else to turn to."

The pause stretches on endlessly. The rain, wild and uncontained now, launches itself against the tin like gravel.

Then, finally, "Piss off and leave me alone."

48

Jennifer glances at McKenzie who's shifting barley and basil risotto around on her plate, eyes fixed in a thousand-yard stare, and Jennifer knows she's thinking about Hank and whether he's out there, dead, and if he is, believing it's somehow her fault. Jennifer nearly tells McKenzie everything but doesn't have the guts.

When McKenzie pushes her plate away and says she going to bed early it's almost a relief.

Jennifer rinses the plates and loads the dishwasher and wipes the bench and tells herself these could be the very last domestic duties she'll ever perform. She lifts her head and looks out the kitchen window and sees Lenise standing on her own front steps. There's a sudden fierce pinpoint of red as Lenise brings the cigarette to her lips then an arc of tiny sparks when she flicks it away. Jennifer expects Lenise to go back inside, but she doesn't, she just stands there and stares at the house.

In the morning she is waiting by Jennifer's car.

"You don't deserve it, but I'll help."

They decide to wait until the next night, hoping the rain would clear, and it does, although dark clouds linger, threatening to deliver more at a moment's notice. Waiting also gives Jennifer time to collect necessary supplies. Earlier in the day she'd driven to Franklin and found a Lowes and purchased a tarpaulin, gloves, masks, rope, bolt cutters, a large container with a lid and wheels, and two flashlights.

At Lenise's suggestion, Jennifer wore a cap to hide her face from the cameras. She also donned a bulky grey hoodie to make herself look bigger, and was sure to keep her head lowered at the checkout. After paying in cash, Jennifer went to McDonalds and flushed the receipt down the toilet. Tonight, with McKenzie asleep, Jennifer waits in the garage. She has the awful feeling Lenise isn't going to show. But a little after 11 p.m., there's a tap on the roller door.

"You're late," says Jennifer.

"Well, I'm here now, so let's get on with it."

They drive in silence. Lenise's stony face stares out the window, and Jennifer thinks of the night they first met when Lenise cradled Baby in her arms in the back seat. Jennifer has the urge to thank her, because even though this situation was in large part Lenise's fault, she could have forced Jennifer to deal with this mess on her own.

It's not long before they reach the Pine Ridge entrance and Jennifer takes the road to the left. Bitumen gives way to shingle, and shadows close in around them. They follow the same route as before, keeping a look-out for landmarks. But with the onset of winter everything's changed. Trees are bare of leaves and even the land looks different in places.

"It's around here somewhere," says Jennifer, hunched over the steering wheel.

"Watch it."

Up ahead a group of college kids mill round a bonfire, bottles in hand. Music thumps and some are dancing. There's a peal of laughter when a guy lobs a can of Axe into the fire making it explode.

"Little shits," says Lenise.

"They're blocking the path in."

"Well, I can see that, can't I?" snaps Lenise. "We'll have to try again tomorrow."

"The search is tomorrow."

"I thought you said it was Tuesday," says Lenise.

"I told you Monday."

"You said Tuesday."

"Okay, Lenise, you're right, like you're always right," says Jennifer. "But that doesn't change the fact we still need to do this tonight."

Jennifer returns to the entrance and heads back to Pine Ridge Road and takes the road skirting the forest. Spots of rain spatter the windscreen.

"Marvelous," says Lenise.

"It's just rain."

Jennifer drives slow, hugging the curb, scanning for a possible way in.

"See I told you. Nothing," says Lenise.

"There!"

Sure enough in front of them is another track, albeit narrow and overgrown.

"You'll never be able to do it."

"We'll see."

Jennifer leaves the road and drives overland toward the opening. It's tight but she does it. The path is rough going and they are tossed about in their seats and Lenise tells her to slow down, placing a hand on the dashboard. Jennifer eases off the accelerator but drives on, into deeper, thicker forest.

"Watch out!"

Jennifer slams on the brakes and they catapult against their seatbelts.

"What the hell is that?"

Something is blocking their path. A septic tank. Broken toilets. Other construction debris.

"Someone doesn't want to pay dumping fees."

Jennifer cuts the engine.

"We can't go any further," she says.

"What now?" says Lenise.

"We walk."

"We'll get lost. Do you even know where we are?"

Jennifer gets out of the car and faces the forest wall. "I think so."

"Don't be a fool. We could be anywhere."

"You'll just have to trust me," says Jennifer.

She retrieves the container from the trunk, hands Lenise the spades and clicks on a flashlight. "Let's go."

They find a gap between a stand of Spanish firs and move forward. Torchlight nods against the vegetation and Jennifer pulls the container behind her, its tiny rubber wheels lurching over roots and rocks. Wind roars like an ocean through the treetops, but down here, close to the forest floor, even the rain can't get through.

They walk for a good twenty minutes before emerging to face a clearing, with more woods on the other side. The wind is instant and vicious and so is the driving rain. It pricks Jennifer's bare arms and she thinks how stupid it was not to bring a coat. She stands on a fallen log and looks out over the land.

"If we can just find the river."

Lenise shouts over the wind. "We're getting lost!"

"I know we're close."

"You don't know that at all!"

Jennifer ignores her and begins the trek to the other side.

"You're going in the wrong direction!" Lenise calls out.

But Jennifer heads across the exposed clearing and Lenise follows. A bitter wind blasts from every direction, robbing them of breath. They avert their faces but there's nowhere to hide and all they can do is keep going and carry up the incline to the other side.

Finally, they reach the embankment and Jennifer puts the container on the ground and stops to catch her breath. Lenise stops too, tries to unwrap the wet, tangled hair from around her neck.

Jennifer picks up the container. "Let's keep moving."

"I need to rest."

"Rest all you want later."

Twenty more minutes and they reach a wire fence.

"It's the border to the orchard," says Jennifer.

Lenise lifts her arm. "Over there."

They cut across the paddock. The sound of rushing water.

"We must be close."

Jennifer does a 360 then sees it. The Arizona cypress. They cross the grass and look down at the grave.

"Something's been at it," says Lenise.

The ground has most definitely been disturbed. A deep gash cuts across the grave.

"What if he's not all there?" says Jennifer.

"There's only one way to find out."

Lenise props the torch in a nook of the pear tree, angling the light directly onto the spot. They slice into the boggy soil and stony mud drips from their spades like excrement, but it's better than the frozen ground Jennifer had been expecting. They dig deeper and deeper into the slop, rain battering the leaves above their heads, the taste of lime and death on their lips. Twenty minutes in, Lenise holds up her hand.

"Careful," she says, staring into the hole.

Jennifer looks over Lenise's shoulder.

"Oh Jesus."

A creamy eye stares back at them.

Throwing the spade to one side, Lenise ties a rag around her face, gives one to Jennifer, and they bend down to finish the job with their hands. They don't get very far because the smell is unbearable. Jennifer can't stand it and stops.

Lenise grips her shoulder. "Think about something else," her voice muffled by the rag. "Think about McKenzie."

Jennifer nods and they kneel side by side and scoop out the mud, gingerly excavating what they had buried all those weeks before. When they are done, Lenise directs the torchlight into the hole.

The lime has done its job well. The process of defleshing had already begun. Chunks of skin had dissolved. Bone too. The fingers on his left hand were gone entirely. The ribcage was empty.

"God," says Jennifer.

"The son of a bitch deserved it. Let's not forget that," says Lenise.

Lenise drags the container close to the rim, gets in the hole and straddles the corpse.

"We need to be careful," she says. "He might break apart."

Together they lift him into the container, folding his limbs in on themselves like a Cirque du Soleil contortionist. Then they fill the hole and leave.

Jennifer pulls to a stop outside the tall wire gates surrounding the abandoned building.

"What is this place?" says Lenise.

"An old fertilizer plant. It was decommissioned back in the 70s after an explosion."

To their left is a rundown three storey office block connected to a large factory in a severe state of disrepair. Windows have been smashed to hollow stars. Loosened roof iron flaps in the wind. Someone has spray painted over the Pergeson Corp sign to say Poisonous Crap instead.

Jennifer retrieves the bolt-cutters from the backseat and opens the chain-linked gates then drives down a dirt road until they reach the back of the plant. They leave the container in the car, shoulder open a door and go inside. The cavernous space is empty apart from pipe remnants scattered over the concrete floor and a large stainless-steel silo lying on its side. Nesting pigeons flutter in the rafters.

Jennifer opens a side door and finds a covered walkway overrun with vegetation. Enormous concrete pipes snake alongside and they follow them into the darkness.

"Where are we going exactly?" says Lenise.

"It's not far," says Jennifer

"I don't like this."

Jennifer glances at Lenise. The whites of her eyes glow brighter than snow.

"Relax, Lenise, we're the only ones here."

"We shouldn't have left him in the car. What if someone pulls up and finds him?" says Lenise.

But Jennifer continues on and Lenise does, too.

"I read an old article once when the whole scandal blew up," says Jennifer. "They kept making the stuff and shipping it off to third world countries even though they knew it was toxic. There's an entire village in Laos which has birth defects worse than Chernobyl."

She falls silent and looks in the distance. The runoff pond. Stagnant and thick and deadly.

"What is that?' says Lenise.

"Our ticket out of this mess."

They walk closer. Jennifer looks for a way in and finds one. An entire section of the fence lies on its side as if it's been driven over. God only knew what else had been dumped here over the years.

They return for the car and, ten minutes later, lay the body out on the lid of the container and push it to the water's edge. They tip it sideways and the corpse rolls into the sludge, the thick oily substance seeping into the remains, pulling the body down into its plummy depths.

Jennifer and Lenise stand on the bank and watch the final shoulder blade slip under.

"That's that, then," says Lenise.

Jennifer casts a look at Lenise, who's gazing at the rippling water. It would be so easy. She would never see it coming and no one would ever know and it would solve another big problem.

"Jenny?"

"What?"

"We should go."

"Yeah."

"Even just standing here is probably bad for our health."

"Probably," says Jennifer.

Lenise stares at the pond. "You're going to leave now, aren't you, move to Florida."

Jennifer pauses and thinks about denying it. "Yes."

"Please don't."

"Lenise, I want you to know I appreciate your help. With everything. You've been a better friend than I ever deserved."

Lenise nods glumly.

"If you say so," she says, turning away to head back to the car.

49

Jennifer switches off the bathroom light and eases herself into the steaming water. At the end of the bath, flames from two soy candles duck and dive from the draft of her body and she rests her head on the folded towel and stares at those flickering lights. They sit in pretty mirrored glass votives, a gift to herself, years before. She had always loved candlelight, how it made everything meaningful and serene, how it changed the simple act of cleaning yourself into an indulgent event.

Her breath comes slow and easy. She feels tired but oddly energized, like she has come through a difficult challenge and lived to tell the tale. An ugly problem had been solved. They would search and find nothing. The body would soon vanish without a trace.

Jennifer draws in a clean and fulsome breath. The blisters on her hands burn and the muscles in her legs ache but tonight has been a good night. Tonight she has slain a dragon.

She thinks of Ethan North. Other, more pressing, investigations would soon demand his attention. The Hank Blake case would fade into obscurity, becoming another face on a database somewhere, another deadbeat dad who never showed up.

Through the tails of steam Ethan's face comes to her. The strong contour of his jaw, the masculine marker of three-day growth, that earnest expression. She closes her eyes and lowers herself further into the soft fleece of juniper and thyme bubbles.

When she is done she slips—naked and fresh and mellow and warm—into her silky cotton sheets and spreads out like a star, right in the middle of the bed, just because she can.

50

Lenise stares into her bowl. A splodge of ketchup sits like a loose turd, center-left, on top of the tee-pee of French fries. The girl with Cody will not stop talking. Blah. Blah. Blah. Words spew out of that pink cupid-lipped mouth blurring into one long monologue. No pausing for breath. No real substance.

Lenise glances at Cody. He is nodding right along with the girl, their two hands resting atop the vinyl gingham in a Siamese fist. Lenise is so tired, so sore and drained from last night's endeavor, she only wishes she had the energy to get up and leave.

It had been a bad idea to come, but Cody had insisted, calling first thing this morning to make plans for tonight. *Melinda wants to meet you.* She'd been in bed with the sheets pulled up over her head trying to forget the fact Jennifer and McKenzie were leaving. She'd told him she couldn't make it, but he wouldn't take no for an answer, so here she was, barely functional, lids drooping like shutters.

The waiter brings Cody's steak and Lenise's stomach swims in acid. She glances at the girl's bowl of Mac n Cheese and sees the buttery rope of a spinal cord.

On and on, the Melinda girl prattles, managing to talk and shovel that macaroni into that big fat hole of hers at the same time. A smear of white sauce has collected in the crease of her mouth. What Cody sees in her, Lenise can't understand. The Americans have a name for her kind— trailer trash. Bad teeth. A mauve bow in her bleached hair. Gold-hooped earrings the size of bicycle wheels. Right now, Lenise wishes little Miss Hillbilly would just shut the hell up.

"When are you coming home Cody?" says Lenise, abruptly.

Melinda gawks at her and stops in midsentence.

"Ma, haven't you heard anything we've been saying?" says Cody.

"The house is too quiet without you."

"You need to listen, Ma."

She slams her hands palm down on the table.

"For the love of God, Cody, I'm trying to tell you I miss you. That's not something I say every day."

"We're having a baby, Ma. We're going to get married."

"What did you say?"

"A *baby*." He looks at her in the way he'd done as a boy. When he would glance over his shoulder to make sure she was watching before he did a big dive or went way up high on the swing or crossed the finish line first.

"Three months gone, today," says Melinda-the-mouth, hand hovering over her belly.

"Is that so?"

"Yes, Ma'am."

Lenise pushes back her chair and gets to her feet.

"Take me home."

"We haven't finished eating."

"Forget it."

She throws down some money and weaves through the other tables toward the exit.

"Ma!" calls Cody.

She collides with someone coming back from the bar and Coke spills all over them.

"Hey!"

"Go to hell," she says, but she's already outside and nobody hears her except the wind.

51

Jennifer finds McKenzie staring out her bedroom window at the cluster of activity in Pine Ridge Forest. Even from this far away, it's possible to make out search and rescue trucks, quad motorbikes, police cars, cadaver dogs, fluorescent vests. There are far more people than Jennifer had been expecting, and it looks like they're going to continue the search into the night because they've just erected a floodlight.

From this distance, Jennifer can't tell if they're searching the burial site but she knows they're close. Her heart skips at the thought that she and Lenise had left something behind. But they had been thorough and swept the area twice before leaving and rain would have washed anything else away.

"Come down for dinner," says Jennifer.

McKenzie refuses to take her eyes from the window. "I'm not hungry."

"You can't stay here all night."

Wind carries the faint rabble of voices, the clipped bark of a dog.

"Come on, hon."

"Where is he, Mom? Why doesn't he call?"

"I don't know."

"Marcus Goodfellow's Dad shot himself in the head because of a gambling debt. No one talks to Marcus now. They post mean things about him on Facebook."

"That's not going to happen to you."

"I don't care if it does. Those haters are jerks."

"Come on, let's go downstairs for awhile, take a break from all this."

Jennifer reaches across to close the curtain, but McKenzie stops her. "I want to see."

"It's not healthy, hon."

"I don't care."

For an instant Jennifer wants to tell her all of it, every last detail, like the smell and the unseeing eye and the weight of his rotting bones in her hands, the complete and utter sense of satisfaction she experienced as he slid into his sour and watery grave.

Instead, she says, "I'll get you some tuna."

It's after ten when the knock on the door finally arrives. McKenzie had long since fallen asleep at the window so it's just Jennifer and Ethan North in his blue puffer jacket and cargo pants.

"Come in," she says. "I've just made coffee."

Without waiting, she walks down the hall into the kitchen and his footsteps sound behind her. She pours him a cup and he holds up a hand.

"I've had enough to keep me going 'til Christmas."

Jennifer rests against the bench and folds her arms. "Well?"

"We didn't find him."

She nods. "I had a hang up call the other night. Maybe it was him."

Disappointment clouds his face, like a parent who's caught a child in a lie. Jennifer chides herself for being such an idiot. To her relief, he changes the subject.

"I saw the For Sale sign out front. I guess that means you're leaving soon," he says.

"There doesn't seem much point in staying. McKenzie's not doing so well."

"She's a great kid."

"Yes, she is."

He stares at her.

"Is there something else?" she says.

"Your bank records, there was a significant withdrawal awhile back."

Her mouth goes dry. "And?"

He shrugs. "It's your money and you're entitled to do what you want with it, but it was a large amount."

"I already told you, Hank drained our joint account. I needed money to live, pay bills, to eat."

"Ten thousand dollars sure buys a lot of ham and eggs."

"What? You think I hired a thug? Maybe a hit man?" she laughs.

He scratches his cheekbone. "I wouldn't blame you if you did. Some would even say he had it coming."

"Well, I didn't."

"Mind if I have some water."

"Help yourself."

She watches him rinse the coffee cup, fill it from the faucet and down it in one go. He places the empty cup on the bench next to hers and stares at it.

"Curious thing. The dogs went crazy in that old orchard, apple or peaches or some crop. We even found a hole that had been dug over. Stunk." He looks up and catches her eye. "You know the smell, when an animal is caught in a trap and left there to rot, except that animals don't bury themselves."

Her heart pounds like a freight train and she's sure he can hear it.

"I don't know what to tell you," she says.

"Oh, no reply needed. Just making an observation, that's all."

He turns to leave and she makes a move to follow him.

"I can see myself out," he says. "Finish your coffee before it gets cold."

52

It must have been after three when something wakes her. Jennifer blinks into the dark and waits for her eyes to adjust. For an awful moment she thinks it's police, come to raid the house, execute a search warrant, take her into custody.

A loud watery *ker-chunk* punctuates the silence. Then another. Maybe she's left the water running in the bathroom. She puts on her robe and goes to check but when it isn't that she heads for the landing and peers out the picture window overlooking the backyard below. A shadowy figure is lying on the sun-lounger hurling something into the pond. *Lenise. Didn't that woman ever stop?* Jennifer goes downstairs and yanks open the sliding door.

"It's the middle of the night. What the hell do you think you are doing?"

Lenise doesn't look up. She just throws another spiky, buck-eyed nut into the water. There's a whole bunch in her lap, and a half-finished bottle of bourbon on the table beside her.

"God damn it Lenise, answer me."

Lenise blinks slowly. "It's a party," she slurs.

"You're drunk."

"So what if I am? Not hurting anyone." Lenise guides the bottle to her mouth, swallows deep then lets out an exaggerated sigh.

"You're being an idiot," says Jennifer.

Lenise straightens up and throws another nut. This time hard and fast. It ricochets off the planter box and bounces back under the sun-lounger. Lenise barks out a laugh, her elbow slipping from the arm rest, splashing bourbon all over the ground.

"Go home, Lenise. We'll talk tomorrow."

"I saw the sign."

"What sign?" says Jennifer.

Lenise purses her lips as if she's just tasted something sour. "Don't play dumb," she says.

"The For Sale sign? Is that what this is about?"

Lenise pats the seat beside her. "Why don't you sit down and have a drink. This can be your going away party."

Jennifer lets out a breath of frustration. "Quite frankly what I do with my and my daughter's life is not your concern. I want you to go now."

But Lenise just laughs. "Or what? You'll call the police?" She staggers to her feet and the nuts tumble from her lap. "You're no fun. This whole fucking neighborhood is a no fucking fun. I should be the one to leave." Lenise takes four halting steps to the edge of the pond and stares into it. "Cody's having a baby. He's getting married."

"That's wonderful."

Lenise looks at her sharply. "Is it?"

"You'll be a grandmother, why wouldn't you be happy about that?"

"He's all I have and now he's going to belong to someone else."

"It's the natural order of things. Children grow up and make their own lives."

Lenise takes a long slug and tosses the bottle into the pond. "You're not going anywhere, Jenny." A slow smile forms on her lips. "I've got evidence."

Jennifer frowns. "What evidence?"

"Your clothes, the knife, your fingerprints on it."

Jennifer takes two steps back, nearly colliding with the sun-lounger. "You're lying."

"Am I?" Lenise eyes glow, triumphant. "I needed to protect myself. Turns out I had great foresight."

"But you'll have to implicate yourself."

Lenise shrugs. "I'll say I found it hidden under some bush."

"I'll tell them you were there."

"You have no proof, they won't believe you," says Lenise, cheeks flushed.

"You're enjoying this," remarks Jennifer.

Lenise moves closer. Jennifer can taste the ether on Lenise's breath. "Face it, Jenny, you've been out-played."

She turns to leave, gets as far as the gate then stops.

"Tomorrow night there's an event at the Gallery that I'm sure McKenzie will like. Tell her to drop by round six. I'll have her back by nine. And don't worry. You know she's safe with me."

53

Jennifer wishes it was just another outrageous Lenise lie but she knows the truth when she hears it. And that smugness. That, I'm so clever I can't even believe it myself look of amazement on Lenise's face. Not to mention the relish with which she delivered the news. Jennifer had never thought to ask how or where Lenise had disposed of the items from that night. She'd assumed Lenise had burnt or tossed them into some out of county waterway.

Her only choice had been to encourage McKenzie to go to Lenise's. For the entire time McKenzie is gone, Jennifer waits at the window, hands bunched into fists, disbelief transforming into anger then into something altogether more visceral.

It's after nine when McKenzie returns. Jennifer knows something is up by the way she takes the stairs two at a time to get to her bedroom.

"Hey, what's the hurry," says Jennifer, catching her daughter in the hallway.

McKenzie turns around. There's a silver stud in her left eyebrow.

"Oh my God, is that a piercing?" gasps Jennifer.

"Lenise says it's important I express myself."

"You're twelve years old!"

"I'm sick of you judging me."

"What's next? A tattoo? Where did you get it done? You have to be over eighteen for that type of procedure."

"Lenise knows someone."

"Lenise."

McKenzie looks at her. "Are we finished?"

Jennifer thinks of the evidence that could put her away for life.

"We'll talk about this later," she says.

Jennifer can only watch, powerless, as McKenzie cuts a path back and forth between their houses, growing ever more distant and unruly. The hatred Jennifer feels for Lenise is like wood rot, growing steadily inside her. Or cancer, metastasizing. Or a sewer line carrying away crap and vomit and tampons and other dead or dying things, down there beneath the layers of asphalt and bedrock where it's lightless and desolate.

She wakes in the night thinking of black things. She wonders what it would feel like to suffocate someone with a plastic bag or push them in front of a moving train. Sometimes she thinks she is losing her mind.

And tonight when McKenzie comes in, Jennifer feels like she's going to scream because it's after six and the lasagna is cold but instead she pretends she's the most reasonable mother in the world and simply says, "You're late."

McKenzie looks at the food.

"You know I can't eat that. It could be contaminated."

"It's tuna."

"That's not the point. I need my own can."

Jennifer slaps down the slotted spoon a little more loudly than she intends.

"You know, it's not easy to come home after a long day's work and cook a meal no one eats."

"No one asked you to do it."

McKenzie retrieves a single serve tin of tuna from the cupboard and gets her plastic bag of cutlery from the kitchen drawer.

"I'll be upstairs if anyone needs me," she says.

Later, when Jennifer is about to scrape the lasagna into the trash, she gets an idea. She puts the food into a Tupperware container and crosses the road and knocks on Lenise's door.

"Can we talk?" says Jennifer.

"We've got nothing to say."

"Just for a moment."

"I don't see the point."

Jennifer doesn't move. Lenise sighs and lets her in.

"I brought you something." Jennifer holds up the lasagna then puts it in on the coffee table. "I understand why you kept the evidence. I'm not angry at you. We were both under a great a deal of pressure. But this thing with McKenzie has got to stop."

"No one's forcing her to come here."

"You know what I mean."

"Do I?"

"You're playing mind games, manipulating her. She's become impossible."

"And you think that's my fault?"

Jennifer can smell the cooling lasagna. Condensation has formed on the lid.

"You can't expect me to live with this guillotine over my head." She looks at Lenise. "Give me what you have, all the evidence. It's the decent thing to do." She pauses. "What if I didn't go to Florida?"

"I'm not an idiot, Jenny. As soon as you have it, you'll be off like a shot."

"I give you my word," says Jennifer.

"Oh no, we're past that now."

"You're being unreasonable."

Lenise pushes Jennifer toward the door. "This conversation is over."

"Come on, Lenise."

"Don't come here again," she says. "There's nothing left to say."

"She's not your daughter."

"Get out."

"I won't let you take her!" Jennifer picks up the lasagna and throws it at Lenise's head. She ducks and it lands on the wall behind her.

"Have you lost your mind!" Lenise gapes at the pulp sliding down the wall.

"Take a good look, Lenise, because the next time I won't miss."

54

Theoretically, the evidence could be anywhere, stowed away in a benign bus station locker or buried beneath some Wisconsin landmark, but that isn't Lenise's style. She'd want to keep it close, in the house, where she has easy access, where it's weatherproof, where she can grab it at a moment's notice and wave it in Jennifer's face.

Saturday afternoon McKenzie announces she's going to the mall.

"You're too young to go by yourself."

"Lenise is taking me."

"Of course she is."

"Don't start."

Jennifer waits until they leave and ducks across the road. From memory, the spare key was kept around the back, buried in an old coffee can filled with bottle caps. Lenise had shown Jennifer after the first incident with Hank in case she ever needed to get inside in a hurry. And there it was, right behind the garden hose.

Jennifer fishes inside the can and the caps rattle against the tin but she can't feel any key so she tips the contents onto the grass and fans them out. Nothing.

She tries both the front and back doors just in case they're unlocked. No luck. She searches for another opening, testing each window for loosened latches, but everything's secured tight.

Then, up there on the second floor, the bathroom window is open with the slimmest of gaps. The window itself is tiny, not much bigger than a shoe box, and Jennifer can't be sure she will fit, but it's the only chance she's got.

She gives the trellis a shake. The wood is thin and brittle in places. The honeysuckle once so lushly tangled between the elfin triangles is, to all intents and purposes, dead. She checks that the timber is screwed securely to the house then gets a toehold and hoists herself up. The dead plant spikes her palms and the wood trembles under her weight. But she continues upward like a rock climber, toe-hand, toe-hand, vigilant for any loose screw, any fracture in the weathered wood.

About halfway up, she freezes. The sound of a vehicle. She risks a glance over her shoulder and realizes just how exposed she is. Even though she's on the non-street side of the house, anyone who looked up would see her here, a grown woman stuck between the first and second floors, clinging to a trellis. The CenturyTel van draws near and she presses her body close to the house and prays for the vehicle to pass. It does, carrying on up the road, turning left into Raybourne Street.

She continues upwards, mindful of the time, picking up pace, the trellis creaking beneath her. When she reaches the bathroom window, she sees just how small it is. She pulls it open as far as it will go and pushes her head and shoulders through until she is half-in half-out, her midriff pressing awkwardly into the aluminum sill. Below her is the toilet, lid shut. The rest of the bathroom is neat and silent and smells of lavender. Her upper arms scrape against the wood as she squeezes through and she knows in a few short hours there will be bruises.

Jennifer dismisses the bathroom as a possible hiding place and goes downstairs instead.

Methodical is best. She begins with the laundry, searching behind the washing machine and dryer and cabinets then moves on to the kitchen, which takes forever because of the large number of cupboards to check, then into the living room where she inspects the ottoman with the flip-top lid, boxes in a book case and old steamer trunk in the corner. When that produces nothing, she goes upstairs to the attic.

She hadn't thought to bring a flashlight. But she sees there's no need because on the opposite side is a small, dust-crusted window which lets in enough light to show that, apart from a large mummified rat lying on top of a wooden rafter, the space is empty.

Disappointment washes over her.

She slips the manhole cover back in place, careful to wipe away fingerprint smudges with her sleeve, and returns the ladder upright.

She stands on the landing with growing unease. They would be back soon. She hurries to the two spare rooms, hunts through both, finds nothing, then moves on to the final location. Lenise's bedroom.

Jennifer pauses at the door. Lenise's most intimate space. Compared to the rest of the house with its homely objects and nods to Lenise's African past, the room is bare. There's nothing on the walls, no photographs, no paintings, no artifacts, just one chest of drawers and a nightstand next to a neatly made double bed. Laid out across the foot of the bed are a pair of plain cotton pajamas, and a checkered cloth dressing-gown graying at the cuffs.

Jennifer hunts through the orderly wardrobe, examines a shoe box of documents and looks behind three short piles of folded sweaters. She rummages through the dresser, between the inner-sprung mattress and bed, then under it. There's no sign of the evidence anywhere.

Frustration courses through her. She's never going to find it.

Something catches her eye. The carpet against the wall on the far side of the room. A barely perceptible rise. She goes over, bends down and runs a finger along the seam. To her amazement, the edge of the carpet lifts up. She flips back the triangle, exposing unpolished floorboards, three of them, loose to the touch.

Heart humping in anticipation, she stands up and presses her heel on the right end of the boards and they lift up. She stacks them to one side and looks into the hole. Apart from a bent nail and a bunch of wood dust it's empty.

Sometime after midnight the phone call comes.

"I know you were here," Jennifer can almost hear the smile. "You'll never find it."

Then the flat dial tone. It's as if all the oxygen has been sucked from the air.

55

Jennifer blinks into the fading light. She's finished work early and needs a place to think, so she's come here to Lake Shore Park, a vast green space bordering Lake Mendota close to Wisconsin University. Jennifer can't see into the lake like she can in the warmer months, when the water is clear as glass, when she can pick out the large grey river stones, the shimmer of a fish, the crisp glint of a soda can. Today there's thickness and murk and leaves floating on top, and a smell, as if something has soured beneath the tangle of black river weed.

Out in the center of the lake she sees a sailboat and a man moving about on deck. He must be cold. The sails are fat with wind, the water choppy, the skies brooding above him. If there's a storm coming, he's ignoring it.

For a second, she swears the ground beneath her bumps as if she is on a jetty and not a park bench fixed to a concrete platform, which is itself, fixed to the hard earth. Just to make sure, she glances down at the ancient seat, with its wooden slates and hexagon screws and paint tiers of blue, white and green and maybe black. Beneath her fingertip someone has etched words. Chicken Salt. She looks closer. Chicken Shit.

Jennifer stands, turns her back on the lake, pulls her coat tight and takes the path lined with willows and river birch and white oaks. She hears the crunch of running footsteps and moves to the side to let the runner pass.

"Jennifer!"

She turns around. Detective North, flushed and breathing heavily.

265

"Rosemary said you might be here."

"Did she."

"Yes."

"The clinic gets stuffy."

She continues on and he falls in next to her. "It's a nice spot."

"Summer is better. Everything's so lifeless in winter."

"Resting, not lifeless. Getting ready for rebirth."

"Poetic," she says.

He zips up his coat. "I wouldn't go that far."

She wonders what he wants, whether she had screwed up again, whether Lenise had finally dropped her in it.

"You haven't left for Florida," he says.

"Not yet."

She can feel him staring.

"How's McKenzie?" he says.

"Fine."

"Really?"

"No."

"Counseling?"

"She won't go."

"Listen, about before. I gave you a hard time with the money thing."

She shrugs. "You're just doing your job."

He pauses. "You came to us," he says.

"Yes, I did."

"And why would you do that if you had anything to hide?" He waits. "Then again maybe it was to throw us off, maybe you were being clever."

"Clever?"

"Yes."

"I couldn't imagine anyone pulling the wool over your eyes, Detective."

"It happens."

"I find that hard to believe."

He scratches his bottom lip with his thumb. "I'm not bullet proof."

She looks at him.

"I saw you with your father," she says.

He stops beneath a Californian Redwood and looks into the woods. "Pop wanders," he says. "Dementia."

"Sorry."

"It is what it is."

"He lives with you?"

"Of course."

"Why do you do this job?" she says. "Do you get a rush from catching the bad guys?"

"That's got nothing to do with it. I told you before. It's about the search for the truth."

"What are we doing here Detective? Are you trying to lull me into a false sense of security?"

"I wouldn't say that."

"Is this your way of eliciting some sort of confession? Some friendly chit-chat on a woodland walk? Get the suspect to open up, drop her guard? They teach you this on some Quantico course?"

"Suspect?"

"Well, I am aren't I?"

"I'm not sure, but I know you're holding something back."

"You're imagining things."

He nudges a rock with his tan brogue.

"It's true what they say, you know, you can tangle yourself in knots so much you forget what you've said before and end up giving yourself away. The truth is so much easier. The truth is better for everyone."

"Is it?" She walks on then stops. "What if I told you something? Would you have to report it?'

He looks at her evenly. "Depends on what it is."

"That means yes."

"I can help you."

"What if I don't need your help?"

He touches his collar. "Your daughter. She deserves to know what happened to her father."

"Leave McKenzie out of this."

Overhead a bird flits from branch to branch, watching them.

"It's too late for that," he says.

She turns away.

"I have to get back."

As she strides off he calls out, "The thing about chickens, Jennifer, is that eventually they come home to roost."

She finds the place. The apartment block is not much more than a framework yet. The graphic on the sign shows pictures of up-market condos and urges people to get in quick. They look nice. All open plan and floating staircases. Maybe there's an apartment like this in Florida for her and McKenzie.

A crew of about twenty in steel-capped boots and hard hats and high visibility vests are doing various jobs. Jennifer gets out of her car and walks onto site, ducking through the temporary fencing. It's noisy with the radio blaring, the band saw whirring, the nail gun popping. She feels obvious but no one seems to notice her.

It takes awhile to pick him out. He's deep in concentration, nailing planks to a side wall, about six levels up, hooked in with a climber's harness. She walks over and calls up to him, raising her voice above the din.

"Can I talk to you?"

Cody looks down. Confusion clouds his face.

"I'm working." Then, "Something happened to Ma?"

"She's fine. I just want to talk to you."

"My break's in twenty minutes."

"I can wait."

She takes a seat by the temporary office and is told to shift by a grumpy man in a flap jacket because it's too dangerous. She moves near the fence and the pallets of wood and plastic bags of insulation and a huge wheel of cabling.

Cody unhooks himself and climbs down the ladder and disappears into a port-a-potty then comes over, flicking a tab from an energy drink.

"What's this about?" he says, knocking it back.

"Your mother told me you were working here. Oh, and, congratulations," says Jennifer, "on the baby. Lenise couldn't be happier."

"She said that?"

"Of course."

He bites into a granola bar.

"Do you know what you're having?" she says.

"Girl."

"I'm sure you'll be a good father."

"You don't even know me."

She nods at the construction site. "You're working hard. That's a good start."

"What's this about?"

"Your mother and I have become friends." She pauses. "I know it's weird, with the dog and everything, but it just worked out that way."

"What's that got to do with me?"

"I want to offer her a job at my optometry clinic, as a receptionist."

"So do it."

"I can't have her working for me if there's work permit issues, I'd lose my license. I didn't want to ask her directly yet because well…you know how she gets…offended."

"We're not illegals, if that's what you're worried about."

"You're both entitled to work?"

He picks a raisin from his teeth. "Yes."

"Your green cards are legitimate?"

"I said yes."

He gets up and throws the granola wrapper and can into a wheelie bin.

"I have to go."

She goes after him. "And your father?"

"And my father what?"

"He's here too, in the States?"

Cody stares at her. "She never told you?"

Jennifer shakes her head.

"My father disappeared when I was ten."

56

Jennifer is locking up the clinic for the night when Lenise corners her, coming out of nowhere.

"Really, Jenny, fishing around for information on my immigration status, that's a new low."

Jennifer heads for her car. "I've tried reasoning with you, Lenise."

"You seem to forget what I've got."

Jennifer thinks about her "woman alone" pocket alarm and wonders if she can bash Lenise with it.

"How could I when you love throwing it in my face every five seconds."

Lenise looks affronted. "You think I like being so hard? You've forced me into this position."

"Blackmail? Extortion? No one's forced you to do anything. You like the control."

"It's not like that."

"What else would you call it?"

Lenise seizes Jennifer's arm. "Just stay away from Cody."

Jennifer turns around. "Now you know what it feels like."

"This has got nothing to do with him."

"Imagine if he found out."

"You're bluffing."

"Try me." Lenise's grip hardens but Jennifer doesn't flinch.

"Just give me the evidence, Lenise, and we can both walk away and get on with our lives. That's all it takes."

"He wouldn't believe you."

271

"Tell me, Lenise? Where's your missing husband? Oh yes, Cody mentioned that too."

For a second, Lenise appears taken aback. "That's none of your business."

"What did you do to him?"

"Nothing he didn't deserve."

"You're beginning to develop a bit of a bad habit, don't you think?"

"Don't push me."

But she can see that Lenise is shaken.

"No, don't push *me*," says Jennifer, opening the car door and getting in. "You're not the only one who can play dirty."

The next day Jennifer follows Lenise. Last night had hopefully spooked her enough to move the evidence, but when she emerges from her house dressed in that ridiculous cowgirl outfit there doesn't appear to be much hope of that. Jennifer decides to track her to the grocery store anyway, just in case she goes somewhere after her shift.

Jennifer parks three rows back from the entrance behind a goodwill bin so there's less chance she'll be noticed. Once Lenise goes inside there's nothing to do but wait so Jennifer uses her phone to search the internet to see if she can find anything about the husband. But it was so long ago and she doesn't even have a first name and there's nothing in any newspaper archives, and missing people in South Africa weren't exactly rare.

For the next four hours, Jennifer watches people come and go. She's dying for the rest room and wishes she hadn't had that third coffee but there's no other choice, she has to hold on and wait.

It's a relief when Lenise emerges. She's changed into regular clothes and Jennifer watches as she gets in the station wagon and pulls out of the parking lot. But Lenise doesn't take the left onto Benmore Street which would lead home but instead turns right onto Rugget Road. She follows the wagon the short distance to the mall then trails Lenise inside on foot.

When Lenise disappears into a baby shop to look through several racks of infant clothing, Jennifer hangs back, pretending to check her phone by the escalator. A short while later, Lenise comes out without buying anything and heads for Gloria Jean's where she loiters as if she's waiting for someone.

Jennifer ducks into a nearby Footwear Buzz, picks up a glitzy stiletto and tells the shop assistant she's only browsing. Then she sees McKenzie appear and join Lenise, her smile widening into a hi.

It's raining by the time Jennifer pulls into the drive. She stays in the car, shakes a cigarette from the pack and puts it to her lips. A tap on her side window makes her jump. Detective North's face appears through the fogged glass. She lowers the window.

"Mind if I come in?" he says, stomping his feet to ward off the cold.

She shrugs and he slides into the passenger seat, rain-soaked and pink-cheeked. She catches him looking at the unlit cigarette between her fingers.

"Turning over a new leaf," she says.

His skin glistens and she can smell the wetness, like fresh peat and socks.

"Quitting's a bitch," he says.

"It certainly is."

He scratches the side of his unshaven jaw and stares at her. "You okay?"

"I'm fine." Then, "I don't know."

She feels tears well and does her best to hold them back. "I mean sometimes there doesn't seem much point to it all, does there?" she says.

"To what? Life?"

"Yeah." She rolls the cigarette through her fingertips.

"What about your daughter?"

A vein of rainwater runs down his sleeve, drips off his cuff and splashes on to the toe of his boot.

"I think I'm losing her."

"Parenthood's tough."

"Understatement of the year."

She takes a breath and lets it out. "I've done things I'm not proud of."

She feels the weight of his stare.

"I think we're all guilty of that," he says.

"Even you?"

He pauses. "I need you come down to the station."

She freezes. "Do I need a lawyer?"

"You tell me."

"Can't we talk here?"

"The station's better. There's something I need to show you."

She takes her own car, following his unmarked sedan along the treeless route to the station. When they get there, he takes her to a private room and tells her to wait. The room is different from the one McKenzie had been in. This one is more utilitarian, with plain, vinyl-backed chairs, a veneer table, puke-colored cinderblock walls. A poster about a needle exchange program is fixed to a pin-board.

Detective North returns holding a file and takes a seat.

"You need to talk to me Jennifer, tell me what's really going on."

Jennifer's heart pounds in her throat. "I don't know how many times I have to say it. There's nothing to tell."

"If someone's got a hold on you, I can protect you."

"I don't know what you're talking about," she says.

"You were going to tell me something the other day at the forest but something held you back."

"You're mistaken," she says.

He flips open the folder. "Your neighbor, the woman." Jennifer feels her throat closing in. "She's a strange fish."

"Lenise? She's okay once you get to know her."

"How come I don't believe you?"

"Believe what you like."

"What can you tell me about her?"

"She helped that night when he tried to kill us. I'm grateful to her for that but I've already told you all this."

"And that's it?"

"Yes."

"Did you know she's wanted for questioning back in South Africa about the disappearance of her husband?"

"What's that got to do with me?"

"That's two vanishing husbands, by my count."

Jennifer laughs. "You've quite an imagination."

"Pop always said I could be the next Stephen King."

"Maybe I should call my lawyer," says Jennifer.

"You're free to leave at anytime."

"I'm just saying, you seem to be straying into territory here that I don't understand."

He looks at her. "What's going on? She help you out with your husband?"

"No."

"I mean give you some pointers? Maybe she planned it."

He stares intently at her.

"I'm close aren't I?" he thumps the table. "For Christ sake, Jennifer, I can't help you if you don't tell me anything."

"There's nothing to tell. You're going down the wrong rabbit hole. Hank is gone. He's picked up and he's never coming back and I don't know why you just don't forget about him and move on to something that matters, some other woman's husband who deserves your time and attention."

He closes the file. "We took a look at his truck. It was wiped clean." He takes a sheet from the file and pushes it across the table. "Except for this."

It is an image of a fingerprint.

"It belongs to Lenise Jamieson."

57

Jenny is up to something and Lenise doesn't like it. She was growing, Jenny, changing from the weak-kneed person that Lenise first knew. There was a strength to her now, a tenacity that wasn't there before. Lenise couldn't help but admire it.

Jenny approaching Cody had unnerved her. It fired a protective instinct she'd rarely, if ever, experienced. She couldn't risk Jenny breaking into the house again. Lenise needed reinforcements, a German Shepherd or some similar breed would be ideal. She had once seen a big dog like that attack a man. The idiot seemed to have forgotten that every white in South Africa owned dogs to patrol their grounds and when he climbed the gates of a compound, he was met with a trio of savage canines. She'd been passing in her car as he clawed his way back over the iron gates and ran around in circles on the road in front of her, screaming and clutching a chunk of skin that was his own calf.

Back home there were institutions specializing in breeding and raising canines especially for that purpose. But there was nothing like that here in America as far as Lenise knew, so she was reduced to coming to a place like this, a corner store pet shop, with puppy mill dogs, weak defective animals, bred to sit on your lap or run after frisbees. She'd just have to train one up herself as best she could.

Near the front of the store, she finds puppies. In particular, there's one tiny pug bitch behind glass shredding newspaper and tossing dried up turds all over the place. Lenise looks at the price. One thousand dollars. Expensive and not exactly what Lenise is after but she reaches over to pet it anyway and the cute tyke nudges her hand with its pushed-in face.

"Princess, aren't you?"

"She likes you."

"I was looking for something more robust. Maybe a Rottweiler or pit-bull."

"I heard they can turn."

She veers round. Detective North shoots her a smile.

"More of a cat person myself," he says. "Can you come with me please?"

"What's this about?"

"We can go in my car."

He drives in silence, glancing occasionally in the rearview to look at her in the back seat. She does her best to remain composed but can feel herself shaking.

"Will this take long?" He doesn't answer. "Because I start work in an hour."

They get to the station and he shows her into a cold plain room.

"I'm thirsty," she says. "I need water or tea."

He ignores her and sits down.

"I may not be born here," she says, "but I still have rights."

"Tell me about your husband."

So Jenny had talked.

"What about him."

"Where is he?"

"I have no idea."

"You left South Africa fifteen years ago, just after your husband went missing, is that correct?"

"That had nothing to do with me."

"Is he dead?"

"I hope so."

He raises an eyebrow.

"A lot of people wanted him gone," she says. "He was a bastard."

"Like Jennifer Blake's husband?"

"I don't know what you're getting at."

He opens a file and passes over a sheet with a fingerprint on it. "That's yours. Found in Hank Blake's truck."

"Rubbish."

"We matched it with your immigration records."

"It's a mistake."

He pauses. "Jenny and I spoke yesterday."

"Good for you."

"I'd like to hear your version."

"Whatever she told you is complete and utter bullshit."

"Is it?"

She pauses and looks at him and it dawns on her. This is what they did wasn't it? This was how they tricked innocent people into giving false confessions. It was called being led down the garden path. He points to the fingerprint.

"Explain that."

"How do I know you didn't put it there," she says.

"So that's how you're going to play it."

"You take me for a fool."

His posture softens and he switches tact. "Look, I understand, things got carried away, went a bit too far.

We've all got it in us. No one is immune. I know that. I'm not making judgments about you or taking the moral high ground here, but this has to be resolved, right now, today."

"I sleep very well at night, thank you."

"You spend a lot of time with McKenzie."

"You've been spying," she says.

"It's my job to know what's going on." Then, "We could arrest you."

No body, no witness, no time of death.

"That's a stretch," she says.

He looks at her for a long time then nods. "Alright," he opens the door. "You're free to go."

She gets to her feet.

"Of course I am," she says.

58

Jennifer waits at the kitchen window for Lenise to get home. Sometime after six the battered station wagon pulls up and Lenise gets out and disappears inside the house. Jennifer gives it ten minutes then takes the path round to Lenise's backyard and raps twice on the ranch sliders. Lenise appears, her face a study in raw fury. Jennifer experiences a strange sense of satisfaction. The sharks were circling and for once Jennifer wasn't the only one bleeding.

"You messed up royally," says Jennifer. "You need to fix it."

Lenise grabs Jennifer and pulls her into the far corner of the patio. "You told him about my ex," she hisses.

"Let go of me."

Lenise bangs her back against the wall, gets right in her face. "You're playing a dangerous game, Jenny."

"He came to me. He already knew. He ran a check after finding your fingerprint."

"I don't believe you," says Lenise.

"I don't care what you believe."

Lenise moves closer. "You could be wired for all I know."

"Don't be an idiot," says Jennifer.

"I wouldn't put it past you."

Lenise yanks at Jennifer's clothes, slaps her down for a listening device.

Jennifer pushes back. "You're being ridiculous."

"Where is it?"

"Get off me!" Jennifer breaks free and lifts up her shirt, spins around. "See? Zilch. Satisfied?" she says.

"No."

Lenise hunts the yard, batting at the bushes and searching the flower pots for cameras or microphones.

"Lenise, there's no one else here."

"Why would I believe anything you say?"

"You left your fingerprint behind. You did it to yourself. And it implicates me," says Jennifer.

"They've got nothing."

"A fingerprint in the truck of a missing man isn't nothing."

Lenise points a knuckle in Jennifer's face. "Don't even think about turning on me. Your prints are all over that knife and my version is so much more compelling than yours. I only helped with the body after *you* killed him, I'd be accessory after the fact, but that's all. I'm not going to prison or back to South Africa."

Jennifer pauses. "I've never seen you so scared."

"Shut up."

Jennifer begins to laugh. "Like a scared little bitch." Jennifer laughs harder, her breath trumpeting, and God it feels good, like that third glass of wine when your limbs go elastic and there's a flutter in your chest. "All your scheming and there you go, leaving your fingerprint behind like a total dunce. You can't stay in Wisconsin now, can you? At the very least you'll get deported. Maybe you should run off, disappear before they come for you. Go on, run along now, get out of my life."

Lenise looks at her and seems to deflate. "You're right."

Jennifer stops laughing. "What do you mean I'm right?"

"It's no use, we're both finished," says Lenise.

"You can't just give up."

"I'm out of ideas."

"You've got to think of something," insists Jennifer.

Lenise drops into the garden chair. "There is one thing."

"What is it?" says Jennifer.

"Let me take her. You're the one they want. What's the point in both of us going down?"

"You can't be serious," says Jennifer.

"I'll look after her. We'll go some place far away where no one can find us, where the authorities can't touch her. I'll keep her safe."

Jennifer is incredulous. "My God, you're not kidding."

"She's better off with me. You know that."

"I'm her mother."

Lenise looks at her. "She despises you, Jenny."

Jennifer recoils. "That's not true."

"I'm sorry. I know that hurts. But she told me."

Jennifer feels winded.

"You're making that up."

Lenise turns away, walks the length of the patio and lifts her face to the sky. "At the end of the day I don't need your permission, do I, Jenny? I can do what I like."

Jennifer feels a rush of nausea. "You're out of your mind."

"There's an easy way and a hard way, Jenny."

"Stay away from her."

"The easy way or the hard way?" says Lenise. "It's up to you."

"You're not taking McKenzie anywhere," says Jennifer.

Lenise opens the ranch sliders and pauses before going inside. "Thanks for stopping by."

59

Once there was a fire in an old weatherboard house on the block where Jennifer used to live. She was small, preschool small, when her mother grasped her hand and hurried her out onto the sidewalk to look at it, this formless, blazing surf the color of tinned Spaghetti-Os, with its furious roar and snapping crackle, and the terror of its heat, which Jennifer thought would boil her blood.

She yelled at her mother to take her home but her mother firmly shook her head.

"You need to see this, Jennifer Marie."

Soon other people gathered along the street, eyes wide with awe, watching the growing inferno. An upstairs window exploded and flames licked the guttering through the broken glass. Everyone gasped and a lady with tea bag eyes yelled, "I think I see someone!"

In the crowd there was a guy with an afro and he pulled off his t-shirt and bunched it to cover his mouth and ran right into that house. Everyone waited but he never came out. Then a fire truck pulled up and a man in a yellow hardhat stepped down and the kid on the BMX with one bare foot on a pedal and the other planted on the ground pointed at the house.

"Hey, mister, there's a guy in there."

The hardhat man put his hands on his hips and made a sucking noise with his cheek.

"It's fully involved. No way, no how my men are going in."

Instead the firemen uncurled their hoses and sprayed the blaze with giant fans of water which misted Jennifer's face.

Someone said that's a real shame and people began to walk away and the tea bag lady murmured "I thought I saw someone" and finally her mother's hand tightened around hers and they went back up the street toward home.

"See, Jennifer Marie, that's what you get when you go playing with fire."

Jennifer stares at the ceiling, and pulls the cover up around her shoulder. Years later when Jennifer talked about the fire, her mother had seemed pleased.

"You remember that."

"Sure, I was terrified. And that guy who went in and never came out…"

Her mother had frowned.

"What man?"

And then her mother's face cleared and she nodded in a knowing way.

That was her mother: always ready with a lesson to ward off the otherwise inevitable badness in Jennifer. No matter how good Jennifer tried to be, her mother's skepticism met her at every corner. She was always tossing Jennifer's room for some imagined sign of aberrant behavior—hidden cookies, damning diaries and later, condoms and weed. And when she would find nothing she would accuse Jennifer of being devious for hiding things so well.

As far as Jennifer could remember the worst thing she ever did was get her ears pierced without permission at Smith's Pharmacy when she was twelve, but to her mother, even this small infraction was clear evidence of Jennifer's poor character and so justified no TV for a month and, even worse, removing the diamante studs so the holes in her lobes would close up.

Perhaps her mother was right, perhaps Jennifer was bad all along and only her mother could see it.

Jennifer gets out of bed and pulls on her robe and goes to McKenzie's room.

"Knock first," murmurs McKenzie, burying her face in her pillow.

"You're coming with me," says Jennifer.

"I'm sleeping."

"It's Saturday and we're both alive, with two good arms and two good legs."

"What's wrong with you?"

"There's some place I want you to see."

By the time they reach Hoyt Park the sky is the color of bone. Jennifer drives up the winding road until they reach a little used perch on the eastern side. They get out and climb the steps to the wooden lookout with its three-sixty-degree views across Madison and out over the east.

"Now watch this."

The sun emerges from the horizon like a marigold.

"That's something isn't it? The color?"

"Yeah."

"Did you know the human eye can distinguish between 10 million different colors? Think about that. *Ten million.*"

Birds wheel through the sky and it's just so beautiful that Jennifer wishes they could stay up here, the two of them, bathed forever in this golden light.

"My mother always said a sunrise makes you appreciate the world and your place in it." Jennifer feels the wind change, a cold slipstream, barreling in from the north and she rubs her arms. "She could be tough, but she meant well. You would have liked her."

McKenzie walks around the lookout, scanning the world below.

"He isn't coming back is he?" she says, sneaker toeing the kickboard.

Jennifer fixes her gaze on Lake Mendota.

"Let's not talk about him, just for now, okay? It's so nice here, with the sun, me and you."

McKenzie picks a loose splinter on the wooden railing with a thumb nail. "We used to play poker for candy. You didn't know about it because of your sugar vendetta. But it was fun." A spot of blood appears on her thumb and she smears it into the wood. "We used to do a lot of fun things like that."

Jennifer turns back to face the sun, stares at the lone orange eye upon them.

"New beginnings, hon. Every day you can begin anew. It's a choice."

Jennifer angles the car into the garage and cuts the engine. She looks at McKenzie.

"I love you, hon. You know that."

"Why are you acting so weird?"

"I'm not."

"All that sunrise stuff. Have you been smoking weed or something?"

"I just have the feeling good things are about to happen."

"Oh, so now you're psychic."

Jennifer pauses. "We need to get organized for Florida."

McKenzie's fist curls. "I thought you were over that."

"It's time to put things in motion. Properly this time."

"You know I don't want to go."

"It'll be a fresh start, hon."

"I don't care about fresh starts. I want to stay here."

"It's not what's best for us."

"I'm not going anywhere until we know where Dad is." McKenzie storms into the house and Jennifer follows.

"We can't put our lives on hold because of him," says Jennifer.

McKenzie spins round. "Did he do the same things to you?"

"What?"

"Did he touch you like he touched me?"

"Oh, McKenzie, hon, what good would it do?"

McKenzie comes close, eyes burning. "*Tell me.*"

"Please, stop this."

McKenzie shoves Jennifer's shoulder. "Answer me!" McKenzie shoves her again, with both hands, on both shoulders. "I said answer me!"

"I won't," says Jennifer.

McKenzie turns away and the fight seems to leave her. "I didn't want to do those things," she says.

"I know."

"I didn't." McKenzie places both hands across her mouth and begins to sob. "Why didn't you stop him?"

"I didn't know," says Jennifer.

"But you should have seen," presses McKenzie, tears streaking her face.

"Oh God, you have to believe me."

"But it was your job to see."

"Oh, hon."

McKenzie stares at Jennifer. "He went to you, after. You must have known. I used to wait, hope you would do something. I tried to tell you but you never listened."

"Stop this."

"Because you didn't want to hear."

"That isn't true."

McKenzie takes two steps toward Jennifer. "The truth is I hate you more than I hate him."

"You don't mean that."

"Oh, but I do."

60

She stands in the dark kitchen, hipbone against the edge of countertop, the only sound, the buzz of the fridge. Jennifer lifts the smoldering cigarette to her lips as she stares out the window. She draws deeply, letting it fill her lungs. The rush is welcome and numbing and freeing.

Outside the wet road shines. Rain ceased falling hours ago but the temperature has plummeted and everything is turning to ice. By morning daggers will hang from the streetlamps. But right now the chill is exactly what she needs and she stands there in her bra and underpants, wearing the cold like a suit.

Across the street, Lenise's house is silent and lightless, the ear of the satellite dish cupped to the sky.

On the bench, next to the soft pack of Camels, is the gun. Jennifer traces the cool steel terrain of the weapon, with its enamel, twice-baked coating and well-oiled interior. Inside there are ten copper-tipped missiles, snug as beans inside their nooks, ready to come to life.

She can see everything, even the inner workings of her own body. The taut floss of her veins mooring muscle and bone. The strings of her eyeballs flexing this way and that. The vitreous fluid like silk behind her lids. Every nerve stands on end, like seedlings rising to meet the rays of the moon. She drains the cigarette, savoring the harshness at the back of her throat, then wipes the butt back and forth in the wet sink and pushes it down the plug hole where it will come to rest with the other detritus in the S-bend.

Using the spare key Lenise had given McKenzie, Jennifer enters her neighbor's house. She climbs the stairs, opens the bedroom door and puts the gun to Lenise's throat. "You know what I want."

Lenise's eyes fly open. She's tries to sit up but Jennifer presses the muzzle in further. "Don't."

Lenise blinks at Jennifer. "This makes me sad, Jenny. Especially when we've been through so much together."

"Tell me."

"You act like I was against you. I was never against you."

"Where is the evidence?"

"Alright," says Lenise. "I took it to the plant."

Jennifer parks in front of the gates and pulls Lenise from the car and they follow the open sewer lines through the back fields toward the plant. The night is blacker than black and Jennifer can't see her own hand in front of her face. She's worried Lenise may try something funny so she warns her to stick close to the wall, and pushes Lenise in the hip with the gun, and they move quickly along the trench until they find the opening to the empty building and enter.

"Where?" says Jennifer.

Lenise lifts her chin to the office that overlooks the factory floor. "Up there."

They climb the steps and reach the landing.

"That one." Lenise points to the office on the left.

Jennifer opens the door. Bird shit. Dust. A trace of phosphorous. Jennifer waves the gun at Lenise.

"Show me."

Lenise enters the office and crosses the floor, stopping at a pair of balcony doors overlooking the forest.

"What do you suppose it was like," says Lenise, glancing through the dirty glass, "working here day after day in that poison? Do you think they went mad after a while? You know, agent orange mad, and had offspring with no brains and mysterious new forms of incurable cancer?"

"Where is it?"

Lenise looks back at Jennifer. "I only ever acted in your best interests, Jenny."

Jennifer laughs. "You did what was best for Lenise."

"I know you think that, but it isn't true." Lenise pauses. "I'm sorry to tell you, Jenny, but you were a bad mother."

"You don't know anything."

"I know you weren't there when she needed you the most."

The words burn and Jennifer snaps. "I didn't have any idea about what Hank was doing and you know it."

"The point is that maybe you should have." Lenise's eyes blaze. "Hurts, doesn't it? To know that you've failed, that you're a disappointment to yourself, that your daughter's going to grow up knowing her mother let her down in the most terrible way."

"Shut up," says Jennifer.

"You don't know how lucky you are to have her. Oh you give lip service to it, but you really don't know."

Jennifer lifts the gun. "*That's enough.*"

"Go on," says Lenise, facing her. "I want you to."

Jennifer's heart pounds, the gun shakes in her hand, but she doesn't lower it. "The evidence first," she says.

"I would never have used it."

"I don't believe you."

Lenise nods sadly. "Of course you don't."

She bends down behind the desk and pulls out a black duffle bag. "It's yours. Take it. No catch. It's all there."

Jennifer looks inside and sees bloodstained clothing and the knife wrapped in a rag.

"It's so easy for you," says Lenise. "You've got McKenzie. You're beautiful. You'll move away and make a new life for yourself, find someone who loves you. I'll be stuck here working some shit job with no one to come home to."

"Perhaps that's exactly what you deserve," says Jennifer. "Did you ever think about that?"

Jennifer slings the duffle bag over her shoulder, turns to Lenise and lifts the gun.

Lenise looks back at her. "I'll save you the bullet."

She throws open the balcony doors. A rush of wind almost blasts them off their feet. Jennifer lifts a hand to shield her face from the flying grit.

"What are the hell you doing!" she shouts over the roaring wind.

"You can go now, Jenny."

Lenise steps backward onto the ancient platform and her hair takes flight and her eyes gleam. In an instant, Jennifer realizes this is not what she wants. Lenise wiped out, another person lost to this entire, sorry mess.

"Come back inside. You're going to fall!" she yells.

Even with the howl of the wind Jennifer can hear the wood screech like a sinking ship. Lenise takes another step back and the wood creaks and Jennifer can see that ruin of a railing dangling over the edge offers no protection.

"*Lenise, don't!*"

But Lenise keeps moving until she's hard up against the rust-blistered barrier. "I set you free, Jenny."

Then the wood tears open.

"Look out!" cries Jennifer.

Lenise screams as her right leg smashes through the platform. She stares at Jennifer, stunned, then watches in terror as the rest of the timber begins to give way around her.

"Oh God!"

Lenise shudders down once, then twice, until she's armpit deep in a hole and kicking in the dead space above the ground.

"Jenny, I don't want to die!"

"The railing," shouts Jennifer.

Lenise extends her arm and grips one of the metal rods. Jennifer yells for her to hold on then lies down on her stomach and reaches for Lenise's wrist.

"Please don't let me die."

The railing shakes and squeals and two screws pop and plummet to earth and Jennifer is in danger of falling herself. Lenise's wrist is mere inches away as Jennifer snakes further out onto the platform, feeling the timber buckle and squawk beneath her. Then, mercifully, her hand locks around Lenise's wrist and she pulls. But gravity is stronger.

"Jenny!"

"Hold on!"

Jennifer's shoulder feels like it's going to pull apart. Then, out of nowhere, she has a surge of strength and feels the heat of adrenalin flood her body and she hauls Lenise up through the hole, pulling her clear to the safe ground of the office floor.

Lenise begins to sob. "I knew you wouldn't let me go."

They lie there shaking and breathless and spent.

Finally, Jennifer gets to her feet. She picks up the bag, pausing at the door to look back at Lenise. But there's nothing left to say.

61

Jennifer lets herself in through the garage and walks to the foot of the stairs and pauses there, veiled in the darkness like a robber in the night. Satisfied that McKenzie was still asleep, she hurries to the lounge, kneels down at the hearth's edge and opens the glass hatch.

A tepee of kindling is perched on crumpled fists of newspaper and she takes the lighter from behind the mirrored candle holder, set three places aflame and picks up the bulging Savemart bag. The plastic has split and terry cloth protrudes from a small tear. She reaches inside and withdraws the first item. Her bloody t-shirt, the marl grey one she'd bought five years ago for some awareness campaign about breast cancer or global warming or child poverty, the one with the white heart on the front made up of identical tiny white hearts, the one she had found so cute and trendy and soccer-Mom chic, the one now spoiled with the blossoms of her dead husband's blood.

She throws it into the fire and it shrinks, the heart melting like snow in a blaze of flames that turn from pink to green to blue.

Her eyes begin to water. Nylon. Cotton. Something else. It hits her. Burning blood. She fights the urge to throw up and fans the door back and forth and the t-shirt rages until it's nothing more than an ashen peony rose.

She feels lightness, a blissful lightness, as if a terrible weight has been lifted, then remembers that it isn't over yet.

She tips the bag upside down, digs through the remaining items. Four blood-stained rags and a knife wrapped in a torn bed sheet. She stares at the knife, nestled there against the brushed cotton, and runs a fingertip over the hardened drips of blood on the cherry wood handle.

She picks it up. Such an ordinary object for such ordinary things. How many times had she taken this knife to the stiff crust of a ciabatta loaf or the tough skin of a winter tomato or the wax rind of a Gruyere wedge. Even the aluminum cap from a bottle of Merlot had once met the slice of this blade.

So too, her own hand. Chopping basil and red peppers had once resulted in a nasty gash between her forefinger and thumb requiring an ER visit and stitches and a lecture from Hank about proper kitchen safety practices. "You need to take better care. You're always in such a hurry."

They'd bought it from a late-night shopping channel binge in their early days. The two of them had fought over which one to get. She wanted the smaller cheaper knife with the free placemats, but he insisted on high end one, the one with its own state of the art sharpener, surgical grade, Cohen and Kennedy chef's knife. His was fifty bucks more expensive than hers, but he'd been right, it had proven to be an excellent knife and had lasted through fifteen years of kitchen duties, until that last day, when it had disappeared right into his chest.

"What are you doing?"

The voice rings like a bell. Jennifer does not turn round. She hears breath, slow and deep, feels eyes search her back.

"You don't want to be here," says Jennifer.

"Mom?"

"*Just go,*" Jennifer pleads.

298

It's then she finally turns around, setting the knife down on the hearth, getting to her feet.

"Sweetheart."

McKenzie's face is raw with confusion. "Is that a knife?"

McKenzie steps forward from the doorway to take a closer look, but Jennifer blocks her. "*Don't.*"

"Let me see."

McKenzie tries to push pass, but Jennifer stops her with an embrace and presses her trembling lips to her daughter's ear.

"Please go back to bed, hon. Do as I say, just this one time, okay? You do that and everything will be good, I promise you. Just turn around, walk up those stairs and go back to bed. Please, please, please, just do that for me."

McKenzie's chin shudders in the groove of Jennifer's collarbone. "*Mom*," she whispers, "there's blood."

Jennifer holds tighter, stroking McKenzie's hair, breathing in that sleepy, child-woman scent, not wanting to let go, this baby, her tomboy, the true north of her life. If only Jennifer could start again, go back to the day she first brought her home, cradled in the safe alcove of her arm, when life was about the first opening of brand new eyes, a tiny maple leaf hand splashing the bathwater, dewy gums sucking the cloth ear of Mr. Bun.

McKenzie twists out of Jennifer's hold and takes two full steps backwards. "You made me think he ran away," she says.

"Don't do this."

"You made me believe it was my fault."

"It's not what you think."

McKenzie slams her fists into her thighs. "What Mom? What do I think?"

Jennifer shakes her head. "You've got it wrong."

McKenzie presses her hands to her temples. "Oh God, oh God, I'm going insane."

She bends over, unable to catch her breath. Jennifer places a hand on her shoulder, but McKenzie shakes it off. "You killed him."

"No."

"Stop lying."

"It was an accident. Lenise—"

"Lenise what?"

"She and I...He was going to hurt us and we just wanted to scare him and it got out of hand. Oh God, McKenzie you have to believe me."

"Liar!"

"It's true."

McKenzie pauses. Cinders slip through the iron grilles of the grate. "I don't even know who you are."

"Oh, McKenzie, I love you so much, please," implores Jennifer.

"Get away from me!"

McKenzie swings out blindly and Jennifer goes down, falling backward, the softest part of her skull smashing against the corner of the hearth. The world goes quiet and grey. Then Jennifer opens her eyes and McKenzie is gone and so is the knife.

62

By the time Jennifer gets to the front door, McKenzie is on her bike disappearing up the road. She's heading east, out of the neighborhood and into town. Jennifer stands there in a daze listening to the bike tires hiss curses at the bitumen. It's an effort to focus. The bang to the head was fierce. Her skull feels like it's submerged in a pressure cooker and black dots fly like arrows in front of her eyes.

She wills one foot in front of the other, gets in the car and tries to catch up to the winking pedals. They suddenly veer left and disappear down a cycle way. Jennifer circles the block and finds the exit, but by the time she gets there McKenzie is gone.

"Hon, please don't do this."

She starts to cry and her vision blurs as she scans the roads, pavements and driveways. It is all so incredibly bleak, too many dark and dangerous places. She pictures McKenzie, pedaling face first into the biting wind, tears turning to ice on her cheeks, knife clutched in her hand. *Think.* Where could she be?

Jennifer checks all the obvious places. The school. The library. The skate park. The tennis courts. No sign of her anywhere. She glides past dark alleyways, the off limits back lots, the badlands sites and under the bridge places.

The streets are mostly empty apart from an old lady in an anorak walking a terrier and, over by the substation, a shifty guy in a grey hoodie who glances briefly into her headlights revealing a face of finger-picked lesions.

She turns left and sees the Walmart parking lot and a group of older Korean kids hanging out by a pimped up maroon Concord, playing around with subwoofer settings, knocking back dollar beers.

"Have you seen a girl come through here on a bike?"

"No one like that."

"You sure?"

Abruptly, Tupak blasts from the Concord, drowning out her voice, and she moves on.

For over two hours, she drives up and down every side, back, and main street she can think of. It gets close to 4 a.m. and Jennifer grows frantic.

She spots an empty drive-through and a kid around nineteen grimly trying to wrangle burger wrappers into a black sack with a trash-picker. She winds down her window.

"Did you see a girl come through here on a bike?"

"Say again."

"Twelve, wearing pajamas, purple with white daisies, have you seen her?"

He reaches up and scratches a flaky patch of eczema under his ear. "No ma'am, just some dude on a three-wheeler."

"You sure? Maybe she used the bathroom or something?"

He stares at her. "You don't look so good."

"Is there anybody else inside who might have seen her?"

He shakes his head. "Just me here from two to six. You sure you're okay?"

"Please, this is important."

"I'm sorry. I haven't seen her."

He walks closer to Jennifer's window, dragging his near full sack behind him. "Here," he says, removing what she thinks is a condom from his pocket. Using his teeth, he tears open the foil and hands her the moist towelette inside. "For your face."

She glances in the mirror at her dirty, tear-streaked reflection and takes the towelette and presses it to her skin.

"It's got Aloe in it," he says.

"It's nice."

"Yeah."

She stares numbly through the windscreen. The street sweeper appears around the corner, brushes whirring in the gutters.

"I don't know where she is."

"Who?"

She buries her face in her hands and cries.

"Ma'am, please let me call someone for you."

She lifts her head. "I'll be alright."

"It's no trouble."

"I've got to go."

She pulls out of the lot. Glancing in her rearview, she can see the kid standing there, staring after her, trash-picker in his hand like a bullwhip.

Taking a right, she retraces the route she'd driven earlier, past the tennis courts, skate park, library, school. Nothing. The pressure in her head is unbearable. A searing pain strikes her temple, blinding her completely. She's forced to pull over and throw up in the gutter. Bile spills from her lips. Her insides cramp violently and she throws up again.

She rests her palm on the side door to catch her breath, legs quivering wildly beneath her. She pauses there for a moment, trying to get it together, to dial things back. All around her the sky is brightening, the color of honey, lights are flicking on inside buildings, a new day is coming.

She calls Ethan North. "I can't find McKenzie."

He pauses then says, "I'll meet you at the house."

When Jennifer turns the corner into Pine Ridge Road his car is already there. She hurries from the Nissan and crosses the grass toward the house. A flicker to her left stops her. McKenzie's bike, discarded on top of the holly bush, rear light flashing.

"McKenzie!"

Jennifer runs inside. The living room is empty, fire dead, rags gone.

"In here," the low intonation of a man, coming from the kitchen.

She bursts through the door. Relief washes over her. Ethan North and McKenzie look up from the table, the bundle of bloody rags and knife in front of them.

"Oh thank God." She embraces McKenzie. "I'm sorry. I'm sorry for all of it."

And it feels so good, just to hold her, to know she's okay, and Jennifer doesn't want to let her go, then she hears the voice and is gripped by a sudden awful terror.

"Jenny."

She cannot swallow. She cannot see. She cannot breathe.

"Turn around, Jenny."

McKenzie is trembling. "She's got a gun," she whispers.

Jennifer turns round. Lenise is in the corner, leg bloody and raw, eyes darting, Jennifer's gun wavering in her hand, the one she'd so foolishly left behind at the plant.

"I thought we were done," says Jennifer.

Lenise brushes hair from her eyes with her wrist. "I can't do it." Her voice is low and sad.

"Can't do what?"

Lenise begins to cry. She looks at McKenzie. "Let her go."

Time falls flat and heavy. Lenise cries hard, and they watch her, and that wobbling gun.

"You can't just expect everything to be fine, Jenny. My heart isn't made of stone." Her voice is thin, like she's talking in a tunnel, and Jennifer's never seen her look so bad.

"Give me the gun," says Ethan.

Lenise blinks at him dully. "No," she says.

"You're injured, you need help," he presses.

Lenise snaps. "This has got nothing to do with you."

"You're only making things worse," he says.

"Shut up."

"Do what he says," says Jennifer.

Lenise looks at McKenzie. "What about you, girl? Nobody ever asks what you want."

"I'm scared," says McKenzie.

Lenise's face softens. "Come here."

Jennifer steps in front of McKenzie. "Leave her alone."

"Come on, girl." Lenise lifts an arm and gestures McKenzie over.

But McKenzie shrinks further behind Jennifer. "I don't want to."

"There's no need to be frightened," says Lenise.

McKenzie doesn't move so Lenise hobbles forward, energy clearly flagging, and holds out her hand. "Girl, do as I say."

"Mom, don't let her take me."

But Lenise sidesteps Jennifer and pulls McKenzie to her side.

"Leave her alone!" cries Jennifer.

"Good girl," Lenise kisses the top of McKenzie's head. "Everything's going to be fine, just fine, you'll see."

Ethan North stands up. "Enough."

Lenise points the gun at him. "Be quiet."

He raises his hands. "Think about it. This isn't the way to go."

"What would you know?" Lenise takes a phial from her pocket.

"What's that?" says McKenzie, recoiling.

"It helps people sleep," says Lenise.

The sedative they'd used on Hank. Every bad thing flashes through Jennifer's mind. "Lenise, please."

Lenise ignores her and retrieves a jug from the cupboard, gets some juice from the fridge and mixes the sedative.

"Think about what you're doing," pleads Jennifer.

Lenise pours two glasses. She holds one out to Jennifer. "Drink it."

Lenise nods toward Detective North. "You too. Pick up the glass."

"No," cries McKenzie.

"Don't fret, girl."

"I won't do it," says Jennifer. "I won't leave McKenzie."

"Drink it."

"No!"

Jennifer slaps the glass from Lenise's hand and it goes flying across the kitchen floor. Ethan lunges for Lenise but she's too quick and she swings around and smashes him with the butt of the gun and he goes down, out cold. Lenise pivots to face Jennifer.

"For God's sake," she cries. "Can't you see you're upsetting the girl?"

Jennifer stares at Ethan lying there, unconscious on the kitchen floor, and feels hope slip away.

"Is this what you want?" Lenise thrusts the gun at Jennifer. "A bullet? In front of McKenzie? Because that's where this whole thing is heading. Now pick up that bloody glass."

"No."

"For Christ's Sake."

Lenise stomps over to Ethan's inert body, dragging McKenzie behind her, and presses the gun to his temple.

"You don't want me to do this," she says.

Jennifer looks at McKenzie, poor McKenzie who is caught in the middle, poor McKenzie who deserves none of this, the fear coming off her in waves, eyes pleading with Jennifer.

"Go on," says Lenise. "Drink it."

"No, Mom, don't."

Jennifer picks up the glass. "It's alright," she says.

"Please, Mom, don't leave me."

Jennifer lifts the rim to her lips and drinks and returns the glass to its place.

Lenise nods. "You did the right thing."

McKenzie is crying hard now.

"Sorry, Jenny, truly I am," says Lenise.

Jennifer can feel it take hold. Her head circling, growing heavy, her limbs filling with cement, her heart booming way too slowly inside her ribcage. McKenzie's cries begin to weaken and fade and Jennifer watches their hazy bodies turn to leave. That's when she reaches for the knife and lurches across the room and plunges it into Lenise, right between the wings of her shoulder blades. A shot rings out and Jennifer falls down and she is on her back, breathing hard, seeing the world in cubes. The ceiling. The underside of the countertop. A window segment. The chunk of sky beyond it. McKenzie is stroking and kissing her face.

"I'm alright," says Jennifer. "I'm alright."

Outside it has begun to snow.

63

When Jennifer opens her eyes all she can see is a shard of ice. But when she looks again, it's not ice at all but a tiny window of obscured glass. She shifts her head. She's in a hospital room, in bed, tethered to a drip. There's a trail of charcoal saliva on her pillow.

Taking it slowly, she sits up on her elbows. Somewhere in the back of her mind she recalls multiple quick hands upon her, tearing at her clothes, probing her throat, pinching her wrists, pricking her arms, slapping her face. A jug of water sits on the nightstand and she forgoes the plastic tumbler and grabs the jug with both hands and gulps it back until her stomach swells and she's finally rid of the taste of salt and blood.

She braces herself on the mattress and hauls herself to her feet. Her head swoons and for a second there she thinks she might collapse but she doesn't, rocking back and forth on her heels instead, water dripping from her chin, riding the ground until it steadies under her feet.

The machine of her mind shudders to life, beginning with Ethan North out cold on the floor, the knife in her hand, a bicycle in a holly bush. Did she actually stab someone? She has no memory of who exactly but deduces it must have been Lenise, but she can't know for certain because all the facts are out of sequence and jumbled together. She could have stabbed Ethan North or even McKenzie.

That awful thought seizes her and she's suddenly desperate to find McKenzie. Clutching the spine of the IV stand, she shuffles towards the door, getting only as far as the end of the bed before her legs begin to buckle.

"Whoa," says Ethan North, catching her.

She looks up at his face.

"You're alive," she says.

"Of course."

If he's alive, McKenzie might not be, so she pushes him off and keeps moving. "I have to find McKenzie."

"You need to rest."

She bats away his hands and heads for the door and shouts at the empty corridor. "McKenzie!"

But there's no sign of her anywhere.

"Hey," says Ethan. "She's fine. I made her take a break. She's in the cafeteria getting food."

Jennifer looks at him.

"You're lying," she says.

"I'm not. God's honest."

She calms down. "I thought I'd lost her," she says.

"The opposite's true—you saved her. You saved me too, for that matter. Now get back into bed."

And she does, slowly.

"Is Lenise dead?" she says.

He pauses. "A few inches to her left and she would have been toast. She has a perforated lung but she's going to be alright."

"It all happened so fast," she says.

"You did the right thing."

"It was an accident, what she did to Hank. She was trying to help me," says Jennifer.

"I know."

Outside two birds fight on the ledge and it's dawning on her, the fact that the secret is finally out and now there are consequences to face.

She looks at him. "So you know the truth."

He nods. "Yes."

"And I'm a bad person, for lying, for trying to cover things up."

"You got in over your head," he says, frown deepening.

"Will I go to jail?"

And he licks his lips and looks at his feet and she thinks it must be bad news.

"They're going to offer you a plea deal, accessory after that fact, improper disposal of a body, three years suspended sentence. You'll be on probation which means you'll need to report."

"I'm not going to jail?"

"Not if you take the deal, "he says.

"What about Lenise?"

"They try her here or send her back to South Africa, they haven't decided," he says.

Outside one of the birds gives up and flies away.

"I know it sounds strange, but she's probably the best friend I ever had."

The door opens. It's McKenzie, that hair so savagely cut returning thicker and darker than before. Ethan excuses himself and leaves them to talk.

"How are you doing, hon?"

"They put a tube down your throat," says McKenzie, hovering in the doorway.

Jennifer pats the space beside her. "Why don't you come sit."

McKenzie positions herself at the end of the bed.

"I thought you were going to die," says McKenzie.

"That was some night."

"Yeah."

"You must have questions," says Jennifer.

"I bought you something from the hospital gift shop."

McKenzie digs inside her bag and takes out an object. At first Jennifer thinks it's one of those Christmas snow globes, but when she looks closer instead of Santa there's a tiny island girl in a grass skirt and a purple lei holding a sign that says Hawaii. McKenzie shakes it and the girl's hips sway and glitter sand cascades around her.

"They didn't have one for Florida," says McKenzie.

"I love it," says Jennifer.

McKenzie shakes the globe again and the sand flutters and the island girl dances.

More books you'll love from
Deborah Rogers...

The Amelia Kellaway Series
Left for Dead
Coming for You
Speak for Me

Standalone novels
The Devil's Wire
Into Thin Air

About the Author

Deborah Rogers is a psychological thriller and suspense author. Her gripping debut psychological thriller, The Devil's Wire, received rave reviews as a 'dark and twisted page turner'. In addition to standalone novels like The Devil's Wire and Into Thin Air, Deborah writes the popular Amelia Kellaway series, a gritty suspense series based on New York Prosecutor, Amelia Kellaway.

Deborah has a Graduate Diploma in scriptwriting and graduated cum laude from the Hagley Writers' Institute. When she's not writing psychological thrillers and suspense books, she likes to take her chocolate lab, Rocky, for walks on the beach and make decadent desserts.